# Welcome Me to

# Willoughby C

# Welcome Me to Willoughby Close

### A Return to Willoughby Close Romance

## KATE HEWITT

TULE
PUBLISHING

# Chapter One

IT WASN'T LONDON. Emily David stood in the doorway of the cottage, part of a converted stables, and told herself to keep calm. The place was clean, everything bright and sparkling and looking quite new. That was something, at least.

She took a step inside, doing her best to admire the wood-burning stove, the granite counters and chrome fixtures in the kitchen, the French windows overlooking an overgrown postage stamp of garden, a tangle of wood beyond. Really, it was all wonderfully quaint.

So what if it wasn't London? It wasn't her flat in a modern, anonymous building where no one knew her name and she preferred it that way. It wasn't London, where people kept their heads down, mobiles clamped to their ears, and did their best not to make eye contact. It wasn't London, where she could melt into a crowd, where her office environment was safe and controlled, where she'd developed a routine that *worked*.

She could deal with all of that. She'd have to. It wasn't as if her boss, Henry Trent, now Earl of Stokeley, had given her that much choice. He was leaving his high-powered position at Ellis Investments to live at Willoughby Manor in Wychwood-on-Lea here in the Cotswolds to run a charity he and his wife had recently set up for children in care. He wanted Emily, as his executive assistant for the last four years, to accompany him.

Emily had balked at the idea at first; she didn't like change, and she wasn't keen on being so far away from the city, although admittedly it was only an hour by train. Still, this felt like another world—the cluster of four cottages around a little courtyard hidden from the narrow road by a dark wood, the crenelated towers of the manor house visible over the tops of the trees.

Henry had done his best to sweeten the offer, giving her a pay rise and free accommodation in the form of this cottage. Eventually, Emily had agreed; Ellis Investments's HR had said there were no other positions in the firm suitable for her and, truth be told, she actually liked working for Henry. Blunt and often terse to the point of rudeness, he never pried, never engaged in idle chitchat, and was almost as briskly efficient as she was. Together, as boss banker and executive assistant, they'd clicked.

But she had no idea if that positive dynamic would continue here, while Henry ran a charitable foundation out in the sticks, and she was meant to help him.

A careful breath in and out and Emily made herself start

to relax. At least the place was clean, she told herself again. It felt like the one positive thing she could hold on to. The moving truck would be arriving any moment, and then she could start putting things in their place. She ran her fingers along the granite counter in the kitchen, frowning slightly. Maybe she'd give everything a quick spritz, just in case.

"Hello?"

Emily turned around to see Henry's wife, Alice, standing in the doorway with a bright smile on her face.

Her boss had married Alice James eighteen months ago, and Emily still didn't quite know what to make of her. She was ridiculously young, a couple of years younger than her own twenty-six, with a halo of white-blonde hair and an angelic smile to match.

She'd certainly started to soften the usually taciturn Henry, turned him into a man who actually *whistled* as he walked, or so Emily had noticed when Henry had come into London for work. She didn't know what to make of that, either.

She hadn't had much interaction with Alice since the wedding, as she'd been in London and Alice had stayed here, in Wychwood-on-Lea, a chocolate-box village in the lovely Cotswolds with all the thatch, charm, and golden stone you could possibly wish for. She'd met her only three or four times, and the interactions had been brief, as Emily had been working and Alice had only stopped by the office to see Henry. Now she forced a smile to her stiff lips as Alice came into the cottage.

"What do you think? Will it do? Henry said you had a nice flat in Earl's Court—"

"Oh, yes, it's fine." Emily spoke a little too quickly. She wasn't in the right frame of mind to rhapsodise about the cosiness of the cottage, the quaintness of the village. Everything still felt new and uncertain and alarmingly fragile. She held on to her smile as she added, a bit belatedly, "Thank you so much."

"Oh okay." Alice was still smiling, but in a puzzled sort of way. Did she think they were going to be instant best friends now that Emily would be living here? Emily couldn't see that happening.

She'd had plenty of colleagues and acquaintances, people she passed the time of day with, or chatted to about the weather, but she didn't really have friends. She didn't *do* friendship, and hadn't since she'd been a child. She couldn't see herself starting now, in this strange place.

"I brought this." Alice brandished the tin Emily now saw she was holding. "Tiffin. It's Henry's favourite."

"Thank you, that's so kind." Emily took the tin and put it on the counter. She realised there must have been something slightly and unfortunately dismissive about the gesture because Alice's smile wavered.

"You're not allergic? It does have raisins. Or maybe you don't eat sweets…"

"No, no," Emily said hurriedly. "I'm sure I'll enjoy it

very much. Thank you." She thought she'd said the right thing, but Alice was still looking a bit…nonplussed. Disappointed, even.

Why, Emily wondered on a silent sigh, did a simple conversation have to be such a minefield for her? Now if they'd been talking about *work*, she'd have been fine. She could talk about spreadsheets and databases and filing systems all day. But a simple bit of chitchat with a woman who was so obviously thoughtful and kind? Her stomach went in knots and her tongue became firmly tied as every instinct kicked in to stay private.

She couldn't help it; it was a habit, one built up over years of careful self-protection. Stay polite, efficient, at a distance, so people didn't look too closely, or ask too many questions. So they don't find out the truth.

It was the way she'd always needed to be, and it was hard to stop now, even when it wasn't strictly necessary, with this slip of a woman who so clearly wanted only to be her friend.

"Okay. Well." Alice tucked her hair behind her ears in a nervous gesture as she kept smiling. "Is the moving truck coming soon? Because I could help you bring things in…"

Emily opened her mouth to say she didn't need any help, then closed it again. "Actually, if you had any spray cleaner and perhaps some paper towel? I'd love to wipe all the surfaces before the furniture is put in."

"Oh." Alice glanced around at the near-sparkling kitchen. "Okay. I have some back at the house. I'll nip up and get it for you."

"Thank you so much. I really appreciate it."

"Right. Won't be a tick."

Alice gave her another uncertain smile and then thankfully left the cottage. Emily let out a shaky breath of relief. This was all going to be so much harder than she'd expected, and that was saying something, since she'd had no illusions that it would be easy.

But every innocuous conversation felt like sandpaper on skin, an irritant, even a danger. It was hard to shed that self-protective skin even when it wasn't needed as much as it had been back in London. After all, her mother wasn't living with her anymore. She didn't actually have anything to hide.

Emily slid her phone out of her pocket and checked it for messages, but of course there weren't any. Her mum didn't do texts, or voicemails, or even phones. No matter how Emily tried to stay in touch, Naomi preferred to surprise her by suddenly showing up, usually with a suitcase and a smile, to stay awhile.

That had been fine in London, when she'd lived in a building where neighbours didn't notice or care. But here in Wychwood-on-Lea? With the helpful Alice popping round, and who knew who else? When Emily had driven into Willoughby Close's courtyard, she'd seen at least one of the four cottages had been occupied, and it had made her stomach clench a little. She couldn't be dealing with nosy neighbours, well meaning though they might be.

While Alice was gone, Emily decided to inspect the upstairs of the cottage. Henry had mentioned two bedrooms, and as she mounted the set of narrow stairs, she saw that indeed there were two—a master bedroom with fitted wardrobes and an en suite bathroom, and a smaller bedroom with a view of the back garden and the meadow and woodland beyond, the silver ribbon of the Lea River glinting under the fragile March sunshine before winding its way into a dark wood. It was, Emily supposed, so very idyllic...if one liked that sort of thing. She didn't know if she did.

She'd grown up in the city, had found solace and safety in crowds, anonymity, life buzzing and pulsing all around her. The quiet here scared her, although she couldn't say why. The solitude felt like a threat, the emptiness an exposure.

Certainly the possibility of nosy neighbours felt exposing. People coming in at all hours, with cheerful hellos and kind, smiling eyes, asking how she was, what she was up to... Emily suppressed a near shudder. It was like something out of a BBC comedy about moving to the country. It was what you were supposed to want, wasn't it? Yet Emily was quite sure she didn't.

"Hello? Emily...?" Alice's friendly voice floated up the stairs. Emily turned from her view of the back garden and headed back down to the open-plan living area. Alice brandished a bottle of cleaning spray and a roll of paper towels with a triumphant smile. "Will this do?"

"Perfect, thank you so much." Emily smiled and took both. As Alice watched, she started spraying. She wondered if she should have waited, but the truck would be here any minute and she needed everything to be clean. Still, perhaps it was a bit OTT.

"So," she said in as airy a voice as she could manage, "how do you like living at the manor? I've only been here for your wedding. That was so lovely…"

"Honestly? It feels like a dream come true." Alice laughed self-consciously. "As naff as that sounds, it really does."

Emily glanced at the younger woman; happiness was radiating from her in an almost visible way, like beams of sunshine shooting out from her fingertips. A shaft of entirely unexpected envy twisted her gut and she spritzed some cleaning spray onto the top of the pristine cooker.

"Well, Henry certainly seems happy. He's stopped scowling, which I never thought I'd see."

Alice laughed. "Yes, he's unbent a bit, hasn't he? That makes me happy, too."

"I'm not quite sure how to deal with him, to be honest." She let out a little laugh. "I really am delighted for you both. Honestly. It's so wonderful to see…" She didn't exactly know how to finish that sentence, and so she stopped, only to see to her horror that Alice Trent was looking at her with something like pity. Did she feel sorry for her, so clearly on her own, solitude radiating from her the way happiness was from Alice? Perhaps Henry had said something. *My poor secretary, darling. She's got absolutely no social life at all…*

Emily's cheeks warmed as the moment spun out and then, thankfully, was broken by the rumble of tyres on gravel outside.

"That must be the moving truck," Alice said with a bright look. "Let me help you move your things in."

"Oh, you don't…" Emily began, but Alice was already out the door. Heaven help well-meaning neighbours. The last thing she wanted was Alice bringing boxes in, reading the labels on the top, asking brightly about things she had no need of knowing. And then unpacking them, touching all her things, putting them in the wrong place, *heavens…*

Emily walked quickly out the door. The truck had pulled right up in front of the cottage, and the burly driver and his equally impressive colleague were already opening the back and starting to unload. Clearly they were on the clock, which suited Emily fine.

"The boxes are marked by room," she said. "If you can put them in the right places?"

"Sure thing, love." The driver gave her a nod and a wink. "How about a cuppa?"

"Oh…right. Yes." Fortunately she'd put some of the most essential kitchen things in her car, a ridiculous rental that Henry had arranged, thinking she'd enjoyed zipping about the country lanes in a navy-blue convertible Mini, the top down to the spring breeze.

And in truth, Emily sometimes wished she *was* the sort of person who would enjoy that—the hedgerows blurring by, the wind in her hair. But the reality was that she was definitely a sensible sedan sort of girl, and driving the Mini from London to the Cotswolds had made her feel both uncomfortable and nervous, especially after she'd googled "convertible safety concerns" at a rest stop.

Still, she was here, she'd made it, and she'd return the car tomorrow even though Henry said she could have it for the week. Since she'd be working at the manor and there was a train station in the village, she hoped she wouldn't need a car anyway.

"Do you want to me to make the tea so you can supervise the movers?" Alice asked as Emily brought the box with the kitchen stuff back into the cottage. She looked so eager to be helpful, so very hopeful, that Emily almost relented.

"Thank you, but I think I've got it in hand," she said as firmly as she could without being rude. "I don't have that much stuff, anyway. I doubt it will take long. But you've really been so kind."

"Oh…" There was no mistaking Alice's disappointment, and Emily's stomach curdled with guilt. She wasn't trying to be mean, honestly; she just…liked to do things on her own. She *needed* to.

"Thank you, though," Emily said yet again. "You've been very kind."

"It's no trouble at all. And I wanted to let you know that

you're invited to come up to the big house for supper tonight," Alice answered, rallying once more, with cheerful determination. "Nothing fancy—just a kitchen supper. Shepherd's pie. You're not vegetarian…?"

Emily's smile was starting to feel fixed. "No, I'm not."

"Well, Henry insists that you come. He wants to welcome you properly. He was busy this afternoon, meeting some potential donors, but I know he wants to see you tonight, check in with how you're settling."

"That's very kind," Emily said after a second's pause. As everything else was. Why did Alice have to be so bloody kind? And Henry, as well? She knew she couldn't say no to her boss, although she dreaded the prospect of making chitchat with Henry or Alice over what would surely be an interminable, if delicious, supper.

Her relationship with her employer had worked because they'd both been efficient, uninterested in niceties. Henry had appreciated her brisk manner, and she'd appreciated his taciturn one, as well as the fact he'd had zero interest in her as a person. Since his marriage, and now his move, that seemed as if it might change, and Emily wasn't sure she could deal with that on top of everything else.

"I do hope you'll like it here," Alice persisted. "I know it's not as busy as London—that's a huge understatement, obviously—but people are so friendly. When you've settled in, you must come over for one of our girly evenings with Ava and Ellie, Harriet and Olivia… Ellie used to live in this cottage, with her daughter Abby. She's married to Oliver now and they've moved out towards Oxford, but she still comes in for our get-togethers. And Harriet was in number two but she and Richard have moved to the other side of the village. Then Ava's with Jace, in the gatekeeper's cottage... She has the sweetest little boy, William." For a second Alice looked wistful. "And Olivia runs a bakery and teashop in town, and she's dating Simon, a music teacher at the primary. They're all such fun. You won't be lonely here, I promise you. There will always be people around, to help, to chat, to have a laugh with. It really is the loveliest place to live."

Emily blinked, taking in all the names, all the socialising. "That does sound lovely," she said with the same sense of inevitable duty and dread that she'd accepted the dinner invitation. Since Alice hadn't set a date for the "girly evening"—shudder—she could certainly back out later.

"Okay." Alice looked around the empty cottage, the movers already stacking boxes by the French windows. "I suppose I'll go, then, if you're sure you don't need me..."

"I'm fine, honestly." Emily softened her words with a smile. "Thank you, though, for offering, and also for the tiffin. It really does look delicious." She took the kettle out of the box, gave it a rinse, and then started to fill it.

"Shall we say seven for supper? Is that too late?"

"Not at all." It gave her a few hours to unpack and sort, at least.

Finally, with a flutter of her fingers, Alice was gone, and

Emily breathed a sigh of relief. She knew Alice meant well, of course she did, but it had been exhausting navigating so many invitations. Quickly she made the movers their tea, and then started shifting boxes.

There really weren't too many—she'd always been one for economy, preferring the clean lines of an empty room than the chaotic disorder of a full one. Half of the boxes were her mother's things, all loaded into the second bedroom for when—or, really, if—her mother ever showed up. Emily never knew when it would be, or for how long.

With a sigh she started emptying a box of books—business manuals and no-nonsense self-help guides that she considered suitable for show in the sitting room; her secret pleasure—sweeping, romantic epics—would go upstairs in her bedroom.

"Ta, love." One of the movers came downstairs brandishing an empty mug. "We're all done here."

"Thank you very much." Emily saw them out, with the requisite tip, before she resumed unpacking. It felt strange to put her familiar things in this new place. She'd been in her flat in Earl's Court since her first pay cheque at Ellis Investments. Admittedly it had only been a let, and she hadn't been particularly attached to the small, boxy flat with its tiny kitchen and even tinier bathroom, but it had been familiar and it had been hers, and right now Emily couldn't keep from feeling a pang of sorrow at its loss.

"Stop it," she told herself out loud, in the firm voice of a primary school teacher. "There is absolutely no reason to feel sorry for yourself. You're extremely fortunate, you know."

And she *did* know. She had a job that was secure and made her financially stable; she had a lovely cottage to call her home; she had a mother who loved her in her own chaotic way, and she was healthy and young and... Her blessings petered out and she blew out an impatient breath. She had this lovely cottage, she continued determinedly, and she was healthy...

She'd already listed those ones. Emily pulled a piece of packing tape off a box and it came away with a satisfyingly loud rip. She was done counting her blessings, as well as feeling sorry for herself, simply because she'd moved to a new place she wasn't at all sure about. She had work to do.

Two hours later the unpacking was mostly done. Her streamlined grey sofa looked a bit out of place in the cosy sitting room, and her angular white dishes seemed rather austere in the glass-fronted cupboards, but Emily didn't mind. She wasn't a patchwork throw or colourful pottery type of person, after all, and she didn't think she ever would be.

Upstairs she'd stacked her mother's boxes in the second bedroom, undecided whether she should unpack them or not. Her mother might be irritated if she did, hurt if she didn't. It was impossible ever to know what reaction she might provoke, or what mood she might find her mum in when she finally did turn up.

Which reminded her, she needed to ring Naomi and let her know her new details.

"Hello?" The musical voice sang out dreamily after the fifth ring, when Emily had been poised to leave a voicemail.

"Fiona? It's Emily David. Naomi's daughter?"

"Emily…" The woman's spacey voice made Emily grit her teeth. Her mother's latest best friend was a hippy in her sixties who somehow made a living selling hand-dipped candles in Camden Market. She also smoked a lot of cannabis.

"Could I talk to my mother, please?"

"I'm afraid she's not here, darling."

Annoyance as well as a tiny pinprick of alarm shivered along Emily's spine as she registered Fiona's insouciant, indifferent tone. "Do you know where she is?"

"No. She's a grown woman, after all. I'm not her keeper, and neither are you." Fiona was still speaking in that away-with-the-fairies voice that made Emily grit her teeth.

"That's true, but you know she has medication she needs to take regularly, so—"

"Oh, medication." Now Fiona sounded scoffing. "Conspiracies by big pharma, you mean."

"Fiona, please—"

"Naomi is much, much better without all those pills," Fiona said firmly. "She's been so much freer, so much happier. You can't have any idea the burdens she'd been under, which have just been lifted—"

Emily's fingers tightened on her phone. "Are you saying she hasn't been taking her medication?" Her voice unspooled like a thread of wire.

"You don't need to worry about her," Fiona declared, all airiness gone, and then she hung up. Emily closed her eyes.

Fiona was just the latest in a long line of her mother's friends—men and women of all stripes and dispositions, drifters and grifters and other lost souls. Naomi picked them up like strays, or perhaps it was the other way around, and they were the ones picking her up. Emily didn't know the ins and outs of each one—there had been far too many—but she knew enough to feel nervous, if her mother had gone off her medication again, even for a day. The last time, three years ago, had been disastrous. Emily did not want to go through something like that again.

And hopefully she wouldn't have to. Fiona had sounded as if she'd had her head in the clouds, or at least in a cloud of cannabis smoke. Emily doubted she knew whether Naomi was taking her medication or not, and when she'd spoken to her mum before she'd left for Wychwood, she'd seemed fine. *Fine.* But where *was* she now?

Emily hesitated, wondering if she should call her father to let him know what was going on, but she didn't think she could bear his defeatist attitude right now, his weary resignation bordering on total indifference.

*Your mother's made her choices, Em. I know it's hard, but you've got to let her go.*

He *would* say that, because his motto had been to let people go, including Emily herself. And yet she knew that wasn't entirely fair; her father had tried. Sort of.

With a sigh Emily decided to leave it for now. She'd call Fiona again after this dreaded supper, and again in the morning if necessary. Not for the first time she wished her mother possessed a mobile, but as with many things, Naomi didn't hold with them.

With only twenty minutes until she was meant to be up at the manor, Emily hurried to change out of her now-dusty clothes. A quick shower just to feel properly clean, and then she pulled on a silk blouse and tailored trousers; she didn't do casual. She pulled her chestnut-brown hair into a neat ponytail, and slicked on some eyeliner and lipstick, because she always liked to look professional. Polished. A glance at her reflection made her nod in satisfaction; she was ready.

As Emily stepped outside the cottage, the last of the afternoon's light was trickling from the sky like golden syrup, puddling on the lane that wound its way up to Willoughby Manor, and touching the bright heads of the daffodils with gold.

It was all so very lovely, Emily thought with something close to reluctance. Who wouldn't want to live in such a beautiful place? Who wouldn't enjoy wandering through the narrow paths she could see twisting through the wood, or along the gently rolling meadows that bordered the Lea River?

Of course, she knew the answer to that question. She wouldn't. And just like with the convertible Henry had thought she'd enjoy tootling about in, Emily almost wished she could be the sort of person who could happily frolic through a meadow, or wander in a wood. Who could welcome the new neighbours of Willoughby Close with friendly enthusiasm instead of a caution bordering on dread. Who could live life to the full instead of cagily dipping a toe in here or there.

Unfortunately, she knew she wasn't that kind of person. And she didn't think she ever could be. It hadn't actually bothered her that much until now; it hadn't bothered her at all. Yet suddenly, when she was faced with the stark differences, she felt her own lack in a way she hadn't let herself before.

Well, she thought, squaring her shoulders as she headed up the sweeping drive to the manor, she was who she was and she didn't intend on changing. Willoughby Close would just have to get used to her.

# Chapter Two

"COME IN, COME in!"

Henry was even more effusive than Alice had been earlier, seizing Emily by the elbows as he planted a most uncharacteristic smacking kiss on her cheek. Where on earth was all this bonhomie coming from? And when would it stop?

Instead of his usual three-piece pinstripe suit, Henry was wearing a pair of battered cords and a jumper that had actual holes in the elbows. Emily did not know what to make of him. She'd never seen her boss like this. He was usually like her—without a hair out of place, any smile one of briskness rather than bonhomie, moving and speaking quickly, wanting to get things done.

Yet now, as he led her down the hallway, still holding her by the arm, he seemed full of relaxed geniality in a way that made Emily feel rather alarmed. She didn't know what to do with this man as her boss, how to be with him.

"I can't tell you," he said as he led her through the ubiquitous green baize door to the servants' quarters of the manor house, "how free I feel, now that I've left Ellis Investments and London behind. I feel as if I've shed a skin. I'm like a new man!" He grinned at her, surprising her yet again.

Yes, she'd noticed that Henry had relaxed somewhat since marrying Alice. A stiff, stern man, he'd most certainly softened a bit since falling in love. But he'd still been Henry: somewhat terse, often taciturn, with comforting protocols in place, and *always* wearing a suit.

When Emily had started working at Ellis Investments, he hadn't called her by her first name for over a year. She'd *liked* that.

This Henry, who kissed her cheek and was practically gambolling down the hall, was a new and unwelcome species. It was as if in leaving Ellis Investments, he'd shed the last of his own self, and she didn't know what to make of the man who remained.

"You certainly seem so," Emily remarked cautiously as she followed him towards the kitchen of Willoughby Manor. So far what she'd seen of the place had seemed elegantly dreary—dark wood-panelled walls, lots of muddy oil paintings and blank-faced statuary. She knew Henry and Alice were transforming the place into a retreat and holiday centre for foster kids as part of their charitable foundation, but it hadn't seemed particularly inviting so far.

Then Henry pushed open the door to the kitchen.

"*Oh...*" The single syllable escaped her in a sigh of surprise as she gazed around the wide, rectangular room.

Latticed windows climbing with ivy let in the last of the evening's light, and the wide stone sills beneath were crammed with colourful hand-painted flowerpots that held a variety of houseplants. A large rectangular table took up the centre of the room, set for three, along with a jug of pink tulips.

An enormous Welsh dresser ran the length of one wall, filled with an odd assortment of china and crockery. The pride of the room had to be the huge bright red Aga that rumbled away cheerfully; Alice was standing by it, her face flushed and happy. A grey cat, looking as soft as cashmere, lay curled up on an armchair in the corner of the room, its purr competing with the rumble of the Aga.

The room was chaotic, messy, with far too many things in it, and normally the disorder would make Emily's toes curl as she struggled not to start straightening everything into neat and pleasingly parallel lines.

Yet for some reason, right then the sight of all that lovable mess caused a painful ache of longing to pulse through Emily that she couldn't understand. The Aga...the cat...the tulips...it was all so unbearably homely, a cross between *Downton Abbey* and *Little House on the Prairie*. She didn't think she could stand it, and she wasn't even sure why. She'd never encountered such a room, or such a feeling, before.

"It's a lovely room, isn't it?" Henry said, taking in her single "oh" at face value. "Alice did it all. She's transforming this lonely old house room by room, aren't you, my love?

Turning it into a proper home."

Henry kissed Alice on the cheek, and Emily forced a smile. Her heart felt as if it were tipping over, and she needed to right it again. Quickly.

"Oh, Henry, really." Alice laughed as she batted him away. "I didn't do much. Glass of wine, Emily?" She nodded to a bottle of red breathing on top of the Aga, just another element of the cosily domestic scene.

"Yes, thank you." She didn't normally drink much at all, but she felt she could use the fortification tonight, which looked to be an interminably awkward evening of Henry and Alice's well-meaning benevolence and her decided third wheeling, not to mention the jumbled-up feeling she had inside that she didn't understand and definitely didn't like.

"So are you all settled in number one?" Henry asked as he poured her a glass of wine. "I hope it suits?"

"It's lovely." What else could she say? Besides, it was. There wasn't a single thing wrong with it.

"And I hope you'll get used to life in Wychwood-on-Lea. I know it's a far cry from London, but people really are friendly. You won't be short of a social life."

"That's what I was saying," Alice chimed in. "I've already texted Harriet to arrange a drinks night out...perhaps next weekend? Then you'll be able to meet everyone in one go."

Emily nearly shuddered at the thought. "That's lovely, but don't put yourself to any trouble—" she said, only to have Alice shake her head quite firmly.

"Not at all! I'm happy to do it. It's always fun to get out and have a drink and a laugh."

Emily wouldn't actually know. She smiled in reply and took a sip of wine, savouring its velvety warmth.

"As I recall, you weren't much of one for night life, were you?" Henry asked as he poured glasses for him and Alice. "Most evenings you were working late."

"I had a demanding position," Emily returned a little stiffly. She had no idea if her position here would be as demanding, but she hoped it would. She didn't know what she'd do with herself, without a job to suck up all her emotion and energy.

"Well, I can't wait to unleash your incredible organisational skills on Willoughby Holidays. That's what we're calling the charity—did I tell you?"

"I think you said something…"

"Wait until you see the office space." Henry's eye glinted with humour that Emily didn't understand. What about the office space…? "Anyway," he continued, "the first thing we want to do is to plan a fundraiser here, showcasing local businesses, for June. A really fun, friendly, but splashy affair. Do you think you can manage it?" The question seemed rhetorical, but startled, Emily nearly spluttered her wine.

"June?" It was already the tail end of March. "That's only two months away."

"End of June," Henry said comfortably. "So more like three. I'm sure you can manage it, Emily. You're the most capable person I know."

But she wasn't a PR person. At Ellis Investments she'd managed Henry's diary, typed his letters, answered his phone, and taken dictation. Skills she'd come to master and take pride in. And yes, she'd arranged flowers to be sent to certain clients, and had booked a bi-annual golf weekend for others, and made sure the meeting room was always stocked with bottled water, pens, and paper, and she'd done that all very well indeed, but organising an entire fundraiser? The prospect filled her with alarm but also excitement. This job might turn out to be even more demanding than her old one, and that surely could only be a good thing.

"And of course you won't have to do it on your own," Henry added cheerfully. "Alice wants to help. She's been involved in the charity from the start, and she's got loads of good ideas."

Alice met Emily's gaze with a shy smile; Emily had a feeling she looked fairly horrified. "Oh, good," she managed, and then quickly took a sip of wine to hide her expression. The thought of working together on such a big project in close quarters made her skin prickle. Henry had always been content to leave her to her own devices, and she far preferred working alone. But maybe Alice would offer her ideas and then toddle off. Surely she had other things to keep her busy.

"I think it's ready," Alice announced, and she withdrew a bubbling shepherd's pie, the mashed potato crust perfectly golden, out of the Aga.

Soon all three of them were seated on one end of the big table, and Henry was doling out the pie while Alice passed around the salad. Outside the shadows were lengthening, the sky deepening to a dark violet. It felt homely and welcoming and yet Emily still felt uneasy. She really didn't do stuff like this, and she still felt weirdly mixed up inside.

"It's so quiet," she said after a moment, and Alice laughed.

"Yes, it is, isn't it? When I first moved here, I was a bit spooked. You could hear the windowpanes rattle and the pipes creak…"

"Alice lived at Willoughby Manor with my great-aunt," Henry explained, "until she died." He and Alice exchanged looks that managed to be both loved up and sorrowful.

"She was quite a character," Alice murmured. "A truly lovely lady."

Emily murmured something back. She'd known Alice had lived with Lady Stokeley—at least she thought she had. Alice had been her carer, which was how Henry had met her. A fairy-tale romance, by all accounts, just as Alice herself had said.

"And how are you finding living here together?" Emily asked. "Are you used to the quiet?"

"Oh, yes. It still feels as if we're rattling around in here, though. We only use a couple of rooms."

"We'll fill them up soon enough," Henry said with a significant look.

"You'll be using the manor for the holidays, I suppose?" Emily surmised, and Alice blushed. Oh. So he hadn't been talking about the holidays.

"That, as well," Henry answered with a chuckle. "But we're keen to start a family of our own."

"When the time's right," Alice said quickly, and rose from the table to refill the water pitcher. Emily detected an undercurrent but she couldn't figure out what it was. She certainly wasn't about to ask.

"Anyway, Emily," Henry resumed, "I promise I won't work you too hard. I want you to be able to explore the Cotswolds, and all Wychwood-on-Lea has to offer." He smiled encouragingly. "It's important, in organising the fundraiser, that you're able to take part in the community life of the village. Get to know all the shopkeepers and local businesses. Be a face in the village."

"So in one breath you tell her that you won't work her too hard," Alice teased as she sat back down at the table, "and in the next you say it's all work!"

Henry grinned, unabashed. "I'm afraid that's how I operate. But Emily knows that?" He raised his eyebrows in query, and Emily nodded back, although her stomach was churning.

Yes, she'd known that. Back in London Henry had regularly pulled fourteen-hour days, and Emily had often worked through her lunch breaks and into the evenings. But her boss seemed to be asking for something rather alarmingly different here—involving herself in the community life of the village? Getting to know all the small businesses?

Did Henry know her at *all?*

Perhaps he did, because he favoured her with a smile that seemed just a bit too knowingly compassionate as he said, "I think this move to Wychwood-on-Lea will be very good for you, Emily."

Right.

The conversation moved on, and Emily nibbled at her shepherd's pie—delicious—as she half-listened to Alice and Henry debate which room to renovate next, and then describe the village's spring fete, complete with an egg hunt and Easter bonnet competition.

It sounded rather idyllic, and yet somehow, combined with the loveliness in the room, from the pie to the wine to the cat in the corner, it was all having the unfortunate effect of making her feel a bit melancholy. Everything about this was outside of her experience, which should have been fine, but for some reason tonight it wasn't.

From the age of seven, Emily had grown up avoiding adults, attention, conversation, or care. Her life had revolved around her mother and keeping them both safe, and while that had had its own rewards, it hadn't been anything like this. She didn't like feeling the lack; in London she never had. Or maybe she just hadn't let herself.

In any case, it was ridiculous to want something like this, or to feel like she'd missed out on something. She knew she'd missed out on the stereotypically normal childhood. That much had always been obvious all along, but she hadn't minded.

Besides, most children didn't grow up in a manor house, with a kitchen the size of a skating rink, in a village that, if Alice and Henry were to be believed, was like something out of *Midsomer Murders* but without the crime. None of it had to make her feel as if she'd somehow been deprived.

"So are you all unpacked?" Alice asked as she brought a sherry trifle to the table, along with custard and pouring cream.

"Mostly. I didn't have that much to begin with, anyway." She'd tried to speak lightly, but Alice was giving her that funny smile again, an uncomfortable mix of puzzlement and pity, as if Emily had just said something normal people didn't. Surely not everyone was a hoarder, Emily thought with a touch of irritation. "You'll have to tell me the best place to buy groceries and things," she said a bit over-brightly, and Alice nodded, and launched into a discussion about the new deli that had opened up on the high street, along with the Tesco on the other side of the village.

The conversation remained thankfully innocuous as they had their coffees, liberally laced with liqueur, and when Henry insisted on showing her the office before she started work tomorrow, Emily tottered on her feet. She hadn't had so much alcohol in a long while, if ever.

She followed him down a dark, rather dreary hallway,

lined with more heavy oil paintings of frowning ancestors and muddy country scenes, before he threw open two wood-panelled doors and flicked on the lights of what had once been the morning room.

"Sorry about the mess," he said rather unrepentantly as Emily blinked. There were piles of papers *everywhere*, along with teetering stacks of books, frames six deep stacked against the walls, and boxes of unidentifiable items scattered around. Someone had cleared a narrow path between all the mess to get to the other side of the room, but that was it. It was her worst nightmare come to life. The stacks of papers, crumpled and disordered…the *dust*…

"How on earth am I supposed to work?" Emily asked faintly, and Henry clapped a friendly hand on her shoulder.

"Alice said the same thing, but you're brilliant at organising, Emily, and I thought since this is mainly your office, you ought to have charge of how it's set up. Order whatever you like, and anything you don't want in here we can put up in the attics."

Anything she didn't want? How about two-thirds of the room's contents?

"The papers need to stay," Henry said, as if reading her mind. "And be sorted. Obviously. I've ordered a few filing cabinets, but I thought you'd want to pick out your own desk and other bits. As for the rest…well, I'm afraid this room became a bit of a dumping ground as we started to renovate a few others, but I know you'll have it in hand in no time."

And organise a massive fundraiser in the next three months, as well? And get to know an entire village's worth of people when she was just about the world's most antisocial person?

"You have a lot of confidence in my abilities," Emily finally said, and Henry nodded in firm agreement.

"Absolutely. I thought you'd relish this kind of challenge."

Emily suspected Henry just hadn't wanted to bother with the mess, but as she said her goodbyes a short while later, she realised she didn't actually mind as much as she might have. She'd been afraid this position wouldn't provide her with the activity and stimulation her work at Ellis Investments had, but if the mess of the room and the promise of the fundraiser were anything to go by, her fears were entirely unfounded. She looked forward to being busy, starting with a *massive* clear-out of her office.

As she put on her coat, Henry offered to walk her back to Willoughby Close, but Emily insisted she could do it on her own. She did most things on her own, after all, and she was looking forward to a quiet walk in the darkness to clear her head.

"Numbers two and three are currently vacant," Alice called as she headed down the drive. "But Olivia is in number four. Do pop in and say hello. She'll be thrilled to have a neighbour."

It was something Emily couldn't see herself doing, and yet she felt that unsettling mix of excitement and melancholy as she walked down the sweeping drive, illuminated only by a pearly, luminous half-moon, back to Willoughby Close. This was certainly a far better commute than thirty minutes on a crowded, smelly train where she was compelled to spritz sanitiser on her hands half a dozen times. And the quiet, which had felt so eerie at first, now seemed rather peaceful.

And yet…Emily knew she wasn't ready for nosy neighbours, well-meaning employers, or working closely with a woman who seemed to be hoping to be her BFF. After years of deliberate self-isolation, hiding in crowds, keeping herself apart, the empty space around her felt alarming. Exposing. But right now, with the darkness so soft, the air possessing a chill but also a hint of spring, Emily felt…not quite hopeful, not happy either, but…something. That was as much as she knew.

Willoughby Close was cloaked in darkness as she walked across the courtyard to number one. Number four, residence of the unknown Olivia, was dark and silent.

Emily let herself into the cottage, breathing in the unfamiliar scent of the place—even the cleaning spray Alice had lent her had a different smell than the one she normally used. It wasn't home, not yet, and she wasn't sure if it ever would be, if she even knew what home was anymore.

She slipped her mobile out of her pocket to check if her mother had called, even though she knew she hadn't. Worry nibbled at the edges of her mind, but she'd had too much wine to let it take over, and she was desperately tired after the day of moving and then the evening up at the manor. She'd think about her mother tomorrow…and she'd certainly ring.

Leaving her phone on the table, Emily headed upstairs to bed.

# Chapter Three

EMILY WOKE EARLY to an unfamiliar dawn chorus of birds and bright sunlight slanting through her curtainless windows. She'd forgotten to draw the blind before flopping into bed last night, most unlike her.

Usually her bedtime routine was carefully orchestrated—slippers lined up by the bed, blind drawn, door closed, clothes put away, outfit for the next day selected and hanging neatly on the wardrobe door.

Last night she'd had the presence of mind—or rather the necessary compulsion—to put her clothes away, although she hadn't bothered picking something out to wear today, for her first day of work. It was Monday, so she always wore a white blouse and navy pencil skirt. At least she had at Ellis Investments.

But what was the dress code for working alone at Willoughby Manor, in a space that looked more like the local tip than an office? Henry certainly didn't seem bothered by formalities any longer, although he'd once been such a stickler for them, but even so Emily didn't like the thought of going to work in jeans, not that she even owned any. She was strictly a power suit type of girl, or at the least a smart skirt and blouse.

Feeling a bit groggy from last night's unaccustomed indulgences, she reached for her dressing gown and belted it tightly around her waist before thrusting her feet into slippers. Her flatmate in uni had joked she had the soul of a middle-aged man, and Emily supposed there was some truth to that friendly aspersion. She certainly liked her dressing gown and slippers.

Downstairs, sunlight spilled through the French windows, bathing the room in gold. Outside a thrush hopped in the dew-spangled grass and a skylark sang sweetly. It was all so perfectly pastoral, it was hard not to stop and savour the moment, as unfamiliar as it was.

From the courtyard Emily heard a car start, and she inched up the blind to see a battered-looking sedan reversing out of the parking space in front of number four. The mysterious Olivia got up early, it seemed. It wasn't quite half six.

Emily moved back to the kitchen and began to make her coffee—two perfectly heaped teaspoonfuls of Illy coffee, never any other brand—in the little cafetière, and then plunged and poured the liquid into her usual white ceramic mug with a pleasingly chunky handle. The normality of the routine soothed her, despite the strangeness of the kitchen, the birdsong outside, the lack of traffic noise and sodium streetlights casting an eerie glow.

It was so *quiet*.

She took her coffee to the utilitarian table for two the movers had left by the French windows. Her mother still hadn't been in touch, a fact that Emily was trying not to let make her feel anxious. It was early still; she'd ring Fiona again before she walked to work.

It was surprisingly peaceful to sit and sip her coffee, gazing out at the untidy little garden. She watched, entranced, as a robin plucked a fat, wriggling worm from the grass and hopped away delightedly. She'd have to mow the lawn, of course, and she didn't have a lawn mower. Perhaps she could borrow one.

Perhaps she'd even plant some flowers, or get a couple of those terracotta planters to put by the French windows. The possibility made something unfurl in Emily, a fragile tendril taking root and starting to grow. This cottage could become far more of a home than her boxy flat in Earl's Court ever had been. More of a home than she'd ever had before, moving from bedsit to rental and back again, all through her childhood.

Nearly half an hour had passed with Emily simply staring into space, and, realising the time with a flash of discomfiture, she sprang into action. It wasn't at all like her to sit and daydream.

In any case, she had plenty of time to get ready, thanks to the lack of a forty-minute commute, and by half past eight she'd eaten, exercised, showered and dressed. She tried to reach her mother again, trying to tamp down on her instinctive panic when Fiona's phone just kept ringing. They were probably both asleep. She'd try again at lunch.

The morning was still fresh and dewy as Emily started walking back up the drive to Willoughby Manor, her navy court shoes clicking on the pavement. She suspected she was overdressed in her silk blouse and skirt, but this was what she always wore on Mondays, and despite the cleaning work she knew the office needed, she really wasn't a casual clothes kind of girl.

"Hi!" Alice greeted her with her usual easy enthusiasm after Emily lifted the big brass lion's head knocker and let it reverberate through the house. "You don't have to knock. I'll give you a key in any case, but feel free to just come in and get started." Her gaze swept down Emily's outfit but she said nothing. Alice was, Emily noticed, wearing jeans and a jumper that had a ragged hem. Both she and Henry looked as if they were now dressing from a charity shop, but Emily liked her tailored clothes, many with designer labels she'd worked hard for. A glossy hairstyle and a pair of heels felt like armour.

"Come on through," Alice said as she led her back to the morning room Emily had surveyed last night. Now the heavy velvet curtains had been drawn back to let in all the light, and the room seemed enormous, with its high ceiling and huge windows. It was also chock full of junk.

"I'm sorry we haven't tidied it up," Alice said with a grimace of apology. "But Henry was insistent. He said you'd want to be in charge of your own domain."

Emily couldn't help but smile at that. It was true, even if she wouldn't have minded a few less bits and pieces filling up the room.

"Where is Henry?" she asked as she put her handbag down on the only available surface, a bookshelf by the door.

"He has a meeting with a potential donor in Reading. He travels so much now. I think I see him less than I did when he worked in London." Alice gave a little laugh, but Emily saw the flicker of unhappiness in her eyes. Not quite a fairy tale, then.

"That's understandable, at this stage. I'm sure he'll scale back once the foundation is up and running properly."

"I hope so." Alice brightened hopefully. "Would you like a coffee? I've just put the kettle on."

Emily pictured it for a moment—the two of them at that big kitchen table, the Aga and the cat, cups of coffee and maybe even some freshly baked scones or muffins. Alice seemed like that type of person. The sunshine would be streaming through the windows, and it would all be so very homely.

"I really should get on," she said, trying to make her tone an apology. "But perhaps later, for elevenses?"

"All right." Alice gave her one of her rallying smiles. "I'll come back then and liberate you from all this mess."

After Alice had left, Emily let out a breath and surveyed the room. It really *was* a mess, and her fingers were practically twitching in her desperation to start cleaning. She *hated* a messy room. Hated it with a passion that she knew bordered on compulsion. She couldn't wait to get everything sorted and spritzed.

The hours passed surprisingly quickly as Emily began to go through the room, sorting papers, piling books, and heaving boxes of junk out into the hall for someone named Jace to deal with, or so Alice had assured her when Emily had asked what to do with all the stuff.

"Wow, you've done so much already," Alice exclaimed as she came up at eleven. "It already looks so much better."

"Yes, it does, doesn't it?" Emily wiped a strand of hair from her cheek. She was feeling a bit dusty and dirty, but at least the room had been emptied. She'd finish wiping down all the surfaces after her coffee.

"Do you want to come to the kitchen?" Alice asked shyly. "The kettle's on and I've made some muffins…"

Just as Emily had suspected. "That would be lovely, thank you." She wasn't particularly looking forward to a heart-to-heart with Alice, but she was desperate for a coffee, and she couldn't bear disappointing her yet again. It felt too mean.

The kitchen was just as Emily remembered, cosy and warm and filled with sunlight. The cat was curled up in the armchair, and Emily wondered if it had moved at all since yesterday evening.

"How are you finding everything?" Alice asked as she poured them both mugs of coffee. "Do you miss London and all your friends?"

*What friends?* "I do miss London," Emily said as she sat down at the kitchen table. "I've lived there for a long time."

"You grew up there?"

Briefly Emily thought of the semi-detached house in Reading she'd called home for six years, and then the parade of places she'd rested her head since. "I spent a lot of time there," she said. She had absolutely no desire to go into her complicated childhood with Alice. She didn't go into it with anyone. Which reminded her...she still needed to call her mum.

"What about you?" she asked Alice. "Where did you grow up?"

"Oh, around Oxford, mostly." Alice let out an uncertain laugh. "I was in care for most of my childhood, so I bounced around a bit."

"Oh." Emily stared at her in surprise. She'd assumed somehow, as she realised she always assumed, that Alice had had the sort of normal, stable upbringing most people seemed to have and Emily hadn't. "I'm sorry. I didn't realise. That must have been difficult."

Alice shrugged as she took a sip of coffee. "It was what it was."

Still...Emily couldn't imagine it, even as she sort of

could. At least she'd always had her mum—and her dad as well, in the background. "Does the manor feel like a proper home?" she asked.

"It's starting to. And I hope it can be a home away from home for a lot of foster kids, perhaps the only one they'll have."

Emily nodded slowly. "The charitable foundation makes a bit more sense now."

"I'm surprised Henry didn't tell you about my background," Alice remarked. "Although actually I'm not. I think he feels it's private, or that I'm embarrassed about it or something, but I'm really not."

"You shouldn't be," Emily returned. "It wasn't your fault."

"No." Alice looked thoughtful. "Although children have a habit of blaming themselves, I suppose. But I made a deal with myself a long time ago that I wouldn't become bitter or hardened by how I grew up. I'm determined always to see the best in people, and I think I do. Mostly."

Which was probably why she was so determined to be friendly with her, Emily realised. It both humbled and exasperated her. She really didn't *do* friends. Didn't know how. And yet Alice was going to keep trying—of that she could be sure.

"I've put the feelers out for an evening out this weekend," Alice said. "I think everyone's up for it, if you're free on Friday?"

"Oh..." Unfortunately Emily couldn't think of a single credible excuse, and yet the thought of going out with a bunch of strangers who all knew each other made her want to back away, palms up. "I'm not sure..."

"No one is at all scary," Alice assured her. "Except perhaps Harriet, but she doesn't mean to be. She's just one of those take-charge sort of people. And Ava is absolutely gorgeous and knows it, but you just get used to it. Ellie is sweet, and so is Olivia..."

They all sounded positively terrifying. Emily's stomach clenched with nerves and she reached for her coffee. "Mmm," she said, because she couldn't think of any other response.

"It'll be fun," Alice said firmly.

The cat rose elegantly from the chair and gave a languorous stretch before jumping neatly down and stalking across the kitchen floor. It was a beautiful animal, a soft, deep grey with eyes the colour of smoke.

"Oh!" The exclamation erupted from Emily as the cat jumped up onto her lap in one sinuous movement, turned around twice, and then settled down to sleep.

"She clearly likes you," Alice said, amused, before she leaned forward, concerned. "You're all right with cats? You're not allergic?"

Was she all right with cats? The answer was not really. She wasn't an animal person, and the thought of the cat's fur and dander and what have you getting all over her made her feel itchy inside, even without a cat actually *on* her lap.

"Um, well, I haven't actually had much to do with animals," Emily managed. She tried to nudge the cat off her but the feline wasn't having it. Her claws dug into Emily's Marc Jacobs skirt and she let out a purr that sounded like a car motor.

"Andromeda, down," Alice said not nearly sternly enough, and the cat merely blinked at her.

"Andromeda?"

"Henry named her. He's got a thing about Greek mythology." Alice shrugged apologetically. "Give her a shove if you really don't like having her there."

She didn't, and yet at the same time Emily couldn't deny there was something weirdly pleasing about the living warmth of the creature on her lap, the purr that thrummed through her so Emily could feel it in her bones. And yet the fur…and the dander…and the *germs*…

She gave Andromeda a little shove, as half-hearted as Alice's command, and predictably the cat didn't move.

"You're stuck here," Alice said, sounding pleased. "While I've got you, why don't we talk about the fundraiser? I had a few ideas…"

"All right, then," Emily said, doing her best to inject an enthusiastic note into her voice. She could hardly believe she was stuck in a kitchen with a cat and a woman who seemed intent on being her friend. It was so strange, so utterly unlikely, and yet…

It *was* just the tiniest bit *nice*. Amazingly. As long as Alice didn't ask her any personal questions, and they kept it about work, and the cat didn't do something disgusting.

"I've got some notes here." Alice took a stack of papers from the Welsh dresser and brought them to the table. "We've been thinking of a village fete sort of atmosphere, very friendly and open, perfect for a family day out."

"Yes…"

"And Henry in particular is keen for all the local businesses to take part, providing the catering, entertainment, et cetera."

"Are there enough local businesses for that?"

"I think so. There are the two pubs—The Drowned Sailor and The Three Pennies—I'm sure they'll both provide drinks. And then there's Olivia's bakery, and the new deli, and Harriet said a mum from the school does clowning and magic tricks for parties. There's a vintage clothing store and a pet store that can set up booths, along with the toy shop that's just opened and the garden centre—it's closer to Burford, but still—will most likely do a plant stall."

"Sounds like you've got it all planned," Emily said, and Alice hastened to reassure her.

"Oh no, not at all. We haven't asked anyone officially, and we'll have to draw up contracts and the literature explaining it all, and I'm sure there are other things you can think of." She gave Emily an encouraging look.

"I'm not sure how," Emily said slowly. "I mean…I'll do

all the admin, of course, but as you know I'm not from around here. I don't know the people or the businesses or even where Burford is, never mind a garden centre near it. Surely someone more local would be better at organising something like this?" She was starting to wonder why on earth Henry had put her in charge, or even why he'd wanted her here at all. He could have easily hired someone from Wychwood, a mum from the school looking for a job, or someone who at least was connected to the community. She wasn't, and she hadn't been planning on becoming so. Not at all.

"Oh, but you'll learn," Alice assured her, and Emily's heart couldn't help but sink a bit. "People really are so friendly. One night at the pub, or at a ceilidh at the village hall, and you'll know everyone."

A *ceilidh*? "Yes, but even so…" Emily found she couldn't finish that sentence because Alice was already shaking her head.

"Don't worry, Emily. You'll see. You'll be part of Wychwood-on-Lea in no time."

Emily knew Alice meant the words to be a comfort, but they were far from it. She didn't *want* to be part of a close-knit community filled with people who would get all up in her business, not that she even had that much, keeping her life private was an instinct she'd had too long to shed now. She couldn't let people in. She didn't know how. And that was a reminder that she really had to ring her mum. She gave

Andromeda a good shove and with a disgruntled look the cat leapt off her lap, leaving a snag in her skirt.

"Thank you for the coffee," Emily said as she rose from her chair. "But I really should be getting back to work."

"Oh yes, of course. But you're welcome anytime. Maybe we could make it part of your schedule?"

Alice looked so hopeful, and in any case Emily realised she wouldn't really mind a coffee break every morning. "That would be nice," she said. "Thank you."

Back in the office, Emily breathed in the smell of cleaning spray as she stared down at her cat-hair-dusted skirt in dismay. She'd nip back to the cottage to change, she decided, and ring her mum from there. It wasn't as if anyone was keeping tabs on her, and she didn't think she could bear spending the afternoon covered in cat hair. She'd ventured enough out of her comfort zone for one day.

She walked quickly back to Willoughby Close; the air had developed a chill and woolly grey clouds were obscuring the fragile blue of this morning, reminding the world that it wasn't quite spring yet.

Back in her bedroom, Emily changed into another navy skirt and silk blouse, putting her cat-hair-covered clothes into a basin to soak. What had she been thinking, having that animal on her lap? So unlike her, even if it had felt a little nice at the time, a living comfort that she'd been lacking for…oh, she didn't even want to think about how long for.

Standing by the kitchen sink, she gazed out at the gathering clouds and rang Fiona, who thankfully answered.

"Fiona, Emily here. May I speak to Naomi, please?"

"You do like to keep tabs on your mum, don't you?" Fiona said with a rather sour laugh. Emily closed her eyes.

"Is she there, please?"

"Oh, fine, hold on." The phone clattered onto a table, making Emily wince and hold her mobile away from her ear. At least her mother was in the flat. That was something. It seemed an age but was probably around five minutes before Emily heard her mother's rather breathless voice.

"Em? Darling? You know you don't need to worry about me. I really wish you wouldn't."

"I just wanted to check in, Mum. You remember I moved out to the Cotswolds this past weekend?"

"Did you?" Her mother sounded indifferently vague, which wasn't really a surprise. "It's meant to be very pretty out there."

"It is. You know you're welcome to stay anytime—"

"Oh, I don't know."

"Seriously, Mum." Life was both easier and harder with her mother in residence, but regardless Emily would always make the offer. She loved her mother, even if that love was tangled and complicated and sometimes didn't feel like love at all. "I've got a spare bedroom, and all the things you left from last time," she persisted, because some part of her had to. "It's so pretty. You can see a river from the bedroom window."

"Mmmm."

Emily couldn't tell if her mother was really listening. "I'm on the edge of a little village. There are loads of walks you could take." At least she supposed there were.

"I don't know if I'm really a village kind of person. But I'm glad you like it, darling."

Emily took a careful breath. "Fiona had said something about you not taking your pills."

"Oh, Emily." There was no disguising her mother's disappointment. "Really, you are not my doctor."

"I know, but—"

"I'm *fine*. You need to be able to trust me, that I know when I need them and when I don't. I'm not going to be irresponsible."

That was up for debate. "But you know the point of them is that you take them consistently—"

"Really, Emily, I don't want to talk about this with you. I'm a grown woman, taking control of my own life, and I refuse to let you keep me from doing that. I will take my medication as and when I need it, and I am the person to decide that, thank you very much." And on that rather vehement note, her mother slammed down the receiver, making Emily wince again.

So her mother was off her medication, or at least not taking it consistently. She let out a slow breath as outside a bird trilled—a sweet, fluting sound. All right, fine, so her mum wasn't taking her meds. That didn't have to be the end of the world. After all, Naomi hadn't taken medication of any kind all through Emily's childhood, and she'd been…well, perhaps best not to think about those days.

Emily pinched the bridge of her nose and closed her eyes. She knew there wasn't much she could do. And maybe it wouldn't be as bad as all that—after all, her mother's doctors had said, over the years, that coming off medication could sometimes be a good thing. Adjusting dosages, learning to live without it, all that advice. And yet the risk felt too enormous, too frightening. But as her mother had said, it really wasn't her choice to make.

Briefly she considered calling her father, but she knew he'd give her his usual patter. *Your mother has to make her own choices. I know it's hard.*

As if.

But there was no point in feeling bitter about that; Geoff David had made his choices too, including a second wife and family. Emily saw him once a year, if that.

She took another breath and let it out slowly, and then she reached for her coat. She needed to get back to work. Work, the usual antidote to feeling sad or stressed or heaven help her, lonely. Except the jury was out on whether her work in Wychwood-on-Lea was going to have the same soothing effect work had had back in London.

Emily had just turned onto the drive from the lane that led to Willoughby Close when Henry's forest-green Jaguar pulled in from the main road. He slowed, rolling down the window.

"Hop in, and I'll give you a lift up to the manor."

"Thank you," Emily said, and slipped into the passenger side. Henry was wearing one of his three-piece suits, which was comforting, and his Jag was reassuringly spotless.

"How's your first day going?" he asked as he started up the drive once more.

"All right, I think. The office is mostly cleaned."

"Already?" Henry gave her a laughingly admiring look. "You're a force of nature."

"I just heaped things in the hall really," Emily replied. "Alice said someone named Jace would deal with it?"

"Ah yes, Jace." Something flickered across Henry's face and then was gone. "He's the caretaker for Willoughby Manor. Married to Ava."

"Yes, Alice mentioned Ava. I can't keep track of all the names."

"Nor can I, really, but I'm sure you'll manage. Your brain is like a computer. Better than AI. You certainly managed to keep track of my schedule back in London."

"Yes," Emily murmured. "Although this feels different."

"It's a bit more hands-on," Henry agreed easily. "You'll have to get out and rub elbows with people, but that won't be a problem, will it?"

Emily glanced at her boss, noting the rather steely tone she remembered well from his former days. Yet when he met her gaze, he smiled at her. She had no idea what message he was trying to send, although she realised she was afraid she could guess.

"I have a list in my briefcase of all the independent businesses in Wychwood, and their owners," Henry said. "Starting tomorrow, I'd like you to pop into each one and say hello. Introduce yourself, and the foundation."

"I was thinking of writing emails..." Emily began, only to have Henry shake his head quite firmly.

"We need the friendly touch, the familiar face."

"But I'm not actually familiar—"

"You will be," he assured her in that same steely tone, and Emily wondered if Henry was doing this on purpose. Had he decided she needed to be pushed out her little feathered nest? Surely not. In their four years of working together, he'd never asked her a single personal question. He couldn't start caring about her now.

"Tomorrow," Henry stated, and Emily knew it wasn't something she could say no to.

"Aye, aye, Captain," she answered with a mock salute, and Henry smiled.

# Chapter Four

"**M**AY I HAVE a word?"

Owen Jones looked up from the till receipts he'd been going through on top of the bar to see a woman he'd never clapped eyes on before cautiously inching her way into the pub on a pair of steel-grey stilettos, her pert nose wrinkled in wary distaste.

She was dressed like a city barrister, in a black pencil skirt and grey silk blouse, both items highlighting a figure that was blow-away-in-the-breeze slender, and yet, Owen couldn't help but notice, still in possession of a few rather nice curves.

Her hair, a deep, glossy chestnut, was pulled back into an elegant chignon, with only a few wisps framing a delicate, heart-shaped face. In short, she was a stunner, and Owen, who had always enjoyed looking upon a lovely lady, noticed—just as he noticed the slight curl of her lip as she met his gaze.

"You can have several, if you like," he told her cheerfully. "How about a whole dozen? That's twelve right there, I've just said." He grinned, enjoying the startled look on her face. She was prissy, this one, and judging from the way her gaze moved around the decidedly shabby pub, a bit of a snob, but neither took away from her beauty.

"Are you the manager here?"

"Manager, bartender, owner," Owen replied as he spread his arms to encompass the dim interior of The Drowned Sailor, with its crowded tables, rickety stools, and an air of well-worn, well-loved shabbiness. "Come on in." She took another step into the pub, closing the door behind her, and Owen planted his elbows on the bar in front of him. "What can I do for you?"

Her gaze darted around the pub before resting resolutely on him. "I think, perhaps, it's what I can do for you." She gave a very small smile, which Owen answered with a grin. Posh, this one, with a voice like the queen, yet skittish too. Clearly she was slumming it here.

"Is that so?" he said, raising his eyebrows. "I'm all ears."

"Very well, then." She came closer, taking an expensive-looking bag of navy leather off one shoulder, embossed with a gold label Owen vaguely recognised from the gentry of the village. Expensive, like the rest of her. "I represent Henry Trent, the Earl of Stokeley and the CEO of Willoughby Holidays Charitable Foundation—"

"You represent?" Owen cocked his head. "Are you his solicitor?" Was Henry starting to swing his weight around? He'd been earl for over a year, after all. Maybe he wanted to put his mark on the village as well as the manor.

A faint blush touched her cheeks with pink, making her look even lovelier. "No, I'm his executive assistant."

"Ah." He folded his arms across his chest as the woman minced her way towards the bar. "What's he wanting, then?" He kept his voice friendly as he always did, but he couldn't keep a faint, instinctive tension from banding his temples.

Owen didn't know Henry Trent, because the great man had never deigned to talk to the likes of him, but he'd seen him buzzing through the village in his Jag, or cutting a ribbon at the summer fete, larking around as lord of the manor. None of it particularly impressed him, although he played along, as everyone else did, because they enjoyed the fact that the new earl and his lovely little wife had settled at Willoughby Manor instead of using it as a holiday home.

His friend Jace, who worked for the man, had told him he wasn't so bad after all, but Owen had yet to be convinced, and he had every bit of reason to be as suspicious of the landed class as Jace once had, before Henry had married Alice James and, according to some, softened a bit.

All this flashed through his mind as he kept his smile wide and waited for Little Miss Prim to speak. Her lips pursed as she stayed where she was, in front of the bar, her bag clutched to her chest as if she thought he might snatch it off her. "You sound as if you don't like him," she observed.

How had she sussed that one out? Owen shrugged one shoulder. "I like everybody, as long as they pay their tab. But

Lord Stokeley doesn't come in here much, so I don't know whether he's good for a pint or not."

Her lips pursed even further, drawn up like the strings of a purse. "Of course he is."

Owen gave another grin. "If you say so, Miss…?"

"David. Emily David."

"Right then, Emily. Do you want to take a seat and tell me what this is all about?" He nodded towards a stool, which she looked at with that now-familiar slight lip curl of distaste. Admittedly, it wasn't the cleanest place to park a bum, but it should do well enough.

"All right." She perched on the absolute edge of the stool, looking as if she could topple off at any moment and deeply uncomfortable besides. Goodness, but she was more than a bit of a ballerina.

"So?" Owen arched an eyebrow, waiting, curious now. What could Henry Trent possibly want with him?

"Willoughby Holidays will be holding a fundraiser up at the manor in late June," Emily began. "And as CEO, Henry Trent, along with his wife, Alice, would like all the independent businesses of Wychwood-on-Lea to take part."

"Would they?" Something in his tone must have alerted Emily, because she frowned.

"It's their hope, not a command," she said a bit sharply, and Owen merely shrugged. He hadn't said it was either. "I have the details here…" She reached for her bag again, fumbling a bit, because she seemed to have some aversion to placing it on the bar. Owen just kept watching and waiting, a smile playing with his lips. He realised he was rather enjoying her discomfort. "Here are all the details." She pushed several paper-clipped sheets across the bar. "The current plan is that Willoughby Holidays will provide a tent and tables for serving, but you'll have to bring anything else you might need... We're asking for businesses to give fifty per cent of their profits to the charity, if possible, but there will be no charge for attending."

"Sounds fair enough, I suppose." Owen glanced down at the sheets but didn't pick them up. "All the businesses in Wychwood... Does that include The Three Pennies?"

"We're hoping so, although I haven't spoken to them yet."

"Because I have to tell you, that's more of Henry's crowd than The Drowned Sailor. But you've probably realised that."

Emily frowned as her eyes, a clear blue grey fringed with luxuriant lashes and expertly made up, scanned his face. "As I said, Henry and Alice are most hopeful that everyone will take part. The fundraiser is meant to be inclusive."

"Very kind of them I'm sure." He meant to sound genial, but he thought a touch of acid had seeped in. Emily drew her slender shoulders back in something like affront.

"I do think it would be a very good opportunity for a place like this—"

Owen let out a crack of laughter that made her blink. "A

place like this?"

"A pub," she stated quickly, but Owen knew she hadn't meant that, just as he knew The Drowned Sailor was more than a little run-down, the only food on offer peanuts and pork scratchings, the most expensive wine coming in at eight ninety-nine a bottle. But that was how he liked it. Wychwood-on-Lea already had one gastro pub with its craft ales and vegan meals. It didn't need another, and he wouldn't change this place for the world—or for Willoughby Manor.

"Right," he said easily, refolding his arms as he leaned back against the counter. "A pub." Unwittingly this prissy woman had prodded a hornet's nest inside him, and he didn't like the feeling. Wasn't used to it. All his old hurts and biases had been buried a long time ago.

They'd had to be, considering he lived in the privileged Cotswolds, in a village that most likely had more millionaires per square mile than Mayfair. Yet for some contrary reason, Emily David—with her sexy, slender figure and her prim and prissy ways—had given that buried bit of him an uncomfortable poke. "I'll consider it, certainly."

"Thank you." She looked as if she wanted to say more, but then decided not to.

Owen leaned forward, planting his elbows again on the old, scarred wood of the bar as Emily David stood her ground, if only just. "Have you asked the other businesses?"

She blinked. Bit her lip. Looked away. So that was a no, then.

"I intend to," she said at last. "And I expect they will all agree. It's for a good cause, after all."

"Is it?" He leaned a little closer, so he was able to breathe in the scent of her understated perfume. Something light and floral. "Because, you know," he said, his voice dropping to a conspiratorial thrum, "you haven't actually *said*."

Emily didn't reply as a blush tinted her cheeks. She looked like she wanted to take a step back but she didn't. Was he flirting? Maybe. Owen liked to flirt, in a deliberately harmless way. It never went anywhere, because he never let it, and everyone in the village knew that and took him—and his flirting—for what they were worth, which was basically nothing. But Emily didn't know him, and she looked as if she didn't know what to do with his flirting, or the way he dropped his gaze to her mouth, lush and pink, and then up again. Her eyes widened and a pulse fluttered in her throat.

"Willoughby Holidays," she said, with a nod towards the papers he'd left on the bar. "As I said before. I...I thought you would have heard of it...?"

"Nope." Although that wasn't quite true. He'd heard that the Trents were forming some sort of charitable foundation, but he didn't pay attention to the goings-on up at the manor. Never had.

"It's a charity for children in care, to give them a holiday at Willoughby Manor, an opportunity to experience country living and home cooking and...well..." She was starting to look flustered. "Henry and Alice Trent started it six months ago."

"Did they?"

"Yes, they're hoping to have their first holidays offered this summer. I thought it was common knowledge in the village."

"Not to me." He straightened with a shrug. "You're not from here, are you?"

"No."

"London?"

"Yes, but I moved to Wychwood-on-Lea recently."

"When?"

She bit her lip again, a movement Owen suspected was thoughtlessly instinctive and yet also, he couldn't help but notice, inherently sexy. "Four days ago."

"Ah." He nodded knowingly, and she frowned, delicately arched eyebrows drawn together, mouth pursed in an adorable pout. She really was beautiful—but in a china doll way, perfect and untouchable. Fragile too, perhaps, although maybe just prim.

"What is that supposed to mean?"

He shrugged expansively. "The village doesn't revolve around Willoughby Manor anymore, although maybe there are those who think it does, like Lord Stokeley. We're happy to help, of course, but we don't come running at the crook of the earl's finger."

"He isn't..." Emily stopped and shook her head. "I'm afraid I've given a wrong impression of Henry—"

"Actually, I don't think you have."

She frowned. "Do you even know him?"

He let out a crack of laughter that had her drawing back, startled. "No, Miss Prim, I don't. And I don't particularly want to, if I'm honest. But don't you worry. The Drowned Sailor will be serving up pints at this precious fundraiser of yours. I wouldn't miss it for the world, even if it puts Henry Trent's nose out of joint."

"My name is David, not Prim," Emily said, and Owen couldn't tell from her tone if she was annoyed by the moniker or she was simply correcting him.

"David. Right. I'll remember that. So what do you think of Wychwood-on-Lea, Miss David?"

She straightened, narrow shoulders stiffening. "To be honest? I haven't had the best introduction."

He laughed again, a booming sound that clearly put her on edge. "True enough. Tell you what. The next time you come in here, you'll get a drink on the house. As a welcome. Although I can't promise champagne."

"Who said I drank champagne?" Her eyes narrowed as she gave him a quelling look. "Or that I'll come in here again?"

Owen just laughed, because he liked getting her back up, and it was all too easy. Still looking discomfited and huffy, Emily slid her bag back on her shoulder.

"I look forward to hearing from you in due course," she said stiffly, and then she was gone, her heels clicking sharply across the slate floor.

As the door closed smartly behind her, Owen smiled and shook his head. He wondered if he'd ever see Emily David darken the door of his pub again, and he realised, despite her prim and prissy ways, he hoped he would.

She amused him, and she also got under his skin. There was no reason, he knew, to have Emily David irritate him more than any other well-heeled Londoner who swanned into Wychwood, and there were plenty with their highlighted hair, Hunter boots, and huge black Range Rovers. Or the men—red faced, Rolexed wrists, too much tweed and swagger.

It was the nature of the place, only an hour from London, yet with the countryside on its doorstep. People came here to play at happy families, country kitchens. They had no idea what life was really like, and normally Owen didn't let it bother him.

But for some reason, Emily David *did*, and that was both interesting and a bit alarming. Why let this slip of a woman get under his skin? Was it because she was attractive, or was it that hint of something beneath her perfect polish—a hint of vulnerability, even?

Although really anything like that should send him running for the hills. Owen didn't get involved with people who needed fixing, because heaven knew he couldn't help them. He reached for the papers that remained on the bar and tossed them next to the till. He'd thought enough about

Emily David for one day.

❋

As THE DOOR closed behind her, Emily released a pent-up breath of agitation. That had *not* gone as she'd hoped. She'd been aiming for an orderly, efficient business meeting—a relaying of information, an enthusiastic agreement. Hadn't Alice and Henry assured her that people in this blasted village were *friendly?*

That man—Owen Jones, according to Henry's helpful list—hadn't been friendly. He hadn't been unfriendly, either. He'd been...well, Emily didn't know what he'd been. Aggravating. Disconcerting. Impossible.

On the surface he'd seemed friendly enough, giving wide smiles and unsettlingly loud laughs, as if everything, her included, amused him. And yet underneath, Emily had sensed something else, something dark and resentful, and it had unnerved her.

Although this whole process unnerved her—trawling along the high street, introducing herself, being friendly. She would have so much rather just sent an email. A phone call, even. But Henry had been insistent. "Face-to-face contact, Emily!" he'd reminded her again this morning. "That's what's needed here."

He'd given her a kindly smile, as if he knew exactly how difficult this would be for her, and that was at least in part why he was asking. Having Henry Trent interested and involved in her life was not something Emily wanted or needed. And yet here she was.

She'd chosen to walk into The Drowned Sailor first because it was at the end of the lane from Willoughby Manor as she'd walked into the village. She'd surveyed the village green with its play area and pagoda, and the high street meandering steeply up a hill with an assortment of businesses on either side, and she'd decided to start here. Now she wished she hadn't.

Surely she could have found someone a *bit* friendlier, some little old lady running a craft shop who would be delighted to take part, or even better, someone who was busy and efficient and simply took the paperwork with a nod and a smile?

Instead she'd got Owen Jones with his laughing looks and strange undercurrent of animosity, and it had been a forceful and rather unpleasant reminder that she didn't do this sort of thing, and she certainly wasn't good at it.

When he'd called her Miss Prim she'd thought, for an instant, that he'd simply got her name wrong. He must think her a complete idiot, among other things. Not that she cared, although the churning in her stomach said otherwise.

A chill wind blew down the street, making her shiver. Even though it was almost April, it didn't feel like spring this morning. The fragile blue skies of a few days ago had turned to pewter, and the syrupy sunlight was nowhere to be seen. Violet storm clouds blanketed the horizons, and the clusters of daffodils lining the village green looked as if they were huddling together for warmth.

Emily hitched her bag higher on her shoulder and belted her coat before she started up the high street. She could do this. She had to. And surely no one would be as unsettling and difficult as the man she'd just met.

The last two days, working at Willoughby Manor, had actually been quite enjoyable. Emily had finished organising the office, so it was clean and spare and just how she'd liked it. With Henry's approval, she'd ordered some office furniture—a desk and chair, a conference table and set of chairs. With the filing cabinets he'd already ordered, the room would be complete.

It had been fun to organise the office the way she wanted to, keeping everything clean and neat, and her daily eleven o'clock break with Alice, while still a bit awkward and uncomfortable at times, was also pleasant. Andromeda insisted on staying in Emily's lap, and thanks to a container of hand sanitiser and a lint brush, she didn't mind quite so much. In fact, she enjoyed it. Mostly, as long as she didn't think about the germs.

Henry was out and about most days, meeting donors, and so Emily had the office to herself, which she also liked. She'd spent half a day filing—bliss—and then another afternoon organising Henry's calendar with different-coloured fonts. Also bliss. Everything organised and tidy and in its place, just as she liked and needed it.

She'd also rung hoping to talk to her mum again, but there had been no answer. And although the anxiety about that could take over if she let it, like a mist creeping over her mind, Emily did her best to keep it at bay. There was nothing she could do about her mum. She *knew* that, she'd understood it for a long time, and yet it was so hard not to try, just as she'd been doing since she was seven. Better, she knew, to focus her energies on colour coding the foundation's files.

Lunch both days had been a sandwich at her desk while gazing out at the beautiful gardens, enjoying the quiet that had alarmed her at the start, as well as the neatly pruned efficiency of the topiary garden—all perfect angles and trimmed edges. Now *that* was a garden concept she could get behind.

All in all, not a bad start, until she'd met Owen Jones. Now she felt completely off-kilter, and half of her—all right, more than half—wanted to scuttle back to Willoughby Close and panic clean—her usual way of dealing with anxiety— even as she acknowledged she needed to keep going. Better to get it all over with in one go, even if it made her grit her teeth.

The wind continued to blow as Emily made her way up the street, past several postcard-perfect cottages of golden Cotswold stone, the trim done in the grey green that seemed de rigueur in this part of the country. Interspersed with the cottages were the local businesses: quaint buildings with bow windows and cute, hand-painted signs.

Steeling herself, Emily stepped into the first one on the left—a boutique pet shop that offered, of all things, a doggy bakery, as well as grooming services and, heaven help her, pet massages.

"Hello?" she called and an elegant, silver-haired woman stepped from the back of the shop, perfectly arced eyebrows raised in query.

"May I help?"

This time Emily was able to go through her patter clearly, and the woman listened with interest, thank heavens. She took the paperwork Emily offered with thanks, assuring her that Wychwood Waggy Tails would take part in the fundraiser, and promising a full array of dog biscuits, birthday cakes, and other canine treats. As she left, Emily breathed a sigh of relief at having one successful outing—and then kept going.

Fortunately, every shop owner she talked to was far friendlier and less alarming than Owen Jones. There was Verity Bryant, a young woman with long, dark hair, a hippy vibe, and a cheerful manner who ran a rather funky knitting shop with lots of colourful wool and psychedelic patterns; Eric Woodley, a dapper-looking gentleman in his forties whose pride and joy was his vintage clothing store, with a selection of 1950s Chanel that Emily duly admired; Joss Thornton, a former carpenter who ran a high-end toy shop where everything was either wooden, organic, or both, and very expensive; and Scarlett Day, who was in charge of a high-end charity shop that specialised in evening gowns, wedding dresses, and hats worthy of Ascot.

Everyone seemed delighted to take part, and rhapsodised about Henry and Alice and their fairy-tale romance. Owen Jones of The Drowned Sailor seemed to be a blessed anomaly.

Halfway up the street Emily saw Tea on the Lea, a cute teashop, and decided to duck in for a few moments' warmth and a cup of tea before asking the owner about participating in the fundraiser. She'd had more chitchat that morning than she usually had in a week or even in a month, and she needed some quiet.

A cluster of tiny, berry-like bells rang merrily on the door as Emily entered the warmth of the shop, and then she came to the counter to browse the offerings of freshly baked muffins.

"Hello, there." A round-faced woman with frizzy hair came out of the back, smiling as she dusted flour from her hands. "What can I get you?"

"A cup of tea and a blueberry muffin, please."

"Staying in?"

"Yes, please."

"Take any seat you like."

Emily murmured her thanks and chose a seat at a small table in the back. The shop was empty, which meant there would be no awkward eye contact or meaningless chitchat.

She could just relax, sip her tea, and work up her strength to tackle the rest of the high street, which included the new deli and the garden centre that was somewhere on the road to Burford.

Of course, she knew it didn't have to be as difficult as she was making it out to be. It probably wasn't for most people. If she'd got the hang of small talk early on, instead of needing to keep herself to herself, perhaps she wouldn't find this such a struggle.

But the fact was she did, and Emily didn't think she'd ever change. She wasn't sure she wanted to, even in Wychwood-on-Lea. She didn't need people the way most others seemed to; she'd had her mum, and that had always been enough. It still was.

"Here you go." The woman placed a teapot, cup, and a plate with a frilly doily and a muffin on Emily's table.

"Thank you—"

"You're not my new neighbour by any chance, are you?"

Emily, who had just reached for the teapot, put it down again. "Er…"

"Willoughby Close?"

So this was Olivia who lived in number four. Of course it was; Alice had said she ran a bakery. "I moved into number one, yes," Emily said as she rallied a smile. "So I suppose I am."

"Oh, how wonderful! I've been hoping to get some neighbours. They're lovely little cottages, but it's a bit lonely all on your own. You're Henry's new assistant?"

"Yes…"

"Welcome to Wychwood-on-Lea." Olivia reached for her hand, which Emily gave after a second's hesitation. "Sorry, your name…?"

"Emily. Emily David."

"Well, it's lovely to meet you. You must come over sometime for a meal or a glass of wine or whatever, really. Then I can welcome you properly."

"That's so kind…" Her standard response.

"You moved from London? How are you finding it?"

"Quiet," Emily said, and Olivia laughed. "And beautiful," she added quickly, not wanting to seem unappreciative of Wychwood-on-Lea's many charms. "It's all very…beautiful." She'd tried to think of another word and failed.

"Yes, it is. And people are very friendly. You'll have all sorts of invitations, I'm sure, don't you worry."

"That's…" Words failed her again. She didn't *want* people to be friendly. Invitations had always been something to dread. And yet, as she gazed at Olivia's smiling face and saw the first flicker of confused doubt enter her eyes, Emily truly wished she wasn't the way she was. Wouldn't it have been nice to enthuse along with Olivia, to reciprocate an invitation, to joke about things? It was how other people acted. She saw them, overheard their easy banter, and yet she knew it was all utterly beyond her, and always had been.

"Well, do let me know if you need anything," Olivia said, her smile faltering again, and Emily nodded.

"Yes, of course I will. Thank you so much."

Olivia retreated to the back room, and Emily gazed down at her tea and muffin, her appetite and enjoyment both ebbing away. Another awkward conversation, another person who looked disappointed.

It hadn't been like this in London. People didn't *try* so much there. Emily had managed to live her life, quiet and small as it was, with few complications and even fewer interactions. And she'd liked it that way. No one asking her about her life, or discovering what it was actually like. She certainly hadn't been as painfully aware of her own deficiencies as she was here, when her polite reserve seemed to throw everyone off, and made her wish she was different.

With a sigh she reached for the little teapot and began to pour. People would get used to her, she supposed. They would have to. It would just take a little time.

# Chapter Five

"NO IFS, ANDS, or buts. You *are* coming. At least for one glass of wine."

Judging from her mischievous smile and the way she was weaving slightly on Emily's doorstep, Harriet Lang had already had one glass, or perhaps several. Her air was determined, her eyes bright, as she gave Emily the look of a woman who knew how to boss people around, even when a bit tipsy. "It's your welcome to Wychwood," she stated grandly.

"That's very kind..." Emily said. She felt as if she'd said those words a million times already—because everyone *was* so kind. In the last three days, Olivia had made her a meal and left it on her doorstep with a bunch of bright daffodils; Alice and Henry had given her an enormous gift basket of local jams and chutneys and other delectable goodies; and now Harriet Lang, who used to live in number two, was inviting her out with a gaggle of other ex-residents for a drink, just as Alice had promised.

It looked like it was going to be hard to say no. Harriet

must have been briefed, because she'd launched into her invitation with the attitude of someone who expected resistance and was prepared to counter it with every means possible. It was seven o'clock on a Friday night at the end of her first week of work, and Emily had anticipated a night of Netflix. She was already wearing her fluffy socks.

"I'm not dressed properly," she said, giving a little, forced laugh. "I've already got into my pyjamas…"

"Then you can get out of them again," Harriet said with the firm cheer of a school matron. "I'm happy to wait. Ellie has to drive in from Oxford anyway, and she's only left half an hour ago. Really, it's fine. And we'll have *such* fun."

Emily seriously doubted that. An evening of drinks with a bunch of strangers who were already all good friends with one another? Nightmare times two. Times a *thousand*. She knew Alice had been arranging for this to happen, but she'd still hoped it would take too much organisation to get this many women together. Apparently it didn't.

"I'm not really a pub kind of person," she tried, but Harriet really wasn't having it.

"Nonsense. Everyone is a pub kind of person, at least once in a while."

"I'm really not." She had a visceral dread of going out with a bunch of chatty women who would ask her all sorts of questions and no doubt look at her askance for her quiet and invariably disappointing reserve.

"Well?" Harriet planted her hands on her hips, blocking

the doorway as if she thought Emily might make a run for it. "You'd better get your skates on." Her matronly manner softened a bit as she laid a hand on Emily's arm. "Really, it'll be fine. We don't bite, I promise. At least not often."

Which was so reassuring. Not. "I guess I'll get changed," Emily said weakly, and went upstairs. Her fingers were trembling as she slipped out of her comfy clothes and put on a pair of black cigarette trousers and a cowl-necked cashmere top in soft grey. She really didn't want to do this. When was the last time she'd gone out of an evening? She couldn't even remember.

She wasn't a complete Billy No Mates, she told herself as she ran a brush through her hair. She had a few friends from her uni days, work-focused introverts like her. They'd mostly just studied together, occasionally grabbed a quick meal. She saw them once every six months or so, if that; once she'd started at Ellis Investments, right after graduation, she'd focused on her job—and her mother—and let that be enough.

Now she tried to tell herself the evening wouldn't be so bad. If they were all friends, they'd chat to each other and she could fade into the background and be forgotten. Hopefully that was what would happen.

Back downstairs Harriet was wandering around the open-plan living area with obvious curiosity.

"You're not much of one for clutter, are you?" she remarked cheerfully. "I wish I could say the same. But with three children and a dog, my house seems forever in a state of mess. This is pretty." She nodded at a decorative glass bowl she'd picked up, putting it back on the coffee table with a clatter. "Shall we go?"

"Er, okay." Emily reached for her coat, unable to keep from glancing back at the bowl. Harriet had replaced it so it was no longer in the centre of the table, which wasn't a big deal—she knew that, of course—and yet…

It looked so *wrong*.

"Emily?" Harriet stood at the door, swathed in a pashmina, eyebrows raised.

"Coming." Quickly Emily moved the bowl back into the centre of the coffee table, breathing a little sigh of relief at the inherent rightness of it. She straightened and glanced back at Harriet, who was, of course, looking at her oddly. Whatever. It was her bowl. Her table. Her house.

This evening was going to be *awful*.

"Let's go," Emily said as brightly as she could and walked out of the cottage.

Several cars had pulled into the courtyard by the time Emily locked up. She managed to hang back in the shadows as everyone greeted each other like long-lost relatives, with exclamations and hugs and smacking kisses on the cheek. Emily held her bag to her chest, managing a smile when people looked her way.

She'd been introduced to everyone and the names had washed over her in an impossible-to-remember tide—Alice and Olivia, of course, and then Harriet; there was also Ava and Ellie, and they were all talking about people she didn't know—babies and children and husbands or boyfriends. Maybe dogs, as well, judging by some of the comments. Everyone seemed to have somebody in their lives, if not several, a happy and chaotic tangle of relationships that felt utterly foreign to Emily.

"Shall we walk into the village?" Ellie—or maybe it was Ava—suggested. "What's it to be, The Drowned Sailor or The Three Pennies?"

"Oh, I don't think I can bear another night at The Three Pennies," another woman said. Maybe that was Ava. She was gorgeous, with a long, tousled mane of golden-brown hair and a throaty voice that made her sound like a film star. "That place gets more stuck-up by the second."

"The Drowned Sailor it is, then," Harriet said cheerfully, marching in front of them all like a suffragette holding her banner.

The Drowned Sailor. Perfect. This already awkward evening was now potentially going to become even more torturous. Emily would most likely see Owen Jones, with his loud laugh and unsettling manner that had been flirty one second, vaguely hostile the next. Talking to him had felt like static electricity; she'd never known when she was going to get a shock. It had left her all weirdly tingly, too.

Emily trailed towards the back of the gregarious group as they headed down the darkened road towards the village.

The sun was setting but it had been raining all day and the sky was already dark and heavy with clouds, the air damp and cold. Emily pulled her coat more tightly around her as she ducked her head against the onslaught of a decidedly chilly wind, despite it being April in just a few days.

"Sorry if we're a bit overwhelming."

Startled, she glanced up to see one of the women had fallen in step beside her. This had to be Ellie, and she confirmed it with a shy smile.

"Ellie Venables. I used to live in number one, before I moved to Oxford."

"Oh...right." Emily tried to think of something else to say and couldn't. Her brain felt as if it were full of cotton wool.

"I moved with my husband Oliver and my daughter Abby," Ellie continued with a quiet kind of pride. Even in the midst of a dark and rainy night, Emily could see the love shining in her eyes, the happiness that surrounded her like a rosy bubble and radiated from her fingertips just as it had for Alice. "But it was a happy home for the two of us, for a little while. And Marmite too, of course. My dog."

"That's...nice." She sounded so *lame*. But she couldn't think of what else to say, and it *was* nice. Still, Emily felt her lack rather keenly as they continued to walk in a somewhat suffocated silence, and a burst of raucous laughter from the front of the group punctuated the quiet night.

"Are you missing London?" Ellie asked in a voice full of

sympathy. "All your friends?"

"I suppose," Emily managed. She felt like a fraud. "It's very different here."

"Yes it is, isn't it? I moved from Manchester, and you would have thought I'd come from the moon. Some of the la-di-da types looked at me as if I were an alien, at any rate, especially when they heard my accent." She laughed ruefully. "But you don't look as if you'd have that sort of problem." She gave a friendly nod towards Emily's camel-hair coat, not exactly the most sensible clothing option considering the rain, but Emily liked to be stylish. It was her protection.

"Oh, I don't know about that," she murmured. When she'd started at Ellis Investments, it had been important to look the part. And she loved the feel of nice clothes—the silkiness of a blouse, the heft of a good coat. Comforting somehow, and solid. Dependable in a way that people often weren't.

As Emily had continued to work and earn and she'd been able to build her wardrobe, she'd also liked the image she presented—someone who was in control, who had made it.

And yet, as she'd taken in Ellie's rueful smile just now, Emily knew the clothes were no more than a costume, a designer wardrobe hiding the deficiencies underneath. She suspected she was far more of an alien here than Ellie-from-Manchester ever could be, not that she'd ever admit it.

They'd reached the village green, The Drowned Sailor twinkling with friendly-looking lights on one end of it, and conversation was thankfully prohibited as they entered the crowded, noisy warmth of the pub and found a table in the back.

Harriet put herself in charge of amassing enough chairs and stools as everyone took off their coats, and Ava announced she'd spring for the first round of drinks.

"Red or white?" she asked the group.

"What about cocktails?" Harriet suggested, and Ava let out a surprisingly dirty laugh.

"Owen doesn't do cocktails, you git."

Harriet rolled her eyes. "Of course he doesn't."

"Why not one of each?" Ellie suggested mischievously. "Red and white? We're a big group, aren't we?"

"That we are," someone else agreed, and laughter and comments flew around as Emily perched on a stool in the corner and quietly tried to make herself invisible.

As the women continued to chatter and laugh, her gaze moved around the crowded pub. The Drowned Sailor did a brisk business on a Friday night—mostly men clocking off after shift work, by the looks of it, some with their significant others. Emily glanced at the bar and a frisson of something unexpected went through her as she saw Owen Jones standing behind it, just as he'd been when she'd come to this pub three days ago.

There was something weirdly magnetic about him, with that quick smile, the booming laugh she could hear even from across the noisy room. His hair was dark and curly, springing up in a wild thatch around a face that looked as if it had seen a few fights, with a nose that had been broken at least once, and an ear that must have got a bit mangled somehow. Although she couldn't see their colour from here, Emily remembered his eyes—a bright, laughing blue.

She watched as he pulled a pint, his biceps rippling with the smooth, assured movement. He had a tattoo all along one forearm, although she couldn't see what it was from across the room. He was built like a rugby player, or even a fridge—a wide, solid chest, firmly packed with muscle. He wasn't particularly tall, but he made up for it in power.

He glanced up from the pint, and to her horror his gaze snagged on hers, as if an invisible wire connecting them had just been yanked. She froze, as trapped as that poor, ubiquitous bunny in the headlights, and a small, slow smile tugged at his mouth as he kept looking. And she, foolish ninny that she was, kept staring.

Finally, after what felt like an absolute age, Emily managed to drag her gaze away. She felt shaky, weak and watery-kneed. What on earth had just happened?

She looked up again, but he'd moved on, his back to her as he did something at the till. When he turned around, his gaze was firmly focused on someone in front of the bar as he chatted and laughed, his gaze not flicking even once in her direction, which brought a swell of relief along with a ridiculous sense of disappointment that Emily could not bear to examine too closely.

She'd never had a proper boyfriend before, something that hadn't bothered her even if it sometimes felt a bit embarrassing to admit to at her age. Most people assumed she'd had loads of boyfriends; apparently it was the norm to be in and out of relationships as if you were trying on clothes, not that she had any idea.

When she was forced to make chitchat in the staffroom or in a shop, Emily usually got along with vague comments and murmurs, resting on the general assumption that yes, of course she'd had relationships. Of course she was just like everybody else.

Ava returned with the wine, passing around glasses and then topping them up, before her golden-brown gaze rested thoughtfully on Emily.

"And we have a special drink for our newbie," she said in a voice that carried much too far. The other women responded with a bevy of excited murmurs and questions.

"Champagne for Emily David." Ava brandished a flute full of bubbles with an arch look. "Owen was insistent."

"What?" Harriet swung round to face Emily, her narrowed gaze like a laser. "Are you keeping secrets? Do you know Owen, Emily?"

"No—that is, not really." Mortified, Emily felt a scorching blush sweep her cheeks. Damn Owen Jones, and damn his stupid champagne. She didn't even *like* the stuff. "I met him when I was canvassing for Willoughby Holidays, and the fundraiser we're arranging."

"Well he seemed to know you quite well," Ava remarked as she handed Emily the glass of champagne. "Insisted on opening a bottle just for you. Said it was compliments of the owner."

"Goodness, that's not like Owen, is it?" Harriet said speculatively.

"I didn't even think The Drowned Sailor did champagne," Olivia half joked, giving Emily a kindly smile. "I'm sure he just did it to be nice, since you're new."

"Yes, of—of course," Emily stammered. She wanted to believe Olivia was right, and yet she couldn't shake the feeling Owen Jones had been mocking her. She took a sip of the champagne, wincing at the bitter taste she'd never liked. Her gaze moved towards the bar of its own accord, and once again she locked eyes with Owen—he clocked the champagne in her hand and gave her a roguish wink. Emily immediately looked away, but Ava, she saw, had noted the entire exchange, and a cat-like smile curved her lips although thankfully she said nothing.

"Wait, Ava, are you actually drinking tonic water?" Harriet exclaimed, narrow-eyed, as Ava took a sip of the soft drink she'd also procured. "*Ava...*"

"No news of that ilk, so don't wet yourselves," Ava announced, holding up one slender hand. She was incredibly beautiful, in an uninhibitedly sexy way, her curvy figure poured into a V-neck sweater and a miniskirt with knee-length leather boots—a similar outfit to what Harriet was wearing, but Ava looked like a pin-up in it. "But yes, we are trying."

This announcement elicited a flurry of squeals and exclamations while Emily silently sipped her champagne, even though she wasn't particularly enjoying it.

"Oh, Ava, really?"

"Jace must be so excited—"

"How are you feeling about it?"

"So *trying*, huh?" This was said with a wink and a bawdy laugh, which caused everyone else to burst into another raucous round of giggles. Emily shrank back a little against the wall, curling her feet around the rungs of the stool. Hopefully no one would notice her now that their attention had moved on.

"So, *Emily*." Harriet turned an appraising eye on her, making her abandon that faint hope and shrink back even further even as she forced a smile. The laughter had subsided, and everyone turned to face her, falling into an expectant silence as they waited for Harriet to conduct her friendly interrogation. "How are you finding working with Henry now that he's loved up with Alice?"

Emily nearly wilted with relief. She could talk about *Henry*. "He does seem a bit softer," she allowed with a small smile, and this, amazingly, elicited another round of laughter and squeals. How were they not all exhausted, or have headaches?

"That's what true love does to you," Harriet pronounced

solemnly but with a wink in Alice's direction, who blushed becomingly. "Did you leave anyone special behind in London, Emily?"

Stupidly, Emily thought of her mother. "No, not really."

"Not *really?*" Ellie interjected with an encouraging smile. "Tell us more."

"Not at all," Emily clarified, her voice coming out a little sharp, like a discordant note in a melody. She saw the women exchange glances and her cheeks began to heat. "No boyfriend," she clarified needlessly, trying to smooth things over and feeling as if she'd failed. This was why she didn't do small talk. She sucked at it.

"Well, perhaps you'll meet someone here," Ava purred, smoothing over the moment in a way Emily hadn't been able to. "Owen's single, and he just sent you an entire bottle of champagne."

"Owen?" Harriet said dubiously, and Ava raised her eyebrows.

"What? Owen Jones is a looker, even if he's not your type, and he's lovely, as well." Ava turned back to Emily. "Don't you think he's handsome, admittedly in a rough-and-ready sort of way?"

"Er..." Emily felt herself blush, and of course everyone noticed.

"Look at her!"

"Ooh, you do like him, don't you, Emily? He *can* be quite lovely..."

"Owen Jones," Harriet repeated in the same dubious tone as before.

"I think you're the one who fancies him, Harriet," Ellie teased.

"Well, Emily certainly does," Ava said with a kindly smile. "I used to work here a lifetime ago. I'll put a word in."

"Oh, don't, don't," Emily said in an impassioned voice, before she could help herself or think better of it. "Please don't," she added, as if she needed more emphasis. Everyone was staring in a horrible mixture of pity and shock.

"Of course I won't," Ava said after a moment, her tone horribly gentle. "I was just teasing."

They'd all been just teasing, of course they had, and Emily hadn't been able to take it. She should have laughed and played along, and instead she felt near tears. She was so *stupid*.

Emily blinked rapidly, trying to recover her composure. Foolishly, she found herself looking at Owen again; he was leaning on the bar, elbows firmly planted, a kindly smile curving his mouth as he chatted to an old geezer in a flat cap and waxed jacket.

"We really are just teasing," Harriet assured her in a kindlier tone. "But Ava's right. Owen is lovely. Salt of the earth, although if I'm honest…" She frowned as her speculative gaze scanned Emily from top to toe. "I don't know if he's your type."

"Whose type is he, then?" someone else returned with a

laugh, and Harriet shrugged.

"I don't know. I just think he might be a bit rough around the edges for our Emily. She's quite the fashion plate." This was said in a friendly tone, but Emily wasn't sure how to take it, or the *our Emily*.

Somehow she'd been subsumed into this tribe, and she had no idea how it had happened. She certainly hadn't put forth any effort, and in any case she wasn't sure she wanted to be included in this group of raucous, well-meaning women. They were far too overwhelming and invasive, and the evening had barely started. Already she had a headache, *and* she'd embarrassed herself, and the champagne she drunk was swirling sourly in her stomach.

"I think I'll just nip to the loo," she said, managing a smile directed at everyone and no one in particular, and she slipped off her stool and hurried to the back of the bar.

She didn't actually need to go to the loo, but the moment of quiet in the tiny cupboard of a toilet was a blessed relief. Emily ran cool water over her wrists and then pressed her hands to her hot cheeks. She *was* blushing. How soon could she go home? Why did she feel as if she could cry?

Everything about this evening—*everything*—had been outside of her comfort zone of routine and solitude. The women's loud chatter, their knowing looks, their ease and familiarity...and Olivia hadn't even put her glass of wine on the beer mat! Emily had watched a ring of condensation form on the table and struggled not to lean over and put the glass where it belonged.

And then of course there was Owen Jones, sending her an entire bottle of champagne, and everyone wondering what it meant, and just the sheer *presence* of him, even from across the bar, and the way her gaze kept straying to him even when she didn't want it to.

She was so, so out of her depth, in so many ways.

Taking a deep breath, Emily gazed at her reflection in the tiny square of mirror, grimacing at the glazed look of panic in her eyes. It was already nearing nine o'clock. Surely she'd put in her time and could make her excuses now?

Deciding on exactly that plan, Emily headed back out to the pub. As she shouldered her way through the crowded room, trying not to actually *touch* anybody, she saw that her newfound friends all had their heads together. As she approached the group, she heard Harriet's carrying voice.

"Well, she is a bit standoffish, isn't she? I suppose it's coming from London."

"Oh, Harriet, you've got a chip on your shoulder about snobs, since you used to be one yourself."

"I didn't actually *say* she was a snob."

"You implied it—"

"She does dress well, doesn't she?"

"I think she's just shy…"

"Shy! With that look of hers that could freeze boiling water?"

"Let's give her a chance—"

"I *am* giving her a chance. I just think she's a bit of a cold fish, that's all."

Emily couldn't bear to hear any more. She whirled around, plunging through the crowd she'd just manoeuvred through, heedless this time of whom she jostled or bumped.

The door to the toilet wouldn't open, and she jiggled the handle uselessly for a fraught second until a gruff voice called out, "Oi! It's occupied, all right?"

"*Oh...*" Emily took a step backward, horrified at herself, feeling like some desperate creature in flight, without thought or care. She glanced back and saw that the women at the table were looking around for her; had someone realised she'd overheard them? The thought of a painfully awkward apology of a conversation made her feel even more desperate, and so when she saw a narrow corridor leading towards the back, she raced down it without a thought.

It led to a small, dank square of courtyard where the wheelie bins were kept, hardly the escape she was looking for, but at least it was a place to hide. At some point she'd need to go back into the pub, but she couldn't think about that just yet.

She couldn't think about any of it—all the things they'd said, the way they'd picked apart her personality, or seeming lack of it. Tears stung her eyes and fiercely she blinked them back. She wasn't going to let it bother her. She'd learned long ago not to care about other people's opinions.

But no matter about that, because right now it *hurt*.

A clatter at the door had her stiffening and then shrinking against the damp brick wall as she blinked in the gloom, drawing in an unfortunately audible gasp when she saw who had come into the courtyard with a plastic bin full of empty bottles.

Owen.

# Chapter Six

OWEN HEARD HER before he saw her—a quick, breathy gasp, a sound of fear. He squinted in the sodium-lit gloom of the courtyard, looking for the source of the sound.

A sniff had him turning around, and then he saw her, shrinking into the shadows, a look of fear, no, *terror*, on her face.

Emily David.

"What the blazes are you doing back here?"

She straightened, eyes flashing so Owen thought he must have imagined that look of fear. "I just wanted some air."

"People who want air usually go out front." He'd meant to sound friendly but somehow he didn't. Goodness, but this woman rubbed him raw, especially when she was looking down her nose at him as she was now.

"I'm sorry not to stick to the norm." Now she sounded positively frosty.

"It's a bit manky back here, that's all." Balancing the bin on his hip, he raked his hand through his hair, expelling a quick breath. "Everything all right?"

"Why shouldn't it be?"

"Sorry." Owen dumped the empties into the recycling bin. Then he wiped his hands on the tea towel tucked into the waistband of his jeans before he turned back to his unexpected guest. "I just thought something must have happened, to have you cowering back here."

"I'm not *cowering*. You just startled me."

Owen planted his hands on his hips as he surveyed her, or as much as he could see of her in the dark.

"So what happened?" he asked. "Did someone hit on you? Because I can have a word—"

"What?" Emily looked shocked and even disgusted by such a suggestion. "No, of course not."

Of course not? She was a beautiful woman in a rowdy pub. Owen wouldn't have been surprised if every geezer in the place hadn't taken notice of her. He certainly had, when they'd seen each other across the room. He'd forgotten how beautiful she was, prissy or not, with her hair falling about her shoulders in soft brown waves, her slate-coloured eyes fringed with luxuriant lashes. She was wearing a jumper that was soft and clinging, and she looked far more approachable than she had the other day, with her briefcase and business suit, although she certainly seemed prickly as hell right now.

"So what are you doing back here?" he asked. He took a step closer to her, and saw the tears sparkling in her lovely blue-grey eyes. The sight of them made some vital organ inside him twist in a way he hadn't expected. He could be a softie, yes, but that was usually with kids and dogs. Old people, too. Not a sexy, prickly woman who had looked down her nose at him the last time they'd met, and was still trying to now. "What's wrong?" he asked, his voice full of a gentleness he hadn't meant to feel, never mind reveal.

"Nothing's wrong." Again with the affront, as if he was insulting her. "Like I said, I just needed some air."

Riiight. Owen didn't believe that for a second, but he had a feeling getting information out of Emily David was akin to blood from a stone, and really, quite similar. There was something cold and closed-off about her that he didn't entirely understand, but he still got the message loud and clear. *Back off.*

"You don't have to tell me if you don't want to," he told her with a shrug. "But if someone in my pub has done something they shouldn't have, I'd like to know about it."

"It's nothing like that." She let out a huff of sound that he supposed was meant to be a laugh but wasn't.

"What it's like, then?" Because clearly something had happened, even if she didn't like to say, and prickly or not, Emily David was hurting and Owen wanted to help her. More than he should do, perhaps, considering how prissy she was. Totally not his type, not that he was even letting himself think that way.

"Nothing, really. And in any case, it's not your concern." She straightened, giving him what he suspected was meant to be a quelling look, but she couldn't quite manage it. "I should go back in." She sounded as if she'd rather stick an oyster fork in her eyeball.

"You don't have to," Owen replied. "There's a gate over there." He nodded towards the far wall. "It leads out to a lane behind the green, by the river. If you need a getaway."

She looked tempted, her teeth sinking into her lower lip in a way that made Owen want to groan. Did she not realise how alluring she was? He had a feeling she didn't, which seemed crazy. Most women as gorgeous as Emily David were well aware of it. Take his former barmaid, Ava. She knew the precise nature of her charms, and used them to full, laughing effect. Owen had been immune, but his friend Jace Tucker hadn't, and now he and Ava were happily married.

But Emily wasn't anything like Ava. Ava was tough and knowing, while something about Emily seemed fragile. Breakable.

"I can't just leave," she finally said, her voice filled with regret. "It would be rude. Besides, I left my bag out there."

"I could get your bag." Who, he wondered, was she afraid of? Belatedly Owen remembered who he'd seen her with—a bunch of relative newcomers to the village—Ava, Harriet Lang, and a couple of others. Not the handsy date as he'd been half-envisioning. "What happened, anyway?"

"Nothing. I'm being ridiculous." With an elegantly manicured finger she dabbed the corner of her eye. "I need to go back in. I know that." She let out a shuddery sigh that made Owen want to give her a hug. He didn't think that would go over well. She had "Do Not Touch" practically tattooed on her forehead.

"They're not a bad lot," he said, feeling for the words as if through the dark. "A bit noisy and nosy, perhaps, but that's it. They won't bite."

She gave another one of those huffs. "That's what they said. And I know they won't. It's not that."

"What, then?"

A quick, darting look at him before she shook her head. "Never mind. It doesn't matter."

"It must do—"

She shook her head, her gaze on the damp, rather grimy slates below. "I heard them talking about me," she said in a low voice he strained to hear.

Oh. Owen struggled for something to say. He really wasn't good with this kind of thing, but because of the look of naked vulnerability on Emily's face, he thought he'd give it a try.

"I'm sure they meant well."

"They said I was a cold fish." He was silent, and she glared up at him, blinking rapidly. "You agree with them."

"Of course I don't. I don't know you well enough to say." Although as an initial assessment, there might be a grain or two of truth in the statement…

"It doesn't matter," she dismissed, sounding as if she were caught between anger and hurt. "I *am* a cold fish, and I don't even care." This was said with a touch of belligerence that made Owen hold up his hands in a peace-making gesture.

"Okay."

"I really don't care. I never did."

"I believe you." Although he wasn't actually sure he did, if her defiant tone was anything to go by.

She drew another breath, and then straightened, a haughty look coming over her face that reminded Owen of when she'd first entered the pub a few days ago, with butter never melting in her mouth. "Never mind. Thank you for your offer."

"It still stands."

"I'm not going to be rude." Her lips trembled and she pressed them together. "You're probably right. They do mean well."

She looked so impossibly vulnerable that Owen had an ache inside, as if someone had punched a fist into his gut. How could a woman be so prissily composed and yet look so unbearably sad? How could she be coolly distant and yet seem so heartrendingly fragile?

It made Owen want to...protect her. Something she un-doubtedly would not appreciate. And something he didn't really want to do. He didn't have a good track record with protecting people.

"All right, then. If you're sure."

"I am." She moved forward, and Owen, realising he was blocking the door, moved to the side at the same time she did, so they were engaged in one of those awkward little shuffles until Emily stepped forward and Owen didn't move, and he had to grab her by the shoulders to keep her from ploughing into his chest.

The second he touched her he felt as if he'd come alive, a hot wire in his hands, pulsing through his blood. The strength of his feeling, his undoubted, impossible-to-ignore physical attraction, shocked him. Yes, she was beautiful, no question, and he always appreciated a good-looking woman, but *this…*

This felt like something else entirely. Something mind-blowing, life-altering, a force both outside of and inside himself that was taking him over in an instant, like a whirl-wind had just whipped through the courtyard. Through him.

*What the hell…?*

❆

HAD SHE BEEN electrocuted?

Emily went stock-still as Owen's hands remained clasped on her shoulders. He was staring at her in blank incomprehension, and Emily felt as if she might be staring back the same way. Although in all honesty she had no idea how she looked. How she felt. The whole evening had been an impossible swirl of tangled emotion.

His hands were warm on her shoulders, his palms strong and sure, the heat of them burning through her jumper, branding her skin.

This was *ridiculous*. She didn't ever feel this way. She couldn't now. She wouldn't even know how. Besides, Owen Jones was completely not her type, if she had a type, which she didn't. But if she did, it wouldn't be this. Him.

*Him...*

His face was close, closer than it had been even a second ago, so she could see the dark stubble on his decidedly firm jaw, the sweep of his surprisingly long and lush lashes as they hid his blue, blue eyes from her view. She'd tilted her head to look up at him, her lips parting, her mind spinning, her heart beating. Everything going at once, a kaleidoscope of motion inside her, a whirl of feeling.

"*Well.*" His voice was caught between a thrum and a growl, and it made her shiver, an impossible-to-suppress ripple going through her that she knew he felt. His hands tightened on her shoulders. Emily's eyes widened as her heart thudded so hard it hurt.

Was he actually going to kiss her? Right here, right now? It was absurd. Impossible. She couldn't even imagine it happening, and yet...

She wanted it to. At least, part of her did. This crazy, racing, out-of-control part of herself that she'd never encountered before, because she'd never let herself be out of control. Not once. Not ever.

Not now.

"*Don't...*" The word was barely whispered, so half-hearted a child could have seen through it, but it had the desired effect. At least, the effect she'd intended it to have, desired or not.

Owen dropped his hands from her shoulders as if she'd burned him and he took a step back. And then another. A cool, composed look had come over his face, making him suddenly seem very remote, and reminding her that she did not know this man at all, and he probably didn't even like her. He certainly hadn't acted as if he had the last time they'd met.

They stared at each for an endlessly uncertain moment; Emily could not think of a single thing to say, and yet she had the weird urge not to end it. She didn't want to walk away.

Then Owen gave a little bow, gesturing for her to go ahead of him, back inside, down the narrow little corridor into the pub. Away from him.

Emily swallowed. She opened her mouth to say something—but what? She'd already said enough. Now that her brain was beginning to function, she realised she'd said far too much. All that nonsense about them talking about her, and being a cold fish...

He must have thought she was ridiculous. Pathetic.

She closed her mouth. Swallowed again. And then she hurried back into the pub, scurrying in her sudden need to escape Owen Jones and all she'd said to him.

"Emily." Harriet looked genuinely anxious as she half-rose from her seat when Emily approached the table. "We were getting worried…"

"About to send out a search party," Ava chimed in with a sympathetic smile. Did she realise Emily had overheard their conversation? Did they all know? Perhaps they'd been talking about that, too.

"Sorry, I just got into a conversation with someone," Emily said, meeting no one's eyes as she sat on her stool in the corner and then glugged the rest of her champagne; someone had poured her another glass from Owen's bottle. She should have thanked him for that, she realised. She hadn't even mentioned it. Her heart was still racing, and in her mind's eye she could still see Owen's face, so close to hers.

*Had* he been going to kiss her? Or was that just the lamentable figment of what had never before been an overactive imagination?

She had to stop thinking about it. Now.

The conversation kick-started again, and Emily made do with murmurs of interest as Ellie talked about her daughter Abby, and Ava about her toddler son, and Harriet about her husband Richard's new job teaching history in a comprehensive near Oxford. Everyone seemed so happy, brimming with life and love and possibility, that Emily didn't need to make much effort, just as she'd once hoped. It seemed everyone had, by complicit agreement or not, decided to leave her alone…which was just how she wanted it.

Wasn't it?

Of course it was.

At half past ten they finally settled up at the bar, and Emily trailed behind, not wanting to meet Owen's eye. She'd refused to look towards the bar even once since coming back from the courtyard, but as Harriet settled the bill, her gaze snagged on Owen and he gave her a wink that everyone could see. Odious man. Odious, impossible, attractive man. Emily pursed her lips and looked away.

Outside the air was still and cold as they began to totter back to Willoughby Close. As no one was in a fit state to drive, they'd made arrangements to sleep over at each other's houses, something that amazed Emily.

They were like little girls planning a slumber party, something she'd never experienced, of course. But still. It boggled her mind that women her age—and even older— could be so friendly and affectionate, wrapping their arms around each other's shoulders as they planned who would sleep where.

If she'd been feeling left out before, she felt even more so now, but of course that wasn't how she was feeling at all, because she didn't even *want* to be included.

Still, it was with a tumult of uneasy feelings that Emily finally made her farewells; Harriet threw her arms around her and mumbled some sort of apology, and Ellie squeezed her hand and said they would have to get together for a coffee soon. Ava gave her another one of her knowing yet sympathetic looks, and Alice smiled shyly. They really were all lovely, and being with them made Emily ache even as she longed to get away.

She breathed out a gusty sigh of relief when she'd finally closed the door of number one behind her, and the quiet peace of her cottage surrounded her. She gazed round the small, neat space, everything in its place, and tried to feel that sense of reassurance and safety that was so important to her.

*Owen. Owen Jones.*

No. She couldn't think about him. Couldn't remember what she'd wittered on about, or how he'd held her by the shoulders, and how, for several heart-stopping moments, she'd really thought he was going to kiss her.

What if he *had* kissed her? Emily had been kissed before. She wasn't that much of a naïve twit. She'd gone to a party in uni and let a bloke chat her up and then kiss her, quite a sloppy affair, just to see what the fuss was about.

In her last year, during a study session, a geeky friend of hers had blurted his true feelings to her, and shocked, Emily had let him kiss her and fumble at her clothes, feeling weirdly distanced from it all. They'd both drawn back before it had gone very far, embarrassed by the whole thing, and the next time she'd seen him they'd been back to being friends.

Then, her third and last experience had been at a leaving do for another assistant at Ellis Investments a couple of years ago. Emily had been chivvied along to a posh wine bar, and a man had chatted her up and then followed her back to the loo when she'd excused herself. He'd been so suave that Emily had found herself pressed up against the wall before she'd even realised what was going on. He'd been an accomplished kisser, and something about the sureness of his manner had weirdly thrilled her, until he'd cupped her cheek and she'd felt the cold, hard metal band of his wedding ring.

All told, it wasn't much physical experience, but then she'd never really been interested in gaining any to begin with. She really was a cold fish.

With another sigh, Emily moved away from the door. The evening hadn't been a complete disaster, she told herself, even though she suspected it had. In any case, most of those women she probably wouldn't see again, no matter what they'd promised.

Ellie lived in Oxford, and Ava was busy with her husband and son, and Harriet sounded like she was the chair of every village committee going. Judging by some of the remarks made, Olivia worked about eighteen hours a day in her teashop, and with Alice she'd already developed a manageable routine of coffee in the kitchen.

It was fine. Yet as she undressed, folding her clothes neatly as she always did, lining her shoes up by the door, it didn't feel fine. Everything about her carefully ordered world felt just a little jumbled, like a picture frame that was only slightly askew. No one else might notice it, but Emily would, and it would eat and eat at her until she straightened it.

As she lay in bed and stared up at the ceiling, all the little remarks and looks of the evening had the same effect. Ava's sympathetic smile. Harriet's bluster. Ellie's attempt at getting to know her. Each one felt like a pinprick, or a little push, making her feel off-balance and antsy.

And then she thought again about Owen, and it was as if that picture frame fell right off the wall. What if he'd kissed her? How would she have responded? Would it have ended there, in the grimy little courtyard, a quick buss of the lips, or would it have been something more, something swoon-worthy, a scene stolen from a rom com?

Would he have—what? Emily couldn't even begin to imagine what Owen might have actually done, if she hadn't told him to stop. Asked her on a date? Or even to go home with him that evening? How did real life *work*?

She didn't know. And for the first time the not knowing, a lifetime of deliberate and necessary ignorance, bothered her. The unhappy weight of it made her close her eyes and will herself to sleep, if only to stop thinking about Owen Jones.

# Chapter Seven

EMILY WOKE ONCE more to watery sunlight filtering through the crack in her curtains and the sweet trill of birdsong. It was half-past seven in the morning, late for her, and she had a whole, empty day ahead of her.

She lay in bed, her eyes closed as she enjoyed the warmth of the sunshine on her face, and wondered how she was going to fill up her day. In London, she'd had a schedule for Saturdays. A routine. Wake up, have her first cup of coffee, exercise, shower, dress. Household jobs all morning—dust, Hoover, laundry. Food shopping in the afternoon, plus any other errands she might need to run, and then in the evening she'd read a book or watch a film.

Once in a very blue moon an old friend from uni would ask her out for a drink or meal, and she'd go, because it gave her the illusion of having a social life and it was nice to see people occasionally. Sometimes she'd go to the park or a museum, stroll quietly by herself, drinking in the scenery.

She supposed she could follow the same sort of schedule here, although the lack of commute meant she'd come home from work early enough to keep on top of the washing and housework so she didn't need to catch up on the weekend. Still, a blitz around the downstairs never went amiss, and she could wash her bed sheets, as well.

What an exciting day she had planned. The sarcastic thought surprised her, because heaven knew, she'd never needed excitement before. Never craved it in the least, after the wild tumult of her childhood. But right now, for the first time, she wasn't looking forward to a day of routine housework, soothing as that had so often been.

It wasn't until she swung her legs over the side of the bed, feet hitting the floor, that the events of last night tumbled back through her brain. How could she have forgotten for a moment? All those women...Harriet's cold fish comment...and Owen Jones. Him, most of all.

Of course a tiny tussle in the courtyard was no major news to him. An almost-kiss might have rocked her world, but for a man like Owen Jones, it was barely a blip on the radar. The thought brought that unsettling mix of relief and disappointment. What did she actually *want*?

It was not a question Emily had ever had to grapple with before, because she'd always been very clear about what she wanted. Safety. Security. Order. Routine.

It was time to get a start on her day, and regain all those things.

Two hours later Emily had exercised, eaten, showered, and dressed, and was spritzing all the surfaces downstairs with lavender cleaning spray when her doorbell rang. Yet another well-meaning neighbour? How many could there *be*?

When she opened the door, it wasn't any of the women she'd met last night, however, but rather a man—possibly the most good-looking man she'd ever seen. He had chocolate-brown hair flopping over his forehead, eyes the colour of whisky already glinting in amusement, and a slow, sexy smile that curved his unabashedly sculpted lips. Emily just stared.

"You must be Emily."

"Yes…"

"I'm Jace Tucker, Ava's husband." Now that made sense. Looks wise, Ava and Jace were perfectly matched. He stuck out a hand, and Emily shook it.

"Nice to meet you," she said formally, although she had no idea why he was here.

Jace slid his hands in the back pockets of his faded jeans, that slow smile of his seeming just as knowing as Ava's had been last night. They really were a pair. "Ava mentioned you'd just moved in and I thought I'd come by and check everything was all right. I'm the caretaker here, so if anything's not going the way it should be, you can let me know. I'll give you my mobile number."

"Oh. All right." Emily hesitated. "Do you…do you want to come in?"

"Sure."

She stepped aside and he ambled in, taking in the sparsely furnished downstairs with one lazy sweep of his gaze.

Emily fetched her phone and then dutifully typed in the contact details Jace gave her.

"Thank you," she said when she'd finished, but Jace didn't move. He nodded towards the living area of the cottage.

"If you'd like a few more chairs or things, I've got some in one of the barns."

"Oh…" She glanced at the single sofa and coffee table stood in the centre of the room on their own. It did look a bit like a downmarket Airbnb, but her flat in London had been tiny. "Well, I don't know if I'd need them, really. It's just me here." She hadn't meant that to sound as woebegone as it did, but Jace just nodded.

"All right, then."

He made to move, and something—Emily had no idea what—made her blurt, "Actually, I suppose I could take a look at them. If you don't mind. Just in case."

"I don't. Now a good time?"

It was only ten o'clock in the morning, the day stretching emptily in front of her in a way it never had before. "Okay," she said.

Five minutes later they were in the front of Jace's messy truck, several paper coffee cups crammed in the drinks holder, and a week's worth of junk mail on the floor of the passenger side.

"Sorry," Jace said with a lopsided smile, sounding rather unrepentant. "It's a bit of a mess."

"That's okay." Emily knew she sounded stiff, but the truck was a *tip*. She edged her foot away from a browning banana peel and after a few seconds of agony she righted a coffee cup that had been slotted into the drinks holder at a terribly awkward angle. How did people *live* like this?

"Bit of a neat freak, are you?" Jace remarked as she bent down to put the junk mail into an ordered pile.

"I like order," Emily allowed, and he laughed.

"All that post is going right in the bin. I just haven't got round to it yet."

"Obviously." He laughed again, and Emily smiled. It felt surprisingly nice to chat like this. It almost felt like banter, although she supposed it wouldn't for most people.

Jace had driven away from Willoughby Close, towards the manor, but then he turned off to the left, down a dirt track that cut through the wood. After a few bone-juddering moments, he pulled up in front of an old stone barn that looked as if it had been there since the Middle Ages.

"This is all the bits and pieces from the manor that nobody has wanted," he warned as he unlocked one of the big wooden doors and began to push it open. "And most of it isn't in the greatest shape. But you can have what you like."

"Thank you." Emily doubted she'd take any of it. She was more about modern, clean lines, things that were new and bright and dust and germ-free. She didn't know why she'd agreed to come at all, except perhaps for the company. Because for the first time, a day spent on her own had seemed just a little bit lonely.

Still, she thought she ought to give the furniture a good look, for Jace's sake, although the pieces stacked willy-nilly in the dim, shadowy barn looked far too big and ornate for her cottage.

She wandered through the jumbled stacks while Jace waited by the doors, arms folded, one booted foot crossed over the other.

"Alice and Henry didn't want any of this?" she asked, and Jace shrugged.

"I don't think so, but actually this lot was put in here long before they came. This was from back in Lady Stokeley's time."

"Henry's aunt."

"Madam." There was a wealth of affection in Jace's voice. "She died over a year ago now. She was the lady of the manor, all right."

"You make her sound like a character."

"She was. Knew her own mind, shall we say, right to the end."

"And she didn't want any of this?"

"I suppose not. So, anything take your fancy?" Jace asked and Emily was about to apologise and say she didn't think so, when she stopped in front of an old rocking chair. Although it was covered in dust, she could still see the fine grain of the wood, the delicately carved swirls and scrollwork on the handles and back. It was a beautiful piece of furniture, a chair meant to be sat in and savoured, and it made her strangely sad to think of it languishing out here.

"You like that one?" Jace asked.

"Oh, I don't know…" She didn't have any need of a rocking chair, certainly, and it was so *dirty*. And yet…an old memory, like a frayed string, tugged at her mind. *Goodnight nobody…*

For a single second, like a time warp, Emily was a child again, her mother's arm warm and solid around her shoulders. They were sitting on a chair—had it been a rocking chair? Or had it just been in the story? *And a quiet old lady who was whispering "hush."* And Emily had felt warm and safe and happy.

"Emily?" Jace's voice, a low murmur, had her blinking. She had one hand resting on the rocking chair, mindless of the dust for once.

"Sorry. I was away with the fairies there for a second, I think."

"So I'll bring the chair?" Jace was already reaching for it. The memory had gone, dissolved like morning mist, and all Emily saw was a dusty old chair that needed some serious cleaning.

"Oh, I don't know…"

"I'll bring it," Jace said decisively, and with one expert tug he'd released it from the tottering pile of furniture without dislodging anything else and was carrying it out to the truck. Emily followed him hesitantly. The chair really was very dirty. She'd clean it, of course, but still…

She'd just reached the door of the barn, Jace ahead of her, when a small, pathetic meow stopped her in her tracks.

"*Oh…*" A tiny kitten, black with marmalade stripes, was crouching at the bottom of a stack of furniture, its ears pricked, its expression wary. "Jace," she called as she bent down to it. "Did you know there's a kitten in here?"

Andromeda aside, she'd never been much of an animal lover, but the kitten looked so small and helpless. She wasn't going to touch it, of course, although its fur did look rather soft.

"That must be one of Trixie's." Jace propped one arm against the doorframe. "She's Willoughby's barn cat, completely feral but likes to make her home out here. I knew she'd had kittens but I didn't realise she'd put them in here."

"What's going to happen to them?"

Jace shrugged. "They'll be all right, feral like her. She'll abandon them, most likely, when they're a bit older, to fend for themselves."

"Abandon them!" Emily couldn't keep a note of horrified dismay from her voice. "But they're so *little*. Surely you can do something?"

Jace shrugged again. "What can I do? They're not tame. They won't be caught or trained. Most likely they'll fend for themselves…or not."

"But they're only small." Emily heard the tremble of emotion in her voice and wondered at it. She was just talking about a kitten, right? She had to be. "They need care."

"They're pretty adept at taking care of themselves. But feel free to help yourself to one, if you like. Try to tame it, if you can."

A pet of her own? Emily drew back. "Oh, I couldn't."

Jace nodded. "I wouldn't worry too much about them, at any rate. They'll do all right."

"So…you just have cats wandering around the property?"

"Well, we're not flooded with the creatures, if that's your worry," he answered with a laugh. "Truth be told, if Ava gets wind of the kittens, she'll probably want one herself. Olivia too, maybe, and Alice, as well. Although I reckon it won't be easy to catch the little blighters." He nodded towards the spot where Emily had spied the kitten. "He's gone back into hiding already."

The kitten was nowhere to be seen, and Emily struggled to suppress the little pang of loss that caused. "I suppose we should get back," she said slowly, and Jace started to pull the door shut. Emily ducked out before he'd closed it, giving one last glance to the shadowy piles of furniture. "Can the cats get out of the barn if you lock it?" she asked a bit anxiously, and Jace gave her one of his slow, sure smiles.

"Don't you worry. They can get in and out of just about anywhere."

Back at Willoughby Close, Jace brought the rocking chair, dust and all, into Emily's cottage, making her wince.

She needed to clean it *immediately*.

"While I'm here," he said as he was about to leave, "Ava wanted to invite you to dinner next weekend. We're having a few locals over—Olivia and Simon, maybe one or two others. Seven o'clock, Sunday night."

"Oh…" There was no way, Emily realised, she could make an excuse. Jace wasn't even waiting for a reply; he'd just assumed she'd show up.

"We live in the caretaker's cottage, through the woods on the right, off the main drive up to the manor. Follow the path till it ends. Bring a torch. And you might want to wear wellies. It's rained a fair bit."

"Oh. Right." He nodded and turned to leave, and belatedly Emily blurted, "Thank you. For everything."

"No trouble."

And then he was gone, and Emily was alone again, but this time with a dusty, dirty rocking chair. She glanced at it, wondering why she'd been so taken with it, and why she'd allowed Jace to bring it back for her. It really wasn't her style at all, and the dust and dirt alone would normally have her shuddering. And yet…

*Goodnight mittens. And goodnight kittens…*

That little marmalade-striped kitten *had* been cute. She hoped it would be okay on its own. It was so little to have to fend for itself, its mother obviously not interested…

She was making this way too personal, Emily realised. It was a *kitten*. And she needed to clean up this chair.

She dusted it first, wiping it down with damp paper towel, admiring the gleam of wood revealed once the dust had been removed. What the chair really needed was a good polish, maybe with some beeswax… The prospect of restoring the chair to its former glory made her smile. She could put it upstairs, by her bedroom window. She pictured herself sitting in it in the evening, watching the stars come out like diamond pinpricks, and was cheered, even as the image filled her with a restless melancholy.

*Goodnight mush…*

Emily bundled all the dirty paper towels into the bin, and then washed her hands and arms up to the elbows before she decided to ring her mother, just to check in. But when she called Fiona's number, it rang on and on, as it often did, and Emily tried not to let it feed her anxiety. They were most likely just out…

Outside the sky was a dank grey, a few raindrops spattering indifferently against the window. Impulsively in a way she normally wasn't, Emily dialled her father's number.

"Em? Everything all right?" He sounded worried, which was understandable, since she normally only called him when something had happened with her mum.

"Yes, everything's fine. I think. Mum's still living in Camden Town, with Fiona."

"Oh, right…" This was said vaguely, because her father did not keep tabs on his ex-wife the way Emily did, something else that was understandable since they'd been divorced for nineteen years. Yet it still made Emily feel a stirring of resentment, a kernel of bitterness that had rooted right down in her soul nearly twenty years ago and kept growing, little by little, with every tired sigh or disinterested remark.

"I am concerned that she's not taking her medication, though, Dad."

Her father sighed, predictably. "It's up to her whether to take it or not, Emily. You know that. She's a grown woman."

"Yes, I do know that, of course." They'd had this conversation, or one like it, too many times. "But she doesn't do well off her medication. *You* know that." Although perhaps he didn't—not really. Her father had been almost completely uninvolved three years ago, when Naomi had gone off her medication, had a psychotic episode, and been sectioned for eight weeks. Geoff David hadn't even rung Emily once, to check how she was coping, never mind Naomi. She'd left him a voicemail and he'd texted back "hope you're okay."

Emily decided to try a different tack. "You know I've moved...?" she said, and Geoff made a noncommittal noise.

"Have you? A new flat...?"

She realised she hadn't even told him about her job, or her move to the Cotswolds, which was telling, really. She didn't tell her father much, but then there usually wasn't much to tell. "No, I've moved to a village about an hour outside of London. Wychwood-on-Lea. I'm working for Henry Trent's new charitable foundation."

"Henry Trent...?"

Her father didn't even remember the name of her boss. It wasn't his fault—not really. They'd just never had that sort of relationship even though they'd both tried, at least a little bit, at the beginning, after her parents had divorced and her father had seemed, briefly, as if he wanted to keep in touch with his only child. Before he'd got new ones.

"My boss," Emily said tiredly. "Why don't I give you my new contact details?" Not that her father ever wrote or rang.

"That's a good idea," he said with the first hint of enthusiasm. Her father, like her, was a man of details and order. Why he'd married Naomi, who had to be one of the most chaotic people alive, Emily had never understood.

"You could visit," she suggested suddenly, once she'd given him her new address. "Bring Amy and Jasper even, if you liked."

"Oh, well." Her father sounded surprised; she'd never suggested such a thing before. She'd only met Amy and Jasper a couple of times, awkward encounters with her father's second family, the children he'd chosen to keep. "Maybe during the May half-term…" It was so half-hearted it hurt. Of course he wouldn't bring Amy or Jasper. They had to be teenagers now, fourteen and sixteen perhaps, and Emily barely knew them. Her half siblings, and yet strangers, because that's how everyone had preferred it.

"Just a thought," she said, the words an apology. She didn't know why she'd suggested it. She certainly never had before, had never wanted to before.

"No, no, it's a good one." To make up for his lack of enthusiasm, he now sounded cringingly jolly. "I'll ask Amanda. We'll look at our calendars."

"Right." Amanda, her father's second wife, was someone else Emily barely knew. Her father had married her several years after their own relationship had fallen apart, when his weekend visits had trailed to monthly, and then to next to nothing, and Naomi had been well enough, or rather Emily had been old enough, not to need to be dumped at her father's flat.

To give her credit, Amanda had tried, buying Emily a set of bath bombs and nail varnish that had been a thoughtful present for a ten-year-old girl, but Emily had hated them on principle. Amanda still always managed to remember her birthday with a card, signing both her name and Geoff's in her loopy scrawl. Yet even she didn't make any more overtures than that, and neither did Emily.

"I'd better go," her father said. "I'm going to the footy with Jasper..."

"All right." That little remark should not have hurt. She'd trained herself long ago not to let those thoughtless comments sting, and besides she didn't even like football.

And yet, somehow since coming to Wychwood-on-Lea, Emily had felt just that little bit rawer. The tiniest bit more vulnerable than she'd ever let herself feel before, and it scared her. Where was her armour? Her strength?

And why, after years alone, a lifetime even, was she letting these kinds of things hurt? Why was she starting to feel so lonely?

·

# Chapter Eight

RAIN SPATTERED THE tall windows as Emily pulled her laptop towards her. Despite the gloomy weather, she was feeling positive—the office was now completely organised, all the new furniture had been delivered, and she'd done the hard bit of lining up all the local businesses to participate in the fundraiser, so there was only admin, organisation, and publicity left to do, which she could complete in the comforting solace of her office.

She'd also managed to avoid Olivia, Ava, and most importantly, Owen for the whole week, limiting her interactions to coffee with Alice and brief check-ins with Henry. Order had been firmly established, thank goodness, and she felt as if her life was back on its necessary even keel.

Nearly a week on, Emily was able to look at the events of that night at the pub as a mere blip on her radar, just as she'd been sure it was for Owen. She'd been feeling vulnerable, yes, because of how new everything was and how friendly everyone seemed. It had knocked her off-balance, but she was fine now. Absolutely fine.

It felt immensely reassuring to realise that—to come home from a productive day of work and have everything just as she needed and wanted it to be; to eat her meal-for-one while reading a book and have that be enough. It was all completely fine.

If she had to convince herself a bit too much of that truth, well, that was simply because she'd been so discomfited by the move to Wychwood-on-Lea, and having everything shaken up, but it really was all just…fine.

She'd even rung her mother on Wednesday, to check in, and Naomi had assured her, albeit a bit breathlessly, that she was back on her medication and not to worry about her at all—she wasn't going to do something silly.

She'd even suggested visiting Emily one weekend, which had made her spirits lift. As challenging as her mum could be, Emily loved her and missed her when she wasn't there. Visits were stressful, yes, but they could also be fun, and it felt, well, good to be with someone who knew her. Who loved her, in her own, odd way.

So that was good, and work was good, and really, it was all just…good. She frowned at the laptop as she scanned the spreadsheet of donors who needed thank-you letter follow-ups. Working for Willoughby Holidays was, in many ways, similar to working for Ellis Investments, although for a more meaningful cause.

"Emily? Do you have a moment?"

Emily looked up from her laptop to see Alice standing in

the doorway, smiling uncertainly. It was mid-afternoon and they'd already had their morning coffee. This was definitely not part of their routine.

"Umm…yes, I suppose." Emily closed her laptop and scooted away from the desk. "What is it?"

"I wondered if you'd mind giving your opinion about something upstairs?"

"Upstairs?" Emily had never actually been upstairs. She'd heard the occasional clatter or rumble from another part of the house, and generally tuned it out. She knew they were renovating the manor to get it ready for the holidays they hoped to offer that summer, but she hadn't given it much consideration beyond that.

"Okay. Although I don't know how much help I'll be."

"I just want a second opinion, really. I don't know if I've got the tone right."

"The tone?"

"Of one of the bedrooms. Come see."

Dutifully Emily followed Alice up the sweeping staircase, past a life-sized portrait of an austere-looking woman—Henry's great-grandmother, apparently—and around the corner onto the first floor gallery, a wide hallway that had been stripped of its formal paintings, the walls now painted a cheerful light green. Alice opened the first door on the left, and then beckoned Emily inside.

"What do you think?" she asked, as Emily took in the renovated room.

It was lovely, airy and bright, with no hint of moth-eaten wall hangings or fusty old furniture. The walls were a light blue, with white, puffy clouds stencilled along the ceiling. Matching curtains framed the view of the gardens outside, and there was a set of twin beds with matching tables and bureaus, along with a bookcase along one wall filled with children's books of varying ages and descriptions.

"It's lovely," Emily said sincerely. "Truly lovely."

"It isn't too...bland?" Alice asked anxiously. She perched on the edge of one of the beds, reaching for a cloud-shaped pillow that she clutched to her chest. "It doesn't look too institutional?"

"Not institutional," Emily said after a moment's consideration. "Not at all. But I might not be the right person to ask. I sort of like institutional."

"Do you?" Alice let out a huff of laughter. "I hate it. After growing up in it, I want everything to be wonderfully messy and cluttered and real. Henry says I'll turn into a hoarder, but at least we have the space."

Which made Emily want to shudder, even as she understood it. Perhaps everyone was a result of their upbringing, whether they wanted to be or not.

"Was it very hard?" she asked after a moment. "Growing up in care?"

Alice sighed and clutched the pillow more tightly. "It could have been worse. I've always known that."

"That doesn't sound very promising."

"No, it was…well, it was lonely, really." She managed a slightly wobbly smile. "Even when my foster parents were nice. And then I was transferred to a care home—teens usually don't get fostered, because of their age. No one wants them and it's just easier to lump them all together in a home. That was easier, in a way, but lonelier, too."

"I'm sorry," Emily said, because she didn't know what else to say. It sounded awful, worse than anything she'd experienced, certainly, and she felt guilty for feeling sorry for herself even once.

"I don't talk about it all that much," Alice confessed. "It's in the past, and I really am so happy now. I don't want to dwell on it."

"I can understand that."

"Can you?" Alice looked at her rather keenly, and Emily knew it was a perfect opportunity to share a bit about her own past. It was an opportunity she chose not to take. "Anyway," Alice said, brushing at her eyes, "I think redoing these rooms is bringing it all back a bit. Reminding me of my own childhood, the rooms I lived in. And I want them to be so much more than that."

"But they will be, because you and Henry will be here," Emily pointed out. "And you'll be lovely and welcoming to all the kids who come—I'm sure you will be. And that's what will make the difference, not what colour the walls are, or what the curtains look like."

"I hope so." Alice let out a sigh. "If we even get approved. Henry's had umpteen meetings with local councils, and we've got to have even more checks because of safeguarding and all that. I just hope this whole thing actually works."

"It will," Emily said firmly. "If Henry has anything to do with it."

Alice laughed at that. "True. He can be scarily determined." She smiled as she replaced the pillow. "Thanks, Emily. I brought you up here for your opinion on the room. I didn't expect to have a mini meltdown on you."

"It's all right."

Alice rose from the bed and walked towards Emily. For a second she thought she might hug her, and she didn't know how she felt about that, but then Alice just touched her hand. "Thank you. You've been a big help."

"Have I?" It was a new sensation, to have helped someone with their sadness. She didn't know whether to believe Alice, but in any case it felt surprisingly nice to think that she might have been helpful. Needed.

"Is it too early to put the kettle on again?" Alice asked. "Or do you have to get back to work?"

Emily hesitated. She *did* need to get back to work, but she could see that Alice still wanted some company, even if it was just hers, and she didn't want to disappoint her.

"Why not?" she said, and Alice's wide smile was like a wave breaking on the shore.

The kitchen was just as comfortable as ever, and as always Andromeda leapt into Emily's lap the moment she'd sat down. She still kept the lint brush in her desk drawer for that reason.

"I'm not usually so emotional," Alice said as she poured boiled water into a big, floral-patterned teapot. "I think it must be because I'm on my period."

"Oh, right." Emily had nothing else to say to that.

"We're trying, you see," Alice said softly, and for a second her face seemed to collapse in sadness before she raised her head and gave Emily a determined smile. "But it's still early days, I know."

Now she was really out of her depth. "I'm sorry," Emily said, knowing the words were inadequate. "That must be…difficult."

"Have you ever wanted children?" Alice asked as she brought the tea things to the table.

"Have I…?" Emily's mind spun as she struggled to think how to answer.

"Sorry, is that too personal a question?" Alice bit her lip. "I didn't mean to pry."

"No, no." It *was* too personal a question, but then just about any question was, and after Alice's emotional revelations Emily didn't feel she could clam up herself. Weirdly, part of her didn't even want to. "I haven't really thought about it, to tell you the truth," she said finally.

"You haven't?" Alice looked surprised. "I mean, most women do, don't they, one way or another?"

Emily shrugged. "I suppose it's not something I ever thought would happen for me."

Alice cocked her head, her expression softening into sympathy. "Why not?"

"Well…" Emily reached for her tea to have something to focus on other than Alice's cringingly compassionate look. "It just isn't something I've…focused on." Which sounded so lame, but what else could she say? Relationships, marriage and babies, kitchen suppers and family holidays, dogs and cats and a clutter of muddy boots in the hall…it was all so, so beyond her. It was what everyone else had, what she'd always supposed everyone took for granted, but it had never been that way for her. It had always felt as far away as the moon.

"Right," Alice said after a moment. "And is that by choice?"

Emily couldn't keep from giving her a startled look. Of course it was by choice. It wasn't as if she had a pair of handcuffs on, was it? If she'd really wanted a boyfriend, she could have got one, surely?

And yet…

"It's just how it's worked out," she said a bit stiffly.

"But it doesn't have to be that way forever," Alice persisted. "You can't be much older than I am—"

"I'm twenty-six."

"Exactly." Alice looked pleased. "There's plenty of time for you to meet someone."

For a second Owen's image flashed into Emily's mind—the dark, curly hair, the glint in those blue eyes, his hands on her shoulders, the entirely unexpected current of feeling that had run through like a bolt of lightning…

"It's not something I'm looking for," she said firmly. "I really am happy on my own."

Thankfully Alice left it at that, and they ended up talking about the fundraiser, and the hope of booking some Victorian arcade-type amusements, and after twenty minutes of reassuring conversation about nothing more than work, Emily headed back to the office.

Yet Alice's question about it being by choice lingered in her mind like a morning mist, grey shreds of fog she couldn't quite banish.

Of *course* it was by choice. If she'd wanted a boyfriend or even a husband, she would have found one. And yet…there was her mother, always in the background, needing to be managed, protected, cared for. Hidden from prying eyes.

At least, that was how it had been in Emily's childhood, but she was a grown woman now, with her own life to live. If she wanted to pursue a relationship, she could. Her mother didn't even live with her anymore, at least not often. Only when she had no other place to go…or she needed her.

So why did a relationship, a real life, feel so utterly impossible? Was it just because she'd never had one before, because she didn't know how?

And was that something you could just *learn*?

The rain was still pelting down as Emily left the manor and headed down the drive a little bit after five, the sky thunderously dark, the wood foreboding as rain lashed the branches of the trees and sent even more drops spattering into the pavement below. She put the hood of her raincoat up, her head ducked low, as she dashed from manor to close, pausing reluctantly when she heard Olivia call from her doorway.

"You must be soaked! I've just put the kettle on. Do you have time for a cuppa?"

Emily blinked through the downpour to see Olivia smiling at her in such obvious welcome, it felt downright mean to say no. And why should she? A cuppa would be nice, and Olivia was no intimidating Harriet.

"Yes, all right," she said, and walked towards number four. Inside the cottage was identical to Emily's own, but completely different in every other respect. Where Emily's was spare and spartan, Olivia's was messy and chaotic—colours clashing in crocheted blankets, throw pillows, and artwork that jostled for space on the walls. A pile of wildly patterned bowls were stacked topsy-turvy by a sink crammed with dishes. A cat was perched on top of an overflowing laundry basket, gazing balefully at Emily as she took in the scene.

"Sorry, that's Mr Hyde," Olivia said as she nodded towards the cat. "He's my bipolar cat. He's either lovely or horrible, and I never know which."

"Ah, right." Emily looked away because she wasn't sure she knew what the expression on her face was. She knew all about bipolar, never mind cats.

"Anyway. Tea." Olivia reached for a big, friendly-looking teapot covered in cavorting elephants. "Builder's brew all right?"

"Yes, thank you." Emily's fingers were practically twitching to straighten the stack of bowls by the sink, or put the laundry in the washer, or anything that would make this room a little less chaotic. But Olivia seemed oblivious to the mess, cheerfully finding two more clean cups from the cupboard, and disregarding the half dozen piled in the sink.

"Ignore the mess," Olivia said cheerfully as she brought their cups of tea to the table. "If you can."

Emily gave a small smile. It would take some effort, but she intended to do just that.

"So." Olivia gave her an alarmingly frank look as she sat down. "I hope Harriet didn't put you off the other night, at The Drowned Sailor. She can be a bit full on, but she means well, honestly."

"It was fine," Emily said a bit woodenly, and then surprised herself by adding, "I know I come across as a bit reserved and cool."

Olivia made a face. "I *thought* you'd heard that cold fish comment. But you don't come across that way to me, Emily. At all."

"Well, that's a relief, I suppose," Emily said as lightly as she could. This conversation was deeply uncomfortable, and she searched for something innocuous to say, unfortunately coming up with nothing.

"You remind me a bit of myself, actually," Olivia said, and Emily nearly did a double take. She and Olivia were miles apart in every way possible—the messy cottage, Olivia's eclectic, hippyish style and frizzy hair, the easy warmth with which she seemed to approach everything. Absolute *miles*.

"I just mean," Olivia clarified with a smile, "that you seem a bit...isolated. Lonely." She paused, sipping her tea as she watched Emily carefully. "Sorry if I'm being too nosy. But I can relate."

*You are being nosy*, Emily wanted to say. She felt, suddenly and surprisingly, really rather angry. What was *with* people here? Why did everyone feel as if they had the right to weigh in on her life, ask prying questions, make absurd judgements? Who *did* that? No one in London, certainly.

Right then she resented Olivia's friendliness, and Alice's kitchen confidences, and even Henry insisting she traipse up and down the high street meeting people because he thought it would be good for her.

She didn't need any of it. She didn't want any of it, as well intentioned as it might have been. She didn't need a bunch of sanctimonious strangers telling her how screwed up she was, or how she should live her life.

"Sorry," Olivia murmured when Emily still hadn't replied. "I think I overstepped a bit."

"Yes, you did," Emily agreed, her voice trembling. "I understand that everyone wants to be welcoming, but I'm actually fine the way I am, and I don't need people telling me how I feel, even if they *mean well*." Olivia flinched, and Emily realised how biting she'd sounded, just as she realised she didn't, in this precise moment, care. "Look, thanks for the tea, but I think I ought to get home."

"Oh, Emily, I'm sorry." Olivia looked at her in dismay, her face crumpling with obvious regret. "Me and my big mouth. I didn't mean to tell you how you feel, honestly. I just thought I recognised a kindred spirit—I've gone through a lot of life on my own and I know how hard it can be—"

"Thanks again for the tea." Emily stood up from the table with a screech of chair legs. She walked out of the cottage on watery legs, amazed at how bolshie she'd been. Well, so much for being friends with Olivia. Cold fish clearly didn't even begin to cover it; she'd turn herself into an absolute pariah before too long, and so be it.

Her fingers were shaking as she turned the key in the lock, and then stepped into the reassuring calm of her own cottage, where everything was in its place, every surface free of clutter and dust. Yet looking around it now, the single sofa and the one bookcase, the kitchen seeming as spotlessly unused as one in an Airbnb, she couldn't help but think how empty it looked. How barren.

She went upstairs to change, drawing the curtains against

the lashing rain and struggling to hold on to some sense of peace and order. Then she caught sight of the rocking chair in the corner of the room, its wood now burnished to a honeyed gleam, an inviting place to sit that made her think of half-forgotten memories of she didn't even know what.

And, quite suddenly, she thought she could burst into tears and never stop.

"Don't be so stupid," she muttered under her breath as she undressed, putting her work clothes back on their hangers, tights in the laundry hamper, understated pearl earrings back in her jewellery box. Everything in its place, and yet the tears were still there, at the backs of her eyes, rising in her throat, refusing to be ignored.

She changed into her comfy clothes, a matching pyjama set, and willed all the emotion back. Who were these people, to tell her how she felt? That she was lonely?

She'd never considered herself lonely before. Not until she'd come to wretched Willoughby Close.

Back downstairs Emily soothed herself with her usual routines—heating up some lentil soup she'd made earlier in the week as she listened to radio four. Tidying up, wiping down the counters, taking her lone bowl to the table with her book, just as she'd always liked it, and still would.

She was just about to start eating when she saw a tiny, drenched form of black and orange huddled by the French windows. It was, or at least she thought it was, the kitten from the barn.

"Oh, no…" Emily rose from the table and opened the French windows, letting in a sheet of rain that promptly puddled on the floor. The kitten looked utterly woebegone and nearly half dead, cold and wet, and tiny.

Gently Emily picked it up in her hands, amazed at how small it was, and then dried it carefully with a hand towel, its fur sticking up in a marmalade-striped fuzz. Its little eyes opened and a tiny pink tongue darted out and licked Emily's hand. She let out a little laugh of surprise.

"You're going to be all right, aren't you?"

The kitten meowed, and Emily felt as if a crack had opened up right in the middle of her heart. Poor, wee, abandoned kitten. Jace had said its mother would leave it somewhere, and so she had…right on Emily's doorstep.

Emily didn't know if it was providence or chance that had brought the kitten to her, but she knew one thing with a bone-deep certainty: she was going to keep it.

# Chapter Nine

JACE AND AVA inhabited a fairy tale, in more ways than one. Emily ducked under a damp branch as she followed the narrow, winding path through the wood, lit only by the feeble beam of her small torch. Did they not have a road to their place? Were they Hansel and Gretel?

She'd been anxious all weekend about this dinner party, and in the last few hours she'd even thought about texting Jace and telling him she had to cry off. She was sick. She was tired. She was painting her nails. Anything to get out of several hours of socialising with people who all knew each other better than they knew her, although the residents of Willoughby Close seemed to like to *think* they knew her.

Yet no matter how nice everyone tried to be, it would be hours of being asked awkward questions, and then coming across as stiff and formal because she didn't know how to be anything else, and had never wanted to try...until now.

The last few days had been both weird and rather wretched, because Emily couldn't shake the guilt she'd felt snapping at Olivia, or even closing down Alice's questions. If she wanted to put people off, she was doing a good job of it, but the truth was she didn't know any longer if she really did want to put people off.

Until she'd been told she was lonely, she hadn't thought she was. *But now…?*

At least she had the kitten. She'd made a little bed for him in a cardboard box lined with a fleece, and then gone to the Waggy Tails pet shop in town on Saturday morning to stock up on rather overpriced kit.

"Oh, you have a cat?" The woman at the till, the same one Emily had asked about the fundraiser, was all delighted enthusiasm. "Cats are lovely. Cool creatures who can take or leave you, to be sure, and they certainly know their own minds, but they can be wonderful companions."

A bit like her then. Partners in crime. Emily had bought feeding bowls and food, a litter tray and a scratching post, and a book about caring for cats. Then she'd trundled home with her purchases, only to have Jace pull over in his truck and ask if she wanted a lift, which she realised she did.

"Still on for dinner tomorrow night?" he'd asked, giving her a lazy smile that made her suspect he knew how difficult she would find the socialising.

"Yes, absolutely," she assured him. It was only later she realised he'd given her an opportunity to cry off, and for some contrary reason she hadn't taken it.

So here she was, battling her way through the forest, un-accountably nervous for the evening ahead, and yet still sort of…*excited* by the possibility of making friends.

When, Emily wondered, had she stopped making friends? Probably when she was seven, when her parents had divorced and her mother had gained full custody. In Year One, Emily recalled, she'd had a best friend, Ivy. They'd walked around school holding hands, and they'd curl up in the reading nook in their classroom and sound out stories to one another. That was all Emily remembered, that and being happy.

The next year she'd been taken out of school, and her mother had home-schooled her for nine months—a form of unschooling that had been more about Emily entertaining herself, with her mother's occasional manic interest—a trip to the zoo, an elaborate chemistry experiment that seven-year-old Emily hadn't understood, the mess all over the kitchen for days…

By spring of Year Two, her mother had been bored of the whole thing and stuck her back in school, a different one, since they'd moved by then. Emily had been lamentably behind and she'd struggled to make any friends. The halcyon days of Year One with Ivy had felt far behind her.

But why on earth was she thinking about Ivy now? Emily ducked under another branch, her stomach clenching as she caught sight of the lights of the cottage, twinkling in the distance. She'd arrived.

Jace and Ava's cottage did look like it belonged to Hansel and Gretel, or was it the witch? It was tiny and impossibly quaint, with gingerbread trim and a funny little turret. It was not the type of house she'd expect a man like Jace to live in, and he smiled in wry acknowledgement as he opened the door.

"You found it all right, then? Followed the bread-crumbs?"

"I was just thinking that," Emily admitted with a laugh. She stepped into the cosy entranceway and Jace took her coat.

"Come through. Everyone's in the kitchen. It's the only room in the house that isn't tetchy."

The kitchen, Emily saw, had been expanded into a large conservatory, to create a lovely, light, open space with a big granite island and a table to seat eight.

"Emily!" Ava smiled, looking delighted to see her. "Now you know Olivia, of course, and this is lovely Simon, the music teacher at the primary…and have you met Owen?" This was said far too innocently, and Emily froze where she stood. How had she not seen him, standing by the stove, a faint smile on his face as he met her astonished gaze?

Why on earth was Owen here? Jace certainly hadn't mentioned him when he'd extended the invitation. Then Emily remembered how it had been Ava who had said he was single and lovely, and who had looked at Emily so knowingly when he'd sent the champagne, and a blush washed over her face like a tide. This was a set-up. A blind date. Ava and Jace, Simon and Olivia, and her and Owen. It was so excruciatingly obvious she couldn't keep from physically cringing.

"Emily and I have met," Owen said easily. "She came to ask if The Drowned Sailor would take part in the fundraiser up at the manor, and of course I said yes. No one says no to Lord Stokeley." If there was a very slight edge to Owen's voice, Emily thought she was the only one who noticed it. Ava seemed oblivious.

"Henry has been going on about that, hasn't he?" she said with a laugh. "How is it all going, Emily? And can we get you something to drink?"

"Fine, so far. And uh, yes, thank you." They made it so easy, as natural as breathing. Chat, laugh, drink, eat. Life was both simple and full. At least it could be. But everything felt mechanical to her, as if she had to tell herself what to do. *Smile. Nod. Take a sip of the wine Ava just handed to you. Try to act normal.*

"It's going to be quite big, this fundraiser, isn't it?" Ava remarked as they all moved into the lounge, where two overstuffed sofas framed a cheerily blazing hearth. "Olivia, are you taking part?"

"Oh, yes. Emily asked me, too." She gave her a quick, friendly smile that felt like an apology, her anxious gaze scanning Emily's face. They hadn't spoken since Emily had marched out of her cottage, and Emily thought she was the one who should be apologising. She tried to smile back. "I was thinking about doing cupcakes again."

"Oh, I adore your cupcakes," Ava said, and Simon put an arm around Olivia as they settled on the sofa.

"So do I," he said, with a knowing smile, and Emily knew there had to be a story there. Had they fallen in love over the buttercream icing?

"Olivia did a Twelve Days of Cupcakes last Christmas," Ava explained. "A different cupcake every day. They were absolutely gorgeous."

"I came in every day for one," Simon confessed with a laugh, "although admittedly it wasn't just for the cupcakes." He and Olivia gave each other another loved-up look that made Ava roll her eyes good-naturedly. Emily's gaze snagged with Owen's and his laughing look had it skittering away again, panicked. This evening was sure to be awkward in all sorts of ways.

"It's always nice to have things that draw the village together," Ava said comfortably. "Especially now they've cancelled the Easter fete."

"Have they?" Olivia looked surprised. "Why?"

"Don't you remember, some louts last year barged in, drunk as skunks, and wrecked a bunch of stalls?" Jace answered. "Unfortunately there's no way to keep them out, with it being on the village green."

"What about the fundraiser? It'll be up at the manor?"

"Yes, on the grounds," Emily said, although she had barely got that far in her planning.

"You'll ticket it, I suppose?" Ava said. "To keep the riffraff out?"

"Of course they will," Owen interjected, his voice light. He was smiling, but his eyes were rather hard. "You can't have just anyone coming up to the manor, can you?"

Emily felt her cheeks warm. "It's not that kind of event," she said, which she'd already told him, that day in the pub. "It's meant to be very inclusive. Everyone is invited, and if there are tickets, it will just be to keep track of the numbers." She forced herself to meet Owen's gaze. He gave her a grudging nod back, and Emily wondered what he had against the manor, or maybe just Henry. No one else seemed to notice it, but she'd sensed a hostility from him whenever either were mentioned.

"And I'm sure it will be," Ava agreed easily. "It's bound to be fab."

The conversation moved on, and Emily sipped her wine, shooting Owen sideways, speculative looks she hoped he didn't notice, wondering again what he had against the manor. Or maybe it was just her. Despite that weird almost-moment in the courtyard, she was starting to think he might not like her very much. He certainly wasn't paying her any attention tonight. A fact that normally wouldn't bother her at all, because she never wanted attention, shied away from it at every opportunity…but somehow tonight it did.

"Right, food's ready, so shall we all take a seat?" Ava said brightly. "Simon and Olivia, you on that side, Jace on the other end…Owen, can you take that seat?" She gave Emily an entirely bland look. "And, Emily, you next...everyone happy?"

Of course Emily had been seated next to Owen. Ava didn't do subtle, apparently, as innocent as her look had been. Emily wondered how anyone could think she and Owen were suited. They were as chalk and cheese as two people could possibly be—he so gregarious and larger than life, she a small mouse hiding in the shadows.

Owen seemed to be thinking the same thing, for he slanted her a wry, laughing look as she put her wineglass on the table and sat in the seat next to him.

"Don't look quite so horrified," he told her with one of his booming laughs. "I don't bite."

"I'm not horrified," Emily said stiffly. "No more than you are, anyway." Now where had that come from? It seemed his barbed comment from earlier had drawn blood, after all.

"Horrified?" Owen raised his eyebrows, amused. "Is that what you think I am? Now where did you get that idea?"

Emily shrugged and reached for her napkin. "I don't know whether it's me or the manor or both, but something seems to have got your back up." She smoothed the napkin across her lap, not quite willing to meet his gaze. She wasn't normally so forthright, and it made her feel all shaky inside. She shouldn't have said anything.

"You're right about that," Owen said after a moment, the laughter gone from his voice. "Although I don't think anyone else has much noticed. But the whole manor set sticks in my craw a bit. I'm not ashamed to admit it, although I generally don't." He sounded so serious that Emily risked a look up. Everyone else was chatting and serving food, heads angled away from them, giving them the illusion of privacy even at a crowded dinner table—something she suspected was completely intentional.

"The manor set?" she repeated.

"Henry and his like. The privileged few, and they know it." He shrugged. "I suppose I've got a chip on my shoulder, but there it is. They go their way and I go mine, and usually it's fine."

"Henry Trent does take a bit of getting used to," Emily said after a moment, when she'd absorbed all that Owen had said. "He's quite abrupt, but I do think he's a good man underneath." She'd never minded her boss's taciturn ways, and it was his new, more effusive manner that had her feeling rather alarmed, but she couldn't exactly explain that to Owen.

"So you don't think he's a snob?"

Emily hesitated. In her four years at Ellis Investments, Henry definitely had been a snob. He'd insisted on only the best of everything—whether it was his Montblanc fountain pen or the Veuve Clicquot she'd order for a celebratory meeting with a client. His suits were straight from Savile Row, and cost in the thousands. And then there was the Jag...

But he was a rich man, and he'd moved in exalted circles, and the guest list for some of the firm's events would have made many a jaw drop. Did it make him a snob? Was he one still? Maybe.

Emily had never minded, because she liked nice things and anyway, her preferred place was on the outside looking in. But that didn't mean it was for Owen.

"I think he's changing," she answered. "I think Alice is changing him."

"The love of a good woman," Owen quipped wryly. "And I know she's had some hard times of her own—she was a former foster kid, herself, or so I heard."

"Yes, she was."

"Henry keeps it quiet, though, doesn't he? The village crack was that he didn't think her suitable at first."

"I'm not sure…" Emily could see how he wouldn't, but it seemed unkind to be talking like that about Alice now.

Owen shrugged. "She seems like a good sort to me."

"She is," Emily said firmly.

"What about you?" Owen asked. "Where did you grow up?"

Such a loaded question, although it didn't have to be. "Reading," Emily said, because it was what she always said and it was where she'd been born. She had lived there for six years, after all.

"Brothers? Sisters?" Owen raised his eyebrows, giving her a faint smile that seemed to say, *a conversation takes two, you know.* Emily reached for her wine.

"No, just me. What about you?" There, she could bat it back at him.

"A whole passel of sisters. Five, actually."

"Goodness. And that was in…?"

"Cwmparc, in the Rhondda Valley, in Wales. Couldn't you tell?" He grinned at her, his eyes twinkling, making her want to look away.

"I figured Wales," she admitted. "The accent is a bit of a giveaway."

"True enough."

"How did you end up in the Cotswolds?"

"Well, I wanted to get out of Cwmparc as soon as I could. There's not much there anymore, to be honest. The mines shut down for good in the eighties, when I was a kid. Put my dad out of work along with just about every other poor bloke in the place." His face set in grim lines for a second, before it relaxed into an easy smile. "So I took the bus east and my ticket went as far as Cheltenham. From there I worked in pubs here and there until I had enough money to buy The Drowned Sailor. Bought it when it was a right dump and got it for a song."

"And the rest of your family?" Emily asked, curious. Two parents, five sisters. She couldn't imagine having so many people in her life.

Owen's face set again and then once more he deliberately relaxed. "They're still all back in Cwmparc, except my father." He paused. "He died a few years ago now."

✻

HE DIDN'T USUALLY talk about his family—the bevy of sisters with their whiny kids and their tired faces, the reproach in their eyes that he'd got out, he'd made it, at least more than they had. He certainly didn't talk about his father, or the fact that he'd died a drunk, beaten to death in a pub fight in Merthyr Tydfil, alienated from his family, only forty-seven years old. Owen had been seventeen.

And he never talked about his mother, or the fact that she blamed him for his father's death, even though by that point he hadn't seen his father for over a year. Owen stabbed a forkful of lasagne, willing the memories away. It was time to ask Emily some questions, and stop thinking about his own past.

"So, Reading," he said. "Only child." He gave her a slanted, speculative look. He could picture it already—the pink, frilly bedroom, the private school, the hockey sticks and horse riding and trips to Switzerland for skiing. She was definitely that sort of girl—part of the manor set he'd already said he despised. He could tell from her carefully styled face and hair, the designer jumper she was wearing that looked like cashmere, the expensive leather boots. Everything about her reeked of money and privilege. "What was that like?"

Emily looked startled, a little trapped by the innocuous question. "Oh, you know…" she said vaguely, and left it at that.

"Actually," Owen answered mildly. "I don't know." He'd grown up in a two-up two-down colliery house on a steep little street overshadowed by a hulking mine shaft. He could remember when the toilet had been at the bottom of the garden, and they hadn't had enough fifty-pence pieces for the gas meter. "Tell me about it," he invited.

Emily stared at him for a moment, a distant look on her face. Was he boring her? Why did he care?

For some unfathomable reason, he continued to let this woman get under his skin. From the first moment she'd looked down her pert little nose at him, to that strangled *"Don't"* in the courtyard, she'd affected him far too much. Made him want to know her, protect her, even. Both notions were laughable. She thought she was above him. Plenty of people had before, and it usually didn't bother him. He didn't let it. So why couldn't he let it slide this time?

"What do you think it was like?" she asked after a moment, sounding cautiously curious.

"Nice enough, I suppose?" He suddenly felt petty and a little bit ashamed. What did it matter, if Emily David had had a nice life, with two parents and a pony? So had loads of others, and he didn't mind.

"Yes, I suppose that about sums it up," she said after a moment, but something about her tone made Owen think it didn't at all. And for an unnerving second, he wondered if he'd got Emily David completely wrong.

They finished their meal—a lovely lasagne—without saying much more to each other, and somehow Owen felt as if he'd come off worst in the conversation. It was odd, because he was a let-it-roll-off-him type of guy, and yet he'd been the opposite with Emily, from the very first second he'd clapped eyes on her. It annoyed and alarmed him in equal measure. Why did this slip of a woman cause such a reaction in him?

After a mostly silent meal, Emily rose to help clear the plates, even though Ava insisted she didn't have to. Owen had a feeling she was avoiding him, and he could hardly blame her. Something in his manner had been a bit aggressive, even though he hadn't meant it to be.

"What do you think of Emily?" Jace asked in a low voice when the women were organising dessert and Simon had gone to take a phone call from his sister.

"It's a bit obvious, isn't it, mate?" Owen replied. "You get two single people in this village and everyone's pushing you together no matter what."

"You know how it is," Jace returned affably. "You don't have to do anything about it, but there seemed to be some sparks flying."

Yes, there were definitely sparks. There certainly had been when'd touched her. Still Owen shook his head. "She's not my type."

Jace arched an eyebrow. "Or you're not hers?"

"They're one and the same, I reckon."

Jace lifted his beer bottle to his lips as he rocked back on the legs of his chair. "Actually, I don't think they are."

"What's it matter to you?" Owen returned. "You're not usually one to play matchmaker."

Jace shrugged, grinning. "When you've found true love yourself…"

"Oh, stuff it." Owen spoke good-naturedly enough, but he meant what he said. He enjoyed flirting, and he'd gone on a fair few dates, but he wasn't in the market for a real relationship, the kind where people got hurt, where he hurt them. Definitely not.

Perhaps that was why Emily David affected him the way she did, creating in him this unsettling mix of attraction and aggression. He saw her standoffishness and it irritated him, and then he sensed her fragility and felt both intrigued and wary. Who was she? And when would he stop caring?

# Chapter Ten

"WELL?" AVA'S VOICE was a carrying whisper as she took a bubbling and golden apple crumble out of the oven. "What do you think?"

Emily decided it was best to play dumb. "It looks delicious," she said with a nod towards the crumble.

Ava let out one of her throaty laughs. "Not this, you ninny," she said. "Which I think you know full well."

"You are being a bit obvious," Emily felt compelled to say.

Ava placed the crumble on the worktop, her eyebrows raised. "Life is short. What's the harm in being obvious? Subtlety is entirely overrated, in my opinion." Emily thought she disagreed with that sentiment, but she decided not to say anything. "Look," Ava said, lowering her voice so Olivia, fetching bowls, couldn't hear. "I know it's hard when you've been on your own a long time. You're used to fending for yourself, and that can feel good. Safe. And I'm willing to admit that maybe Owen isn't the right bloke for you, but he is a lovely guy and whatever happens, he'd be a good friend.

We can all use a few of those, don't you think?"

"Er, yes, I'm sure," Emily managed after a second's pause. How did Ava know she'd been on her own a long time? Had she been talking to Olivia? Why did everyone seem as if they knew her, and they had the right to say so? It left Emily feeling as if she were naked. Exposed and vulnerable, and she didn't like it at all.

"It takes one to know one," Ava said softly, in reply to her unasked question, and then she picked up the crumble and brought it to the table.

Dessert was a jollier affair than dinner, with everyone chipping in and the conversation moving from topic to topic with lightning speed—rugby, the new playground on the village green, the fact that The Three Pennies was now offering rooms.

"That doesn't cramp your style, Owen?" Simon asked with a smile. He was a gentle-looking man with slightly longish dark hair and kind eyes. He clearly adored Olivia.

"Not at all. The Three Pennies has an entirely different clientele than The Drowned Sailor, as I'm sure you know. And I wouldn't let a dog sleep in the rooms above the pub." Owen let out one of his booming laughs. "I may have a slight problem with damp, but I'm sorting it out."

"I can help you with that, mate," Jace said, and Owen smiled and nodded.

"I'll take you up on that."

They were all such good friends, their conversation so

natural, they made it look easy, just as the women had when they got together. Talk, laugh, eat, drink. Repeat. Everyone else could do it, Emily thought, so why couldn't she? Of course, she'd never wanted to quite so much before. She'd been happy on her own. She still was.

A week or two in Wychwood-on-Lea didn't have to *change* her. She didn't have to let it. And yet it had been so much easier to be anonymous and alone in London.

"I suppose I should get back," Emily said when the dessert plates had been cleared and the decaf coffees drunk. It was past ten and she realised she was longing for the peace and quiet of her cottage, sterile though it might be, even as she'd strangely enjoyed the banter flying all around her, without taking part in it. Socialising, even though she was rubbish at it, was exhausting.

"Oh, you can't go through the wood alone," Ava exclaimed, and Emily knew what was coming. "Owen, why don't you walk her back? It's miserable going down that path late at night. Like being in some haunted fairy tale."

"I'm fine," Emily said, a bit more sharply than she'd intended, because Ava couldn't have pushed them together more obviously than if she'd had a clamp.

"I'm happy to do it," Owen replied. "Besides, it's a shortcut to my place."

That seemed to settle the matter, and Emily said her thank yous and goodbyes rather stiffly while Owen waited in the hall. How long were the well-meaning folk of Wychwood going to keep forcing her and Owen together? Were they the only two single people in the village?

The rain had thankfully stopped as she and Owen headed out into the night, the sky dark and stormy above, the moon hidden by clouds. Emily pulled her coat more tightly around her.

"You really didn't have to walk me home," she said, managing to make it sound more like an accusation than an apology.

"I know," Owen answered easily. "But they never would have been satisfied otherwise."

"It's a bit irritating, isn't it?"

"Is it?" he asked affably, and Emily gave an uncertain laugh.

"I only mean...well..." She swallowed as she focused on the narrow path winding ahead of them, lit by Owen's far trustier man-sized torch than her own small one suitable for a handbag.

"What *did* you mean?" he asked when she faltered and trailed away to nothing. "Out of interest?"

Emily was grateful for the darkness that hopefully hid her scorching blush. This conversation was so out of her element. "I only meant that it's not as if you even like me," she said a bit defiantly, and then quickened her pace, ducking wet tree branches and muddy puddles with alacrity born of desperation.

"You said that at dinner," Owen said as his long strides

kept him level with her. "And I really don't know where you got the idea."

"You don't deny it, then?"

"I don't think I know you well enough to say," he responded as he did his best to walk next to her even though the path really only fit one person.

Emily wanted to drop the conversation, even as some contrary part of her wanted to push it. "You've seemed to have something against me from the start," she pointed out as reasonably as she could. She was *not* going to sound hurt, because of course she wasn't. "Is it because I work for Henry Trent? Or is it just me?"

"It's not you. I admit, I have a bit of a thing about the la-di-da types." He paused. "It's not entirely fair, I know. I'm sorry."

"You think I'm a la-di-da type?" She couldn't keep the disbelief from her voice.

"You know what I mean."

"No, I don't."

He gestured to her clothes, clearly meaning to encompass so much more. "You had a privileged upbringing, and you've looked down your nose at me since you first walked into my pub. I'm not blaming you for it, and I'm not saying it justifies my response, but there it is."

*Privileged upbringing?* Emily didn't know whether to burst into laughter or tears. She did neither, just kept walking, longing to get home. Owen Jones didn't know her at *all*, and why should he? She'd never given him the chance.

"Am I wrong?" he persisted as he kept up with her.

"It doesn't matter."

"Why not?"

She shrugged impatiently, ducking so a wet, thorny branch didn't thwack her in the face. "All I meant was that it's a bit awkward, being pushed together like this, considering."

"Considering what?" The question sounded like a challenge. Emily started to stammer.

"Well, just…I mean…that you don't…that we…"

"Yes?" Owen prompted. He sounded as if he was enjoying her fluster.

"Oh, look, you know what I mean," Emily finished a bit lamely. *She* didn't even know what she meant.

Owen took a step closer to her, and for some reason she was standing still, caught in both the proverbial and literal headlights, or at least torchlight. Then Owen lowered the beam so they were both in darkness. By the light of the moon she could only just make out his face and the hooded intent she saw there.

"But it does matter," he said quietly. "Because of this."

"What…" The word came out in a breath as he put his hands on her shoulders, just as he had that Friday night, and again it was like she'd put her finger in a socket, everything twanging with painful intensity, her whole body electrified and alive. Did he feel it too? Was that why his hands had tightened on her shoulders?

"I don't dislike you, you know," he said, his voice a low thrum, and Emily twitched away from him, or tried to.

"It doesn't matter."

"You don't like me, though, do you?" Owen said, a friendly enough challenge, and unwillingly Emily raised her gaze to meet his. Mistake.

The intensity she'd been feeling dialled up another notch, or three. Her blood beat, her heart pounded, and there were parts of her body that she didn't think about very much that were now tingling. Her breath hitched. Audibly.

"Actually," Owen said, "I don't think *disliking* each other is the problem here, is it?"

Before Emily could reply, not that she would have known what to say, he kissed her.

She froze underneath his touch, everything rigid with shock even as her body flooded with awareness and pleasure. His lips were soft and warm, his touch achingly gentle...at least at first.

After that first exploratory hello kiss, he took a breath and so did she, and then he was kissing her again, harder this time, and that was wonderful too—it was all so *amazing*, as if every single part of her had come alive, and somehow her back was against a tree and her arms had come around him and she was kissing him back in a way she'd never kissed a man before.

His body was as solid and powerful as she'd thought it

would be, and it felt incredible pressed against hers as the kiss went on and on. A proper kiss, not just a buss or a brush, but a life-changing moment. At least for her.

Then, in the middle of that wonderful and heart-stopping kiss, her phone buzzed in her pocket. There was only one person who would call her at eleven o'clock at night, and Emily twisted away from Owen as she grappled for her phone.

"Emily…" He looked both dazed and bemused, but she barely took in his flushed cheeks or rumpled hair as she swiped to take the call.

*"Mum?"*

"Is this Emily David?"

The officious-sounding voice had her blinking in surprise. "Yes…"

"I'm calling from St Pancras Hospital. You were listed as the next of kin for Naomi Rawlings?"

Emily swallowed dryly, her hand clenching the phone, everything in her tightening. "Yes…is she all right?"

"I'm afraid I can't say over the telephone, but I think, if possible, you should come to the hospital as soon as you can." *Dear heaven.* Emily closed her eyes as she tasted bile. "Miss David?"

"I'm here." Her voice sounded thready. "I'll come right away."

"Come to the Ruby Ward, in the Huntley Centre. It's a locked ward, but if you give your name, they'll let you through."

"Ruby Ward," Emily repeated numbly. "All right. Thank you." She ended the call, staring into space vacantly for a few seconds. It had started to rain, and she felt the dampness on her cheeks like tears.

"Emily?" Owen touched her shoulder, his tone now one of gentle concern. "What's happened?"

"My mother's in the hospital." The words felt thick and awkward in her mouth. "I need to go straight away."

"I'm so sorry—"

She nodded mechanically, already walking ahead, desperate to get back to her cottage now. She'd pack a bag, call a cab…

"Where is she? Which hospital?" Owen asked as he hurried to keep up with her.

"St Pancras, in London."

"There won't be any trains to London until the morning," Owen said as they emerged from the wood onto the lane that led to Willoughby Close. "Do you have to go now?"

"*Yes.*" The word came out savagely, like an accusation, but Owen took it in his stride.

"Then let me drive you," he said calmly. Emily whirled around to face him.

"You don't…"

"I haven't had anything to drink tonight, I'm fine to drive. And there are no trains at this time of night," he reminded her in that same calm, even tone. "Not from Wychwood."

"I'll get a cab to Oxford—"

"Do you really want to spend fifty quid on cab fare, and then be on a train with dodgy drunks late on a Sunday night?" He smiled at her, a compassionate curving of his lips that made Emily want to cry. She felt far, far too fragile right now. "Let me drive you."

"But you have work—"

"I don't open the pub until noon, and I can get someone else to do it anyway. Why are you resisting so much, Emily?"

Because no one ever did nice things for her, and he'd just kissed her, besides. She had no idea how she felt about him, about anything.

"All right," she finally relented, because with every second that passed, she was delaying getting to her mother. "Thank you."

"I'll go get my van and pick you up at Willoughby Close."

"All right. Thank you." He nodded, and then he was jogging off towards the village, and Emily was walking blindly towards number one, everything in her pulsing with panic. *Her mother in hospital. A locked ward.* What had happened? How much danger was she in?

Back in her cottage, a little meow greeted her as her newly acquired kitten wound its tiny body around her legs.

"Oh, goodness, I'd forgotten about you." She scooped

the kitten up and pressed her cheek against its soft fur as it purred in pleasure. "I really need to give you a name." Would the kitten be all right overnight? Guilt and worry racked her. She wasn't fit to have care even of a kitten.

And as for her mother…

*You didn't take care of her, either.*

Tears pricked Emily's eyes and she blinked them back. She filled the kitten's food and water bowls and then threw some clothes into a holdall. She'd text Alice, asking her to look in on the kitten while she was gone. Emily knew she'd be more than happy to help.

She'd just shrugged on her coat when a light knock sounded on the door, and she opened it to see Owen ready and waiting, his car, a beat-up van, idling in the courtyard.

"Ready to go?"

"Yes, I think so." Her fingers trembled as she locked up and then followed Owen to the van. It was the classic nondescript white van used by builders and plumbers the country over. Owen opened the passenger door for her, and took her elbow to help her up.

"Sorry, it's a bit of a tip."

A bit? Jace's truck had been spotless in comparison. Yet for once Emily was too rattled and anxious to care about the mess of disposable coffee cups and newspapers on the floor, or the thick dust coating the dashboard.

The van had a bench seat, so there were only a few inches of space separating her and Owen as she reached for her seat belt and he climbed into the driver's side.

"Thank you for doing this," Emily said rather stiltedly as they headed out into the dark, rain-washed night. Wychwood was silent, the village green cloaked in darkness, the only lights coming from The Drowned Sailor, which clearly still had some custom.

"You're sure you don't need to be at the pub?"

"I had the shifts covered tonight anyway, because of the dinner. It's fine."

She nodded, trying to keep her teeth from chattering with cold and fear, but Owen noticed and reached to turn up the heating.

"Are you cold?"

"A bit." But more than that, she was scared. She had no idea what she'd find when they got to St Pancras, what state her mother would be in. Would it be like last time? Would it be worse?

"Do you know what's happened to your mum?" Owen asked after a few moments, when they'd left the village behind and were heading towards the A40.

"No." She wasn't about to go into her mother's history, the medication she must not have been taking, after all. She swiped the screen on her phone and typed *Ruby Ward St Pancras* into the search engine. The result came up instantly—a women's psychiatric intensive care unit. Emily quickly swiped off the screen and looked out the window instead. She could feel each painful thud of her heart.

"Is she in critical condition?" Owen asked quietly, and Emily just shrugged.

"I really don't know. They just said I should come as soon as I could."

"I'm sorry." To her shock he reached over and briefly put his large, warm hand over hers; it was just for a second, but the touch felt even more intimate than their kiss.

*Their kiss*...no, she couldn't think about that now. She couldn't think about anything. She just needed to keep her mind blank and numb, at least until she knew what had happened. What she was dealing with.

Owen must have gauged her mood correctly because he lapsed into a silence that was only broken when they'd reached the outskirts of London, and he asked her to navigate to the hospital by the sat nav on her phone. Housed in a former workhouse, the hospital had an impressive Victorian air, but as Owen drove towards the Huntley Centre, neither of them missed the sign for psychiatric care.

"You can just drop me off in front," Emily said rather brusquely, and Owen looked at her in surprise.

"Let me at least come in with you. You're in no state to face this on your own."

"I'm fine," Emily protested, and once again Owen reached for her hand. She wished he'd stop doing that, even as she wanted him to never stop.

"Emily, you haven't been able to stay still since we got into this van."

"I have—" And yet even as she spoke, she knew he was right. She'd been jiggling her foot and picking at the skin around her nails for the last hour, feeling like no more than a tight ball of nerves.

"I'll just walk in with you," Owen continued in that steady voice she realised she could get used to. Could like, or even crave. "And I'll stay in the waiting room or wherever. Don't worry, I'm not going to pry."

But he already knew too much. Tears crowded her eyes and formed a lump in her throat but she forced it all down. "All right," she relented rather ungraciously. Then she turned and looked out the window, because she didn't think she could bear the sympathetic look on his face for a second longer.

Owen parked the car—the car park was near-empty at this hour—and then they made their way into the Huntley Centre. There were some plastic chairs in the foyer, and thankfully he told her he'd stay there while Emily headed for the Ruby Ward—and whatever waited for her there.

✳

OWEN SIPPED A cup of wretched coffee as he waited for Emily to return. He'd been sitting on a hard plastic chair in the entrance of the Huntley Centre for the better part of an hour, and his eyes felt gritty with fatigue. Whatever he was feeling, though, he knew Emily had to feel worse.

He wasn't an idiot, and it was obvious that this was a

psychiatric facility, and that Emily didn't seem at all surprised to be there. It explained her hurry to answer the phone, and the panicked way she'd answered. Owen had been feeling a bit bemused, that she'd broken their kiss to take a phone call, but it was certainly starting to make sense now.

And yet nothing made sense. Emily's mother in a psychiatric unit? And where was her father? What about that oh-so-privileged upbringing? Owen was starting to suspect he might have got the entirely wrong end of the stick when it came to Emily David, and he didn't know how he felt about that.

But then that was something he didn't need to think about now. Right now he just needed to think about Emily, and what was best for her. That protective instinct he'd been fighting against had kicked in big-time when she'd taken that call, and he'd realised how frightened she was. Unfortunately, that protective instinct hadn't helped him—or anyone else—in the past.

With a sigh and then a wince, Owen drained the rest of his lukewarm, mud-coloured coffee. It was two in the morning, and he had no idea how long he'd be sitting here, or what would happen when Emily came back.

And then there she was, walking down the corridor on stiff legs, her expression stony and closed. Owen rose from his chair, crumpling the paper cup in one hand.

"How is your mum?"

Emily's shoulders twitched in what Owen thought was meant to be a shrug.

"She's sleeping now. They said I should come back in the morning."

"Then you need a place to sleep tonight." She stared at him blankly, and Owen thought she had to be in shock. "Do you have friends…?" he prompted, thinking she could call someone and kip on their sofa. She'd lived in London until a week ago, after all. But Emily let out a strange huff of laughter.

"No."

Owen decided not to press. "Then you need a hotel room." He reached for his phone and started to search. "There's a Premier Inn just around the corner. I'll take you there." Emily didn't reply. She still had that blank look in her eyes, and so Owen took her by the elbow, steering her gently towards the door.

She came unresistingly, as meek as a child, silent and accepting. Her docility frightened him, and it felt like a punch in the gut. He'd seen Emily David reserved, and annoyed, and flushed with passion, but he'd never seen her like this, almost as if she were a husk of a person, unaware of him or her surroundings as he led her back to the van.

They drove in silence, Emily staring blankly ahead, to the Premier Inn a short distance away. Emily waited in the van while Owen went to check if there were rooms.

"Just one room, sir?" the attendant asked, as alertly as if

it were not three in the morning.

Owen hesitated. He knew instinctively that Emily would want her own room, just as he knew she shouldn't be alone at a time like this. "One room with twin beds," he said firmly.

Back in the van he told Emily they had a room, and she lifted her dazed gaze for the first time. "Are you staying…?"

"Yes."

Something flickered across her face and was gone. Owen couldn't tell if she was pleased or not, but he was decided. He wasn't going to leave her like this.

Upstairs Owen swiped the key card and then stepped aside for Emily to enter before following her in and closing the door quietly behind him. She turned to him, startled.

"Don't you have your own room?"

"They only had the one room left." He felt no guilt about lying; he suspected Emily would want to insist on having her own space, and he had no intention of giving it to her. "There are two beds," he pointed out, and she just nodded.

The room was small and utilitarian, with a window over-looking a ventilation shaft. Now that they were both inside, Owen could acknowledge it was going to be very close quarters. Even so he didn't regret his decision.

Emily used the bathroom first, and emerged in a pair of leggings and a T-shirt that emphasised her slender form and reminded Owen that these were *very* close quarters indeed.

As she walked by him, he smelled the light, floral scent of her perfume.

By the time he emerged from the bathroom a few minutes later, self-consciously clad in a T-shirt and his boxers, Emily was already tucked up in bed, her knees to her chest, her back to him.

Owen climbed in the other bed and closed his eyes as he tried to relax. He didn't think he'd ever been in a more surreal situation.

❋

EMILY DIDN'T THINK she'd sleep, not after everything. Even with her eyes shut, images danced across her agonised mind: her mother lying in the sterile-looking hospital bed, restraints on her wrists and ankles, doped up to the gills. Her face had been bloodied, her skinny arms covered in bruises. The nurse had explained as succinctly as possible what had happened— how the police had been called after Naomi, in the grip of a psychotic episode, had attacked someone in the street before trying to kill herself, dragging a broken bottle across her wrists.

Emily had listened, silent and dazed, taking in every detail even though it felt as if they were bouncing off her brain. They'd been here before. Not this room, not even this hospital, but this place, oh yes. Her mother having a psychotic episode, attempting suicide, needing to be restrained, drugged up and deadened. Yes, they'd been here before.

And it was a place Emily hated. Why hadn't she seen the warning signs? Her mother going off her medication, and then insisting she was back on it... Emily should have known. Of course she should have. She'd chosen to believe her mum, to let it go, because it had been easier. Because she'd been both too scared and too tired to consider the agonising alternative. And now her mother was in intensive care, and she was here, and it felt as if her whole world had fallen apart. Again.

Her brain and body both ached as the images continued to flash through her mind—not just from the hospital but also from her childhood. A kitchen full of broken dishes. Her mother crying silently in the bath. Waking up to the manic movements of her mother deep cleaning their flat at two a.m.

At some point, mid-memory, she must have fallen asleep, deeply and dreamlessly, because the next thing she knew she was waking up to bright sunlight and the sound of the shower running. She was alone in the hotel room. Owen's bed looked rumpled, the pillow possessing a dent from where his head had been. If she put her hand there, she thought it would still be warm. Not that she would do something so weird, of course.

Emily sat up slowly, swinging her legs over the side of the bed. She felt tired and hungover even though she hadn't had much to drink last night. Her head ached and her mouth was dry and as she sat there, listening to Owen humming quite tunefully in the shower, she remembered what an idiotic zombie she'd been last night, too dazed to take anything in, letting him lead her from pillar to post like she was ill or brainless or both. What must he have thought of her? What did he think of her now? *Why did she care?*

And yet she did care, even if she didn't have the emotional head or heart space to dwell on it, or the kiss that had been interrupted by the call about her mother.

That kiss…

For a second Emily closed her eyes as she remembered how lovely it had felt to be in Owen's arms, his mouth moving so surely over hers. It had felt both thrillingly exciting and wonderfully safe, which was a combination that didn't make sense and threatened to do Emily's head in. She couldn't think about that kiss now.

The door to the bathroom opened while she was still sitting there, staring vacantly into space and sporting a serious case of bedhead.

Owen emerged from the steamy bathroom with a towel slung around his shoulders, his dark hair damp and curly. He was dressed in a fresh rugby shirt and a pair of jeans; he must have had spare clothes in the van, not that Emily had paid any attention. He gave her a concerned smile now.

"Did you sleep all right?"

"Erm…" Emily pushed a hand through her hair as she tried to make her brain feel less fuzzy. "Yes. I think so. Surprisingly." Owen nodded, his sympathetic gaze scanning her face, making Emily realise how she looked. Sleepy and messy, in her pyjamas, exposed. More vulnerable than she ever wanted to be, and that wasn't even thinking about last night and what Owen must have seen and surmised from the hospital...

"They have a breakfast buffet downstairs," he said as he rubbed his hair with the towel, his dark hair springing into curls like the wool of a lamb. "And then we can head back to the hospital. Is there a certain time they're expecting you?"

"The visiting hours start at ten." Although what state her mother would be in then, Emily had no idea.

"All right. It's only a little after eight now. We've got plenty of time."

"Okay. I'll take a shower, then." She grabbed her clothes and then sidled past him with an awkward smile; this whole situation really was incredibly weird. She'd never been in one like it before. It had always been just her and her mum, and when her mum was sick, it was just her.

Having someone else involved felt very different, and Emily wasn't sure she even knew what to *do* with Owen. She wanted him to leave her alone, and yet at the same time she wanted him to stay. Clearly her emotions were all over the place.

A long, hot shower definitely made her feel better, though, and once she was dressed in one of her armour-like outfits, tailored trousers and a button-down blouse, with her hair and make-up done, she felt ready to face the day—and her mother.

Owen raised his eyebrows as she emerged from the bathroom in her polished state. "You look like you're ready to chair a board meeting."

"I might go into work later," she said, which made her realise she hadn't actually texted Henry to let him know she wouldn't be showing up in less than an hour. When she reached for her phone to text him, though, she found the battery was dead. She'd forgotten to charge it last night, which was so unlike her.

"I'll call Jace," Owen told her easily. "And he can let Henry or Alice know."

Emily knew she didn't have much choice; she didn't actually know Henry's mobile off by heart. Still, she didn't like feeling so out of control, even with such little things. Wordlessly she nodded, and then listened, cringing inwardly, as Owen spoke to Jace.

"Hey, mate, could you do me a favour? Emily's in London to visit her mum in hospital and she's not going to be able to get into work today. Could you let Alice or Henry know? Thanks." As he disconnected the call, he raised his eyebrows. "What's wrong?"

"Everyone's going to be wondering," she said, feeling as if she were squirming inside. "What's wrong with my mum...why you were the one who was ringing..."

"Is that so bad?"

"Yes." The word burst out of her. "I'm a very private person."

"Yes, I can see that." He gave her a measured look. "You don't have to go into detail with everyone, but people want to help, Emily." He paused. "I do."

"You are helping." She reached for her bag and began stuffing her pyjamas into it. "You drove me here, after all." She kept her head lowered, her face averted from his as she zipped up the bag. "Why don't we get some breakfast?"

# Chapter Eleven

OWEN WATCHED AS Emily sat down across from him, having just been to the breakfast buffet. She had a plate with some fresh fruit and little bowl of yoghurt, and a cup of coffee, which she placed precisely to the top right of her plate. Knife and fork were set in parallel lines on either side of the plate, and it wasn't until she had everything arranged just so that she looked up and caught him staring. She frowned.

"What is it?"

He nodded towards her food. "You've got a little routine going there, don't you?" He'd meant it teasingly, but colour flooded her face as she looked away.

"I like things a certain way."

"Yes, I can see that." He eyed her speculatively as she gave her fork one last tweak and then spread her napkin in her lap. Emily David was proving to be far more of a conundrum that he'd originally thought. The last twelve hours had certainly shown him that. Her mother...her vulnerability...their kiss.

Their kiss, Owen acknowledged, had been mind-blowing. Life-changing. He'd kissed a fair few women in his time, but no one, *no one*, had made him feel like that. As if the top of his head was coming off and his heart was expanding to fill up his body. It had been sweetness and fire and yearning and completion all at once, and it had just been a kiss. He didn't know whether to be terrified or elated. He decided he was both, not that he was going to reveal either emotion to Emily anytime soon. He had a feeling she'd be completely freaked out, and he might be, too.

But that kiss certainly put today in perspective, because coming to London wasn't so much about offering a favour to a friend, but supporting a woman he was already starting to care about. Which was something else he wasn't going to be telling Emily anytime soon.

Because that really did freak him out.

"So what's the plan?" he asked as he dug into his plateful of bacon and eggs. "Go to the hospital, see your mum…?"

"Yes." She took a sip of her coffee, her gaze lowered. "I'll need to meet with her care team and see what their thoughts are. I imagine…" She paused, her throat working. "I imagine she'll have to stay in hospital for some time."

Which begged all sorts of questions. What was wrong with her mum? What had happened? Owen decided not to ask. Emily clearly didn't want to volunteer the information.

She lifted her gaze, her slate-coloured eyes wide, her expression direct and resolute. "I don't know how long I'll be, so it's probably best if you return to Wychwood. I'll catch a train back."

So that was him told and sorted. Owen didn't reply, just kept watching her thoughtfully. Unnerving her, clearly, because she put her coffee cup down and narrowed her eyes. "What is it?"

"I don't have to be back to the pub anytime soon." Darren, his second-in-command, had offered to open and man the bar this evening if needed. "I don't mind staying with you until you know what's going on."

Emily pursed her lips, her expression setting into something intransigent. "Thank you, but I don't think that's necessary."

She was shutting him out and he didn't want her to. Frustrated, Owen didn't reply. He knew there was no point in pressing, but it still irritated him and hell, *hurt* him. What was happening here? They barely knew each other.

And yet already something bound them together, something deep and important, and it wasn't just a kiss. Hell if he wanted to name it, though.

They ate the rest of their breakfast in silence, and then headed back up to the room to gather their things. Owen asked her if she wanted to book another night, but Emily shook her head.

"I do need to get back to work. And Wychwood is only an hour by train. I can come in as needed."

At checkout, Emily insisted on paying, and annoyed,

Owen said they'd split the bill.

"You wouldn't have come if it hadn't been for me," she protested, and he shook his head.

"We both slept in that room. We'll split it." Even if he wanted to pay for the whole thing himself.

Emily's heels clicked across the floor as she headed outside to the car park. Owen watched her unhappily; she seemed brittle and remote and a million miles from the tousle-headed woman, sleepy and warm, who had woken up this morning and looked at him with a dazed sort of sadness. That woman had been approachable, someone he could talk to and trust.

This woman, with her sleek, styled hair, her perfect make-up, her silk blouse and narrow trousers, was not. This Emily was like a model or a socialite, or perhaps a powerful businesswoman. Someone whose path he would never cross, and if it did, she wouldn't spare him a second glance.

She certainly didn't spare him one as she made her way to the van and then climbed inside, her face angled to the window as they drove back to the Huntley Centre in silence.

Once again Owen waited in the foyer while Emily disappeared into the ward. She'd thanked him for taking her there, and Owen suspected she meant it as a farewell but stubbornly, stupidly perhaps, he wasn't ready to go. So he waited, goodness knew for how long, for Emily to come back. What would happen then, he had no idea. For now he was content enough simply to wait.

"YOUR MOTHER IS physically stable, but she is refusing treatment or medication."

The consulting psychiatrist, a bearded man with a quiet yet no-nonsense manner, gave Emily a direct look as she nodded mechanically.

"As a result of this, we are intending to section her under section two of the Mental Health Act. She will remain in this facility for twenty-eight days, for observation. Fortunately, the woman your mother attacked has dropped charges, so she will not face any prosecution."

Emily swallowed dryly. She hadn't even thought about her mother being prosecuted. Last time something like this had happened, there had been no criminal charges and the twenty-eight days had been extended to six months, before her mother had agreed to take her meds and shown signs of being mentally stable enough to be released into Emily's care.

"May I visit her now?"

"Yes, and our hope is that will be a positive experience for both her and you." Emily swallowed again. Her throat felt tight and sore. She wasn't sure about it being a pleasant experience. "It will be important to stay in communication with the nurses and ward manager, to make sure your visits continue to be helpful."

"Yes."

The psychiatrist cocked his head, his gaze turning sympathetic. "And it's also important that you have the support you need."

Fleetingly Emily thought of Owen. He was probably heading back to Wychwood by now, glad to be shot of her and her crazy mother. Why had she pushed him away? Yet what else could she have done?

"I'm fine," she told the doctor firmly. It was what she always said, every time. There had never been the slightest chance of saying—or feeling—anything else. "But I'd like to see my mother now."

Thankfully the restraints were off her mother's wrists and ankles as Emily was let into her room, the door locked behind her. Naomi's eyes fluttered open as she approached the bed, and then her mother stiffened before struggling upright.

"Emily. *Emily*."

"Hello, Mum." Emily tried to keep her voice incongruously cheerful as she stood next to the bed. "How are you feeling?"

"Emily, darling, you've got to get me out of here." Her mother's hand scrabbled for her arm, fingers clenching around her wrist, ragged nails digging in painfully. "Please. I don't belong here. You know I don't. They've completely overreacted—it's *ridiculous*. I might have to sue."

Emily tried not to wince as she uncurled her mother's fingers from around her wrist and tried to hold her hand instead. "The doctors here want you to get better, Mum, that's all."

"Better? *Better?*" Naomi snarled. "I'm fine. You know I'm fine. I don't need to be chained up like some animal." She held up her hands as if they had handcuffs on.

"You're not chained—"

"But they won't let me go. I'm being *imprisoned.*"

"It's for the best, Mum. You were hurting yourself. You need to get better—"

"I don't!" Naomi shrieked. "I *don't.* You're a liar, you're all *liars.*"

Everything she said was wrong, and yet Emily kept trying. She always did, because the alternative was to give up, and the thought of doing that was unbearable. "Please, Mum, if you'd just—"

"I'm not listening to anything you say," Naomi spat. "If you won't help me get out of here, if you won't even listen to me, then I don't want to see you. I don't want to have anything to do with you. You're not my daughter."

Emily opened her mouth to protest, but then her mother reached for the plastic water jug on the table next to her and hurled it at Emily's head. She didn't duck fast enough, and it hit her cheek as water splattered over her hair and face. Within seconds the door was unlocked and a nurse bustled in.

"I'm sorry, Naomi, but we can't have that kind of behaviour here."

"Make her leave," Naomi demanded. "*Make her leave!*"

The nurse gave Emily an apologetic look and, tucking her wet hair behind her ears, Emily headed for the door.

"I'm going," she said quietly. "I'll see you again, Mum—"

"No, you won't. I don't want you here."

Pressure made Emily's chest feel tight and heavy and she just nodded and left the room. What else could she do? She'd been here before, had faced her mother's incandescent wrath. The nurse would sedate her, and then she'd wake up hopefully calmer, and eventually she'd want to see Emily again. And when she did, Emily would be there. She had to be.

"Why don't you ring tomorrow?" the nurse suggested after she'd left Naomi. "See how she is? Visits are important." She gave a quick, sympathetic smile. "I know they're hard."

"Yes, I'll ring."

Emily ducked into a bathroom to try to repair the worst of the wet, but her hair was sopping on one side and there wasn't much she could do about it. It didn't matter, anyway.

She took a deep breath, willing the force of her emotion back, always back. She knew her mum didn't mean the things she said. It was the mental illness talking. It was something she'd had to repeat to herself many times since she was seven, when a nurse had said it kindly to her. It was meant to help, but in the moment it didn't, at least not much.

As Emily was buzzed out of the ward, she realised it

wasn't even eleven o'clock. She could be back at her desk a little after noon, working on the latest plans for the fundraiser, which included booking with a carnival company that provided high-brow arcade amusements. Another steadying breath, and she forced herself to focus. *Onwards.*

Then she saw Owen.

He rose from his chair, coming towards her with a kindly smile, forehead crinkled, eyebrows drawn together. "Emily…"

She stared at him stupidly. "What are you doing here?"

"I wanted to wait."

And yet she'd told him to go. Emily just stared at him and Owen frowned, looking uncharacteristically and rather endearingly uncertain. "Is that…is that okay?"

"Yes." The single word wobbled and then, to her horror, Emily felt her face start to crumple. Before she could haul it all back, Owen's arms were around her and she was, amazingly, absurdly, sobbing into the steady warmth of his shoulder.

She didn't *do* stuff like this. And yet somehow she was, and even more bizarrely, it felt *good*. It was what she'd needed, the pressure valve on her emotions blown right off, everything she'd held so closely to herself scattered to the winds.

Owen held her in his arms and patted her back and let her cry, all the while murmuring things she couldn't understand—she had a feeling he was speaking Welsh—but sounded lovely and soothing anyway.

And then, after what could have been thirty seconds or five minutes, Emily came to and stiffened in his arms. She'd been making a spectacle of herself. There was snot on Owen's shirt. And she had to look a frightful mess.

She raised her head from his shoulder and then stepped out of his arms. He let her go, his forehead still crinkled as he watched her uncertainly. "Emily…"

"Let's go. I want to go." She spoke abruptly, every instinct for self-preservation kicking in hard and fast. "I want to go right now."

"All right." Easy as always, Owen grabbed his jacket and then they headed outside, back to the van, while Emily wiped her wet cheeks and tried desperately to reassemble the shattered pieces of herself.

"I'm sorry about that," she managed once they were in the van.

"You don't have to be sorry. You're going through something very tough." A pause where she struggled with how to respond. "Do you want to tell me about it?"

The gentleness in Owen's voice threatened to undo her all over again. She hadn't told anyone about "it" in nineteen years. Her mother's illness was the big, hulking secret she carried around always, lugging behind her, letting it control every choice she made. Whether it was kindly teachers, concerned neighbours, fledgling friends…nobody got to know.

Because if they did, bad things might happen. That was what Emily had believed as a child—she'd be taken away from her mummy, or her mummy would be put in a bad place. *We're all right, aren't we, darling? We'll always be all right as long as we have each other.*

Except when they didn't have each other, because her mum, her lovely mum, was in the middle of a psychotic episode, and Emily had to deal with it all alone.

Emily wiped her cheeks again; she realised she was still crying, tears silently slipping down her face as if they had a will of their own. Perhaps they did.

"I don't know if I can," she said.

"Try." Owen smiled at her, his face so full of gentleness Emily let out a choked noise that sounded far too close to a sob.

"Why are you being so nice to me?"

"Why shouldn't I?" He reached across with one work-roughened hand and with the pad of his thumb he wiped a tear from her cheek. "I care about you, Emily David."

Her heart contracted and expanded all at once. Everything felt impossible, so she just shook her head. Owen didn't seem bothered by that.

He dropped his hand from her cheek and started the van. "We'd better get going before I get a ticket. You talk when you're ready."

Which would be never, and yet some desperate part of her wanted to talk. Wanted to tell someone everything, even as she writhed in shame at the thought. What would Owen think about her mother? What would he think about *her*?

They drove through the London streets full of traffic, the sky heavy and grey above. It was almost mid-April but it still felt chilly and unforgiving outside, spring a fragile hope more than a reality.

Emily watched the streets blur by as exhaustion crashed over her. She leaned her head against the window and closed her eyes, thinking she could fall asleep right there.

And perhaps she did, lulled by the movement of the van, the warmth from the heater, because her eyes fluttered open and she jerked upright, to see they were now on the motorway, heading back towards Wychwood. She glanced at Owen, who smiled at her. Again. He was full of smiles, this man.

"You snore," he said, and Emily let out another choked noise, this one closer to a laugh.

"I don't."

"Just a little snuffle. Quite cute, actually. Like a kitten."

*A kitten.* "Oh no," she said, and Owen raised his eyebrows in inquiry. "I have a kitten. I hope he—or she—will be all right. I texted Alice last night…" She reached for her phone, only to remember the battery was dead. "I did text her…"

"I'm sure it will be fine. Cats are amazingly self-reliant creatures. I didn't peg you as a cat person, though."

"I'm not. It's just this kitten was abandoned in my garden by its mmm—mother…" She trailed off, near tears again, and Owen didn't reply. Emily drew a clogged breath. "I'm a mess," she said miserably, and he reached over and placed one hand on her knee, a comforting touch she realised she craved.

"We all are."

"Are you?"

"Yes, absolutely."

Except he didn't seem like a mess, and yet somehow she believed him. She blinked rapidly, drew another clogged breath. "Okay," she said. "I'll tell you."

# Chapter Twelve

OWEN WAITED, HOLDING on to his smile, as Emily took another deep breath and readied herself to say—what? He didn't know exactly, only that he needed to listen. That he needed to seem steady and safe and reassuring, and not freaked out like he actually was.

Because he'd been here before, and it hadn't worked. Someone had trusted him with their pain and heartache and the mess of their lives, and he hadn't been able to do a damn thing. His mother. His father. His sisters. Just about everybody he cared about, really.

Perhaps that was, at least in part, why he was here now, why this mattered so much to him. Why Emily did. Because here was another broken person, another mess, and maybe, finally, he could help.

Maybe he couldn't.

Either way he was here and he was going to listen, because he cared about Emily.

"I don't actually know where to start," she confessed in a shaky voice.

"How about when you realised your mum was ill?" Owen suggested gently.

"I don't actually know when that was. I don't think I can point to a single moment when I realised that this—my mum, my life—wasn't normal." She paused, her head turned towards the window, her gaze pensive. Owen stayed silent, knowing he just needed to let her speak. "I must have at some point, though, because I know that I learned to—to hide it."

"Hide it?" he prompted after a few minutes had slipped by without her saying anything more.

"My parents divorced when I was seven. There was a custody battle that my father lost. Well, he walked away from it, basically. He wasn't willing to have a big fight about it, which he said for my sake. And it probably was... Courts usually side with mothers, anyway."

*Even mentally ill ones?* Owen waited for more.

"When he left, that was, I think, when life lost all sense of normality. I never knew what was going to happen next. What mood my mother would be in, what...what she might be capable of."

Owen's hands tightened on the wheel. That didn't sound good at all.

"And yet sometimes she was so much fun. Imagine having a mum who wakes you up at midnight to make ice cream sundaes. Or takes you out of school to go to the zoo, just because. Or hugs you and tells you she loves you more than anything, and you really do believe her?" Emily gave him a trembling, heart-breaking smile that threatened to slide off her face. "My mum did all those things and more."

"But the other times?" Owen asked after a moment.

"She was—is—bipolar. Severely bipolar, with psychotic episodes." She let out a shuddering breath. "I know that's a mouthful."

It was a hell of a lot more than that. Owen pictured a seven-year-old Emily dealing with that on her own, and something in him wanted to rage.

"But she was treated for it?" he asked.

"Not for a long time. She didn't want to be treated. She loved the highs, and sometimes they lasted a long time. And I think, when I was a little, maybe it wasn't so bad. At least...my dad used to say that's just how Mum was. Spirit-ed. Emotional." She let out a shuddery sort of sigh. "I suppose we didn't have an awareness of mental health twenty years ago that we do now, and the truth is, she could be a lot of fun. She had all this energy..."

Even so. Owen stared straight ahead, his mouth set in a grim line. Hearing this was even harder than he'd expected. How could a father let his seven-year-old daughter deal with that on her own? "How long did that go on?" he asked after a moment. Emily shrugged.

"Oh, I don't know. Sometimes it's all a blur in my mind. After the divorce, we moved a lot. I went to different schools. I became very good at pretending things were normal, which

I suppose means I must have known they weren't, but it's hard to remember how I really was at the time, instead of looking back as an adult. At some point I must have realised—and I don't know when—that I had to shield my mother. Hide her. I think I knew from a young age that it would be bad if people found out. I might have been taken away, or she might have… It had to be this secret."

"That's understandable…"

She nodded slowly before continuing painfully, "I still feel that way, to be honest. I hate the thought of you knowing any of this, and I don't even know why anymore, because obviously it's not like it was when I was a kid." Her voice wobbled a little, and Owen wished he wasn't driving the damned van. He wanted to take Emily in his arms.

"I'm sorry," he said, uselessly. "I'm sorry you went through all that, but I'm glad I know now."

"I don't know if I am. It feels…scary." She let out a shuddery breath as she shook her head. "Anyway, when I was in Sixth Form, my mother had a psychotic episode that ended up with the neighbours calling the police. I won't go into the details, but it meant she was hospitalised for the first time. As I was over eighteen, I wasn't taken into care or anything like that. I just coped on my own, and in some ways that was a relief. To be alone. But I felt sad and scared, too. It was a strange time." She gave herself a little shake, as if to rid herself of the memories. "Anyway, when she came out of hospital, she had a diagnosis and she was on medication, and life felt a lot easier, but also, if I'm honest, duller. The meds evened my mum out, and I missed her, if that makes sense, because of course it was better." Another trembling smile.

"I can understand how you would feel that way." Some parts of Emily's story were strangely and uncomfortably close to his own. He thought of his father's expansive moods, his generous bonhomie, the lightning shift to temper, the festering resentment, and then he pushed it all out of his mind. He couldn't think about his stuff right now. He needed to focus on Emily.

"But at least it enabled me to go to university, because I felt my mum was well enough to be left on her own. And she was, although there were some ups and downs." A pause, telling in its weighty silence. "Then, three years ago, she chose to go off her medication and had a psychotic episode, out of control and suicidal. She ended up in a psychiatric hospital like the one she's in now, for six months. So I really should have seen this coming."

"Emily, you cannot blame yourself for this." She just shook her head, and Owen struggled with what to say, because he knew you *could* blame yourself. Easily. You could and you did. But even so, Emily shouldn't.

"You can't be your mother's keeper."

"Someone has to be."

"Your mother is an adult—"

"You sound like my father." From her tone he knew it

wasn't a compliment. "My mother is mentally ill, Owen. Seriously mentally ill. If I'm not responsible for her, who is? If I can't help her, who will?"

Owen stayed miserably silent. He didn't have the answer for that one. Not for Emily, and not for himself.

"Still," he said, knowing it was unaccountably lame, and she let out a huff of sound that felt like disappointment. They drove in silence the rest of the way home, because although he had so many things to say, he didn't know how to say them.

"Thank you for the lift," Emily said as he pulled the van into the courtyard of Willoughby Close. She sounded horribly formal. "I really do appreciate it."

"Don't," Owen blurted, and her eyes widened as she looked at him.

"Don't what?"

"We're past that kind of thing, aren't we?"

She shook her head slowly. "Owen, you don't even know me."

"But what I know, I like."

"Really?" She sounded both sad and disbelieving, and it made Owen ache even as he considered her point. *Really?* She'd annoyed him when he'd first met her, and although he understood her prickliness now, he still didn't know that much more about her. Did he? Was he reaching out to her now simply because she was fragile, and here was someone he could finally save? Maybe this wasn't about Emily at all. And maybe he couldn't save her.

"Please don't shut me out," he said quietly. "I want to help."

"Thank you, but there's nothing more you can do. My mother will be in hospital for the next twenty-eight days. After that..." Emily shrugged. "I don't know what will happen." She opened the door of the van while Owen watched in hopeless frustration. "Thank you," she said again, and then she got out of the van.

❉

EMILY COULD FEEL Owen's eyes on her as she grabbed her bag and walked towards her front door. She was waiting for him to start the van back up and pull away, but he didn't. What did he *want* from her? He'd been so kind, too kind, but there was nothing more he could do now.

She had to go to work. She had to live her life.

*Even if you're not sure you like the way you've been living anymore? Even if letting someone in just a little bit might have been both the best and hardest thing you've ever done?*

Emily reached for her key and fit it into the lock. It wasn't until she'd shut the door behind her and breathed in the quiet calm of her cottage that she heard Owen's van start up.

A plaintive meow split the silence and Emily looked down to see her kitten—it still needed a name—inching forward.

"Oh, you." She let out a little laugh as she bent down to

scoop the little ball of fluff into her hands. The kitten came willingly, letting out a thrumming purr as Emily cuddled it close. The live contact felt good, grounding her in the reality that for once she wasn't alone. She had a kitten.

*And you have Owen.*

Of course, she didn't *have* Owen. She'd as good as pushed him away with both hands just a moment ago. And yet she knew that if she rang him now—not that she even had his mobile number—he'd come over in a heartbeat. Wouldn't he? Or was she being arrogant or maybe pathetic in even thinking that? Maybe she didn't *have* Owen at all.

Emily let out a sigh as she let the kitten scamper off. It was only a little past noon and yet she felt as if the day had gone forever. She needed to get to work, to ground herself in the soothing routine of administration and order.

A knock at the door, a persistent rat-a-tat-tat, had her straightening again and going to open it.

"Emily."

Emily stiffened as Alice enveloped her in a quick, tight hug before stepping back to scan her face anxiously. "I've been so worried. Is your mum okay? I fed the kitten. What an absolute darling. I didn't even know you had one. Anyway, he's fine. But what about you?" She let out an abashed laugh. "Sorry, I know I'm running on. I do that when I'm nervous."

"I'm all right. I was just planning to come up to work."

"Oh, but you shouldn't! I mean, you don't have to. Take

the day off…"

Emily shook her head. "My mother is sick, not me. I want to work. Keep busy."

"Oh, of course." Emily tried not to chafe at the blatant look of sympathy on Alice's face. "I can understand that. I'm sure I'd feel the same."

"Thank you." She smiled stiffly.

"Are you going now? Shall we walk up together?"

"All right." Emily wouldn't have minded a little space, but she knew Alice meant well. She filled the kitten's water bowl and glanced at the bag she'd left by the door; everything in her wanted to unpack it, sort laundry, and restore order, but Alice was waiting and so reluctantly she left it.

Outside the sky seemed to hang limply over the earth, flat and grey.

"It hasn't been the best weather, has it?" Alice remarked with a sigh. "And they say more rain is forecast. I hope the Lea doesn't flood."

"Has it before?"

"Not since I've lived here, but people talk about it having happened in the past. I don't think it would affect Willoughby Manor or the close, as we're up high enough, but there are lots of houses alongside the river, and some shops too."

"Hopefully it won't come to that," Emily murmured. She didn't have the energy or emotional space to worry about anything else than what was going on in her life right now.

Back in the office, she was finally able to push all her worries and concerns to the back of her mind as she focused on filing—one of her favourite activities—and then sorting some logistics for the fundraiser. It was, she hoped, shaping up to be a fun and wholesome event, with plenty of children's activities on offer, as well as local businesses showcasing their wares. It made her happy to think of it, to think of anything but the fact of her mother lying in a hospital bed, hating her.

Late afternoon, it started to rain, a steady hammering on the terrace outside as raindrops streaked down the long windowpanes. Alice came in with a cup of tea and an uncertain smile.

"I know you want to work, but I thought you could use a hot drink."

"That's kind. Thank you, Alice." Emily looked up from her laptop, blinking a gloomy world back into focus. The tea was welcome.

Emily cradled the mug in her hands, savouring the warmth. For a few hours she'd been able to keep from thinking about everything, but now, with just a moment's respite, memories started to rush in. The hospital. Her mother's look of fury and hatred. Twenty-eight days. *Owen...*

"Do you want to talk about it?" Alice asked cautiously. "It's okay if you don't."

Emily sighed. "There isn't much to talk about, really." She paused, and then, perhaps because she'd done it once already so it felt that little bit easier, she added somewhat recklessly, "My mother's been sectioned. She'll be in a closed psychiatric unit for the next twenty-eight days."

"Oh, Emily."

Yes, there it was, the cringing sense of shame and fear that she'd said it aloud. Again. There was nothing but pity on Alice's face, but still. Emily wished she'd kept her mouth shut.

"I'm sorry." Emily nodded her thanks, and Alice continued hesitantly, "I know a little of what you're going through. My mum...she was a drug addict. I lived with her a couple of times in between being in care and...it wasn't easy." Alice swallowed hard. "Not easy at all."

"I'm sure it wasn't." Once again, Emily realised, she'd assumed, without even realising she was doing it, that someone wouldn't understand. That they wouldn't relate, when they could. All too well. "I'm sorry, Alice. I didn't realise."

"It was a lot of ups and downs," Alice continued quietly. "I wanted to be with her, but then I really didn't. And then I felt guilty for not wanting it...round and round, until it finally wasn't an issue, because I aged out and she lost touch." She sighed. "I don't even know where she is now."

"That sounds really tough." Emily knew the words were inadequate, yet she didn't have any others. Alice's observation had already skated a bit too close to the bone, to the heart. Yes, she understood that merry-go-round of emotions, wishing her mum would get better and wishing she wouldn't, wishing she would be in her life or completely out of it. And the guilt. Always the guilt. She wished she could explain to Alice how she understood, she got it, but the words were jumbled inside her. "Thank you," she said instead, hefting her cup of tea but meaning so much more. It helped, to know someone else understood what you were going through, if not the particulars, then the generalities.

Alice smiled shyly. "Anytime."

❉

IT WAS STILL raining, a steady, depressing downpour, as Emily headed back to Willoughby Close, huddled under an umbrella as the wind blew the rain sideways straight into her face. The world looked chilled and miserable, as well as thoroughly soaked.

Inside she checked on The Kitten—he really needed a name—smiling to see him curled up on top of a basket of ironing. Of course, she'd have to wash it all again, but it was still rather sweet.

After changing out of her wet clothes, she steeled herself for a telephone call to the hospital, something she knew she would have to do daily.

"Naomi is currently sleeping," the nurse said when Emily managed to get through to someone familiar with her mother's case. "After some agitation, she was sedated this afternoon and has been doing much better."

*Because she was unconscious?* "Should I come for a visit tomorrow?" Emily asked, and a telling pause followed.

"I don't think that would be a good idea, no," the nurse said finally. "I'm sorry, but your mother is still quite emotive and agitated. Keeping her to a safe and steady routine is her best option now, without introducing any outside factors."

So that was what she'd become—an outside factor. Emily murmured her thanks before ending the call. Tears pricked her eyes and she blinked them away furiously.

It was foolish to be hurt by this. She'd understood long ago that she couldn't take her mother's hostility or even hatred personally. But it made her wonder if she shouldn't take the love and affection personally, either. Could she trust anything? *Anyone?*

A soft knock on the door startled her out of her unhappy thoughts, and she wondered which well-meaning neighbour was coming for the scoop now.

But when she opened the door, she saw it wasn't a neighbour. It was Owen, his dark curls plastered to his face, the shoulders of his coat dripping with rain, his smile both sheepish and wonderful.

"You're soaked!"

"It's raining."

"So I noticed." Emily realised she was smiling. "Come in."

She stepped aside as he came into the cottage, dripping all over the floor as he shook the water from his hair the way a dog would. "I just wanted to check how you were doing."

Her heart contracted, expanded, spilled over. "I'm all right."

"Your mum?"

"Still doesn't want to see me." She swallowed hard. "I'll call again tomorrow."

"Will you visit?"

"Not until I'm allowed."

"I'm sorry, Emily."

She shrugged, tried to smile, and didn't manage either. "I wanted to say…I'm sorry for being so emotional earlier. I'm not usually…"

"I know you're not." He gave her a crooked smile. "Sorry, but that's been blindingly obvious from the start."

She managed a laugh. "I suppose so."

"How does it feel, letting someone in just a little?"

"Hard." The word scraped her throat. "Good. But I don't… You still don't know me, Owen. I don't understand why…" *Why you're being so nice to me.* His kindness felt both overwhelming and amazing. *Too much.*

"Well, I was thinking about what you said earlier." Owen shoved his hands in the pockets of his faded and well-worn jeans, looking uncharacteristically uncertain, his mouth turned downwards, his blue, blue eyes scanning her face.

"What I said…?"

"About me not actually knowing you. And there's some truth to that, so I thought, why don't I get to know you? And you get to know me? Properly?"

Emily gazed at him uncertainly as she tried to figure out what he meant. "How do you mean…?"

"We go out on a date. Or actually, we go *in* on a date. I'm inviting you to my house for dinner." His smile was wide, his stance confident now, powerful shoulders thrown back, yet the flicker of uncertainty in his eyes made Emily ache. Why was he trying so hard? No one ever had before.

She'd never even been invited on a proper date before, and now that she was, she wasn't sure how to respond. How to feel.

"Emily…?"

"Sorry, I'm just…" She gave a little laugh as she shook her head. "I wasn't expecting that."

"You weren't?" Owen looked a bit surprised. Dates were fairly normal occurrences, Emily supposed, for other people. Getting asked on one probably wasn't that big a deal.

"No, I…I've never actually been on a date before." She tensed, waiting for his reaction. Shock? Pity? Revulsion, as he realised just how backward and inexperienced she really was, having hidden away from everything for so much of her life? How much *work* she was, for someone interested in dating her?

Amazingly, he took it in his stride. His mouth curved wider, his eyes glinting like a promise. "Then it's about time you went on one."

The ease of his response made her smile again, and something that had been hard and tight inside her loosened, just a little. Maybe something could be that simple for once. That easy.

"Yes," she said slowly, smiling as she said it. "Yes, I think you might be right."

# Chapter Thirteen

"AVA...?"

Emily had to nearly jump out of the way as Ava marched into her cottage on Saturday night, a hanging bag in one hand, a bottle of gin in the other.

"Um, it's nice to see you, but what are you doing here?"

Ava turned around, a look of purpose on her beautiful face. "We have work to do."

"We do?"

Ava glanced at her watch. "It's only two hours until your date with Owen. Yes, we have work."

"What...?" All week long Emily had been hugging the secret of her date with Owen to herself. She'd gone to work, chatted with Alice, arranged the fundraiser, held a business meeting with Henry, and said not a word.

Every night she'd walked home, called the hospital—no real change happening there—and made her dinner, cuddled still-nameless kitten and thought about Saturday night, because she was becoming a little bit obsessed. But she still hadn't told anyone, because that wasn't her style, and it felt too precious a secret to share.

"How did you know about it?" she asked and Ava's mouth curved in a cat-like smile.

"I know everything, love. But seriously, Owen told me. He wanted some advice, bless him."

"Some advice!" Her stomach did somersaults at that little bit of knowledge. "What kind of advice?"

"Never you mind. I keep your secrets, and I'll keep his as well."

"I don't have secrets," Emily objected, and Ava let out one of her full-throated laughs.

"As if, darling, as if."

"That you know of," Emily amended and Ava just smiled.

"You keep thinking that, then. I'll pour the gin."

Emily watched, bemused, as Ava marched over to the kitchen and did just that. "You do have ice cubes, I hope?" she tossed over her shoulder as she moved to the freezer. "Ah, I knew you would. And tonic water, too! You're my kind of girl."

Still speechless, Emily accepted a gin and tonic from Ava and took a sip, wincing a little at the tart taste of the gin. Ava had made it rather strong.

"No point in doing it otherwise," Ava said, and Emily nearly spluttered her gin.

"How do you do that?"

"Do what?" Ava asked innocently.

"Read my mind."

"It's an open book. Every emotion is on your face. Now come on. Upstairs so we can get you ready for this date, because I am not having you looking like you're heading into the office."

And without further ado, Ava picked up the hanging bag of clothes she'd brought with her and headed upstairs.

"Wait a second," Emily protested. "Ava, you can't just..."

"I already took my shoes off at the door," Ava said patiently. "I figured you'd have a thing about that. And I won't touch anything you don't want me to, or mess anything up, or heaven forbid, put anything out of alignment."

Emily, halfway to the stairs, stopped and stared. Blinked a bit. "Wait...what?"

"You're OCD. I get it." Ava shrugged. "We've all got our quirks, haven't we? I know I have mine."

"But..." Of course, Emily knew she had obsessive-compulsive tendencies. When you ordered your spices alphabetically, when you deep cleaned on a daily basis, when you had to have your shoes lined up precisely half an inch apart and perfectly parallel...well, yes, you knew. But she hadn't realised other people had. She'd always tried to hide it. And yet here Ava was, stating it as fact, and not a terribly important one at that. "How did you know?" she asked.

"How did I know? Well, the way you lined your knife and fork up by your plate when you were having dinner at ours might have been a clue. Or how you ate your food—so precisely! Everything cut into perfect squares. Or the fact that I've seen you put hand sanitiser on half a dozen times every time I see you."

And here Emily had thought she'd been discreet.

"The kitten is a surprise," Ava continued, nodding at the fluff ball curled up in his bed, sleeping peacefully. "It's nice to know you're not entirely predictable."

"Ouch."

"I'm teasing. Sort of." Ava grinned. "Now drink your gin and come upstairs so we can turn you into the knockout babe you know you want to be."

Well, there wasn't much she could say to that, was there? Already her three sips of gin had mellowed her considerably. And so Emily took another sip, downing half the glass, and headed upstairs.

As she came into the bedroom, Ava had already unzipped the hanging bag and was drawing out the most ridiculous and gorgeous dresses Emily had ever seen.

"I can't wear any of those," she declared and Ava gave her a rather beady look.

"Can't or won't?"

"Both." Emily nodded to a cocktail dress in ruby satin. "That's far too dressy. And I'd look like—a like a high-priced hooker!"

"Not a bad look, in my opinion," Ava mused. "And with a cute little cardigan, it would be fine. But the red might be a bit much on you." She reached for a dress in a lovely, soft blue grey. "What about this one? It will make your eyes pop."

The dress was more modest than the ruby one, but still far sexier than anything Emily had ever owned. Besides a very boring LBD for work functions, everything she owned came in two pieces or twin sets. Fashionable, but functional.

"I don't know," she answered hesitantly. "To tell you the truth, I thought it would be a bit more of a casual affair…"

"You don't *do* casual," Ava pointed out. "Not like other people, anyway. Do you even own a pair of jeans? Try it on." She held out the dress and after a moment, feeling as if she had suddenly started to inhabit someone else's life, someone else's body, Emily took it. She drank the rest of the gin, her head swirling, as she went into the bathroom and started to undress.

This was *crazy*. She never did stuff like this. She never had people to do it with. And yet here she was, fingers fumbling, Ava humming in her bedroom. What was *happening* to her?

She shrugged out of her work clothes, folding her skirt and top as a matter of necessity as well as habit, before slipping on the dress. It was a soft knitted fabric that slid sensuously across Emily's skin and clung to what curves she had. When she looked in the mirror, she swallowed hard, because already she was looking like someone else. She was starting to feel like someone else, as well.

Ava rapped on the door. "All right in there?"

"Yes…"

"Come out and show me, then."

With one hand pressed to her stomach to steady her nerves—as well as the gin—Emily opened the door. Ava's eyes brightened as she surveyed her appearance, her lips pursed.

"Very nice. Understated but definitely sexy. Yes."

"I don't know if—"

"But you need a belt." Ava ignored her hesitant objection as she riffled through her bag and came out with a black patent-leather belt with an ornate gold clasp. "Let's try this." She slipped it around Emily's waist before she could protest, giving her a quick smile as she did. "This is going to be fab, Emily. Really. Especially when we do your hair and make-up."

"Hair and make-up?" Emily could not keep the alarm from her voice.

"Of course. Can't have one without the other, can we?"

"I think this might be overkill," Emily said weakly. "My make-up is usually quite understated, and I don't want to give Owen the wrong idea…"

Ava pursed her lips. "And what would that be?" Emily didn't answer. She didn't even know, or at least she didn't want to say. "Come sit down and I'll do your hair," Ava said coaxingly. "You do know this is my job, don't you?"

Emily looked at her in surprise. "A hairdresser?"

"No, not that. Although sort of, I suppose." Ava let out a little laugh. "I started a business helping women go back into the workforce—help them with their training, their CVs, and their clothes and hair and make-up. So many don't even know where to begin, and their self-confidence is at absolute zero." Ava picked up a brush and started teasing Emily's hair out. "Don't worry, it's clean," she said soothingly. "I disinfected it before I came."

Emily closed her eyes. Surely she wasn't that much of a germophobe? Well, yes, she probably was. But there was something surprisingly soothing about submitting herself to Ava's ministrations. As she gently pulled the brush through Emily's hair, she was reminded of the storybook, the rocking chair. *Goodnight brush and goodnight mush...* She felt like a child, and it was both a strange and sweet feeling. She closed her eyes and let herself relax.

An hour later, Emily was ready. She'd been amazed at how long the hair and make-up had taken, but Ava was exacting and Emily had found herself enjoying simply sitting still. Plus she'd had another gin and tonic, and she was feeling decidedly relaxed.

"All right, are you ready for the big reveal?" Ava said as she put her hands on Emily's shoulders and steered her towards the full-length mirror in the bathroom. "No peeking until I say, all right?"

"All right." Emily had no idea what to expect.

"Ta-da!" Ava crowed, and Emily opened her eyes.

For a second, as absurd as it was, she didn't recognise the woman in the mirror. For a second, she envied that woman, because she looked so vibrant and glowing and happy. And then she realised it was her.

"I…" Emily was at a loss for words as she put one hand to the soft, full waves that fell onto her shoulders. Stared at her smoky eyes with a subtle, sexy hint of cat-flick eyeliner, the perfectly outlined lips, the touch of colour on cheekbones that looked far more sculpted than usual.

"It's not too much, is it?"

"No…" Because, amazingly, it wasn't. She didn't look ridiculously overdressed or tarty, as she'd feared. She simply looked wonderfully alive. Emily's gaze dropped to her figure, the knit dress clinging to her curves thanks to the help of the belt. She looked sexy but not too sexy, although it was miles beyond what she was used to.

"What will Owen think?" she asked aloud.

"He'll think you're smokin' hot, because you are, and that he has *completely* lucked out, because he has."

The words caused a thrill to run through her, and yet some old, cautious part of her resisted. "Still, it feels a bit much…" All the old doubts were racing back. She never wanted to be noticed. Yes, she'd used clothes as armour, professional clothes that kept people at a distance. Everything about her right now was saying *notice me*, and that was not her usual at all.

Ava put her hands back on Emily's shoulders as she met

her gaze in the mirror. "Trust me when I say this is not too much. Speaking as someone who did more than the 'bit much' all the time, I know what I'm talking about."

"Do you?" Emily managed a wavery smile.

"Yes, I do. Look, Emily, I understand why you don't want to put yourself out there. I was an expert in self-protection for a long time. I did it differently than you, to be sure, but it still feels the same inside. A way to stay safe, to keep people at a distance. And when it works, you might feel safe, but you don't feel happy."

Her words both exposed and comforted her. Emily kept her gaze on Ava's in the mirror as she asked, "Why did you do that?"

Ava sighed. "Because life dealt me a pretty raw hand for a while. My mother scarpered when I was twelve, and my dad wasn't all that interested in a daughter. I left home at sixteen and ended up working in a club—I won't bore you with the details, but it wasn't the best work, shall we say. Then I ended up temping, and then marrying my boss, and living like a trophy wife for five years, never forgetting it for a minute. When I met Jace…he was the only person who kept trying with me. Who saw me as something other than how I saw myself. And if Owen can be your Jace, even if it's just a small chance…well, I want that for you. I want that for anyone. A lot."

Emily swallowed hard, absorbing everything Ava had said. "It's just one date."

"I know, and that's fine. Maybe you'll just have a nice dinner and that will be that. But you'll have gone out, and taken a risk, and that's almost as important. Life is for living, Emily. Not hiding away, however you choose to do it."

"I'm not actually hiding—"

"Not literally, but there are different ways of doing it. Trust me, I know. Now, m'lady, your carriage awaits."

Emily stared at her blankly. "Carriage…?"

"Well, Jace's truck." Ava gave her a flippant smile. "But he's cleaned it just for you."

To her horror, Emily's eyes filled with tears. "I don't understand why you're doing this for me. Everyone. It's so much—"

"Don't cry," Ava said severely. "Or I will too, and worse, you'll wreck the amazing make-up job I did. I'm doing this for my sake as much as yours, okay? Because it makes me feel better too. And I want to help anyone I can, because I know what it's like to be helped. Lady Stokeley helped me along with Jace, and Harriet and Ellie too. I'd never had friends before I moved to Willoughby Close."

Emily's throat closed as she forced out, "I never had any, either."

Ava gave her a quick, hard hug. "I know. But you do now."

Emily nodded, willing the tears back for the sake of her eyeliner as well as her friend. "Thank you, Ava. For…for everything."

Ava nodded back, her eyes as bright as Emily's as she self-consciously sniffed. "Go get 'em, girl."

Emily tottered slightly in the heels Ava had chosen for her—a pair at the back of her wardrobe that she never wore because they were a bit too high. Her head was still swirling from the second gin, although not in a bad way. She felt pleasantly fuzzy, loose-limbed instead of all coiled tension and nerves, expectant and excited and *happy*.

Jace whistled under his breath as she came outside, the air damp, the sky grey, but at least it wasn't raining.

"Look at you," he said as he hopped out of the truck and went around to open the passenger door.

"I feel like Cinderella."

"Not a bad feeling, then."

"But a bit ridiculous," Emily felt compelled to point out as she clambered rather ungracefully into the truck.

"Nothing ridiculous about it," Jace answered affably. "And all I have to say is, Owen is one lucky bloke."

Emily blushed and said nothing. "I suppose you know where he lives?" she asked as Jace turned out of Willoughby Manor's lane. "He did give me his address—"

"I know it." He slanted her a glinting look. "Owen lives on the other side of the village. The other side of the tracks, as it were."

"Oh." She didn't know what to say to that.

"He's got a pretty cool place, though, don't worry."

The truck bumped along a darkened and deserted high

street—seven p.m. on a Saturday night in Wychwood and not much was happening, except at the two pubs. Then he was winding through several narrow residential streets of semi-detached houses before emerging on a road that led to the open countryside at the top of the village. A couple of industrial-looking garages were on the right-hand side of the road, and when Jace pulled into the car park in front of them, Emily gave him a startled look.

"First one on the right. Ring the buzzer."

"He *lives* here?"

"Yep."

Emily stared at the deserted-looking garages dubiously. "Are you sure…"

"Of course I'm sure. But I'll stay here until he opens the door, just to show you I'm not having you on. Go." Gently he nudged her shoulder. "And have fun."

Emily climbed out of the truck, pulling her coat more tightly around her. Here at the top of the village, the wind blew a bit more briskly. Under the gloomy skies she could see the rest of Wychwood tumbling down a hill, and then the manor on the far side. She glanced back at Jace and he gave her a cheery thumbs-up.

Her heels clicking on the uneven pavement, Emily walked up to the first garage. A metal door on rollers was shuttered tight, and a staircase led up to the first floor, and what Emily supposed was the front door. This all felt very odd. Was this really Owen's house? He lived in a *garage*?

Her shoes made a clinking sound as she climbed the stairs, and then, taking a deep breath, pressed the buzzer.

"Here goes nothing," she muttered as her heart started to thud. *Or, really, here went everything...*

# Chapter Fourteen

A FEW SECONDS later Owen flung open the door, and Emily blinked at him in surprise. He cleaned up nicely, was her first thought. *Very* nicely. Instead of his usual rugby shirt and old jeans, he was wearing a well-starched button-down in a bright blue that matched his eyes, and a pair of dark grey trousers. His hair was slightly damp, curls springing up by his ears, and his eyes twinkled as he smiled at her.

"You made it."

"I did."

"Come in." He moved aside, sweeping an arm out, and Emily took a step inside, drawing her breath in sharply as she took in the home before her. "Oh, wow."

"You like it?"

"It's amazing," she said honestly. They were standing on a mezzanine balcony that ran along three sides of the garage, a huge skylight above them letting in the last of the evening light.

"Follow me," Owen said grandly, and she did, along the balcony, past a sleeping loft that had a king-sized bed that made her blush and look away, and then down a twisting, spiral staircase to the main living space below.

It was all open—a huge granite island in the kitchen, an even bigger sofa across from it, facing a wood burner where a fire crackled merrily. Bookshelves lined the walls, filled with battered paperbacks, and something that smelled delicious was cooking on top of the massive Aga. The space was cluttered and cosy and the opposite of Emily's cottage, and yet just as with the kitchen of Willoughby Manor, she found she loved it. She wanted to curl up in a corner of the sofa and go to asleep, even as every sense and nerve was whizzing with life. As Owen moved past her, she breathed in the scent of his aftershave, something citrusy and clean that made her senses swim all the more.

"May I take your coat?"

"Yes, please."

He slid his hands over her shoulders as Emily shrugged out of her coat, and it took what felt like all her strength not to shiver under such a basic touch. Goodness, but she was affected by this man. Was attracted to him. She'd never, ever experienced anything like it.

"Wow," Owen said softly, and Emily blushed and ducked her head as she saw his admiring glance.

"This is all Ava. She insisted I have something of a makeover."

"You don't need a makeover, but you do look beautiful. As always."

"So gallant." A giggle slipped out of her, sort of like a burp. She covered her mouth before giving a wry laugh. "Sorry. I'm nervous. And I've drunk too much gin."

"Have you?" Owen cocked an eyebrow, amused. "Well, that's probably a good thing, as I can't ply you with alcohol. I don't keep any in the house." He went to hang up her coat, and then to the Aga to stir whatever was bubbling away there.

"You don't?" Emily said in surprise. She slipped onto a stool at the big island and watched him at the stove. "And yet you own a pub."

"Ironic, I know." He shot a quick, glinting smile that made everything in her fizz. Again. "My dad was an alcoholic. I had a few bouts with the bottle myself, when I was a lot younger. And so I swore I'd never touch a drop, and I haven't."

"Wow." She shook her head slowly, absorbing all the information. "I'm sorry about your dad."

"So am I."

"You mentioned before that he'd died…?"

"Yes, when I was seventeen. A fight in a pub. They took it outside and he ended up bleeding to death from a stab wound." He grimaced. "Sorry, I know how grim it sounds. But I figured this was about getting to know each other, so…"

"I'm glad you told me." But even so, Emily was shaken. It seemed that everyone had hard history. Everyone was trailing their emotional baggage, battered and heavy. It had been arrogant for her to think she was the only one, or that no one could understand what she'd been going through. Foolish to feel she couldn't let people in. And yet even as she began to grasp that realisation, she still felt the urge to back away from this. From everything, because it was big and new and still scary. Old habits died hard, it seemed.

"Yeah, well." Owen propped his hip against the island as he gave her a frank look. "You told me some stuff, so I thought I'd reciprocate. We are trying to get to know each other, aren't we?"

"Yes."

"So hit me with something else while I get you a drink. I've got tonic, no gin, non-alcoholic beer, fizzy apple and pear… What's your poison?"

"None of them seem like poison. I'll take fizzy apple and pear, please." She was no longer feeling quite so tipsy, but there was a pleasantly drowsy sensation stealing through her veins like honey.

"Right, so what do I not know about you?" Owen asked as he poured her drink and handed it to her.

"What do you know about me?" Emily parried back, not meaning it seriously, but Owen took it as such.

"Well, let's see." He planted his elbows on the island as he gazed her full in the face, gaze bright yet heavy-lidded, lips curved in a smile that somehow seemed sensuous. That lazy, honeyed feeling inside her increased, even as she felt electrified. How she could feel both at once, Emily had no idea, but she did. Oh, she did.

"What do I know about you?" Owen mused. "I know you're careful. Considerate. Thorough."

"Which is good, if I were applying for a job." Goodness, but she sounded boring.

"Hey, I'm just getting started." He straightened, folding his arms as he gave her a considering look that made her feel as if he were touching her. She willed herself to keep his gaze, even though she felt it right down to her toes. "You're kind but you're afraid to show it. You like routine because it makes you feel safe. You love your mum but sometimes you feel like hating her."

"Don't—" The word came out of Emily in a whisper. She felt as if he'd flayed her alive with his words, as if she was standing naked and wounded before him, and he knew it.

"And I know you're lovely and gorgeous and you don't believe that either," Owen continued steadily. Emily shook her head helplessly.

"I thought you were going to say you knew my favourite colour was blue."

He raised his eyebrows, a smile tugging at his mouth. "Is it?"

"Yes, actually." She let out a trembling laugh, everything still so exposed. "But you didn't know that, and you knew all the other stuff?"

"You never actually said."

"I didn't say any of the other stuff, either."

"I know." His tone was so gentle that Emily didn't know whether to smile or cringe. She'd been here for ten minutes and she already felt completely out of her depth. But she always had with this man, from the moment she'd met him, and somehow it had all been okay.

"I don't actually know what you want from me." She blurted out the words.

"I don't want anything *from* you. I just want to get to know you."

"But why?"

"Because I like you. Because I'm attracted to you, and I'm pretty sure you're attracted to me, if that kiss was anything to go by."

*That kiss.* Just the memory of it had her blushing and squirming, everything fizzing inside her again. "Still," she managed.

"Isn't that enough?"

It was more than she'd ever had before. A lot more. Emily's lips curved into a small, slow smile as she realised she could stop questioning for once. Stop doubting. Why not just enjoy what they had here? "Yes," she said. "I suppose it is, actually."

Owen grinned, and then she was grinning too, and then he clapped his hands together. "Right. Let's eat."

"What is it that smells so delicious?"

"Welsh-Italian fusion cooking," he quipped. "Or actually, my throw-everything-in-a-pot casserole."

He brought the pot to the table and Emily brought her glass. It had been set for two, complete with crystal glasses and linen napkins, as elegant as she could possibly please.

"This is lovely, Owen," she said quietly. "Thank you."

He glanced up as he placed the pot on the table, his eyes crinkling at the corners. "Well, I did want to make an effort. I asked Ava about the table settings, and also what colour shirt I should wear." He laughed self-consciously, a slight blush touching his cheeks that made Emily both soften and yearn. She could really, really start to care about this man. "But we'll see if my casserole lives up to its name."

"I'm sure it will."

Emily wasn't used to small talk, or dates, or sitting at a table in candlelight feeling fuzzy and relaxed in a way that had nothing to do with the gin that had already worn off. Surprisingly, it was all so much easier than she'd expected. So much *nicer.*

Owen regaled her with stories from the pub, and she told him about her ideas for the fundraiser, and the conversation flowed along with the apple-pear fizz.

"So how is that a teetotaller decided to run a pub?" she asked when they'd finished the meal and were washing up, cosily side by side, in the kitchen.

Owen shrugged. "Pubs are what I know. My dad spent all his free time in one, and I fetched him home when I could. Then I started on the same track, until I wised up."

Emily slowly ran a tea towel along a crystal glass to dry it. "What made you wise up?"

Owen sighed. "It's not very pretty." He pointed to his rather rumpled left ear. "I got in a fight like my dad did, except I was the one throwing the punches. Ended up before the magistrate on an assault charge."

"Oh, no…"

"That sobered me up. I was only nineteen. My dad had been dead for two years, and I knew I was going to follow him into the grave one way or another unless I cleaned up my act. So I did. Haven't touched another drop of alcohol since then."

"That's amazing."

He grimaced. "More like necessary. I thought of my dad and I saw into my future. I didn't like the look of it."

"And running a pub?"

"I suppose," Owen said slowly, "you and I are similar in that way. Running a pub is my way of keeping things in control. If I run the rowdiest pub in this village, well then, I know how bad it gets, and I can make sure it doesn't get any worse." He shrugged, rubbing his hand along the back of his neck as he offered a self-conscious smile. "How's that for a bit of psychoanalysis?"

Emily smiled back. "Very clever."

"Not really. I didn't even get my GCSEs, you know." The dishes done, they moved over to the sofa, Emily curling up one end while Owen threw another log into the wood burner before taking the other end. The lights were dim, and Owen had put on some mellow jazz on in the background. Emily couldn't remember ever feeling more relaxed.

"GCSEs aren't everything," she said.

"You got yours, I presume, despite your difficulties at home?"

She let out a laugh of acknowledgement. "Well…"

"Let me guess. Nine A stars?"

"Ten," she admitted, and he let out one of his booming laughs.

"Of course. That's something else I know—and like—about you. You work hard."

Emily ducked her head, overwhelmed by the unabashed admiration in his voice. "I can't remember when I've had so many compliments."

"Then I'll keep them coming."

She met his warm gaze, unable to keep from shaking her head. "It doesn't feel right somehow."

"What doesn't?"

"This. It's too easy."

"Why can't something be easy?"

"I don't know." She hesitated. "Maybe because everything has always been so complicated. And maybe because I'm wondering if…if you're too good to be true."

✱

OWEN FELT THE expression freeze on his face, the easy smile

he'd been giving morphing into something of a rictus. *Too good to be true.*

Well, he was, wasn't he?

And someone as clever as Emily was bound to suss it out. He took a sip of his drink, trying to school his face into something relaxed.

"Well, you know what they say. Don't look a gift horse in the mouth."

She frowned, her forehead crinkling. "Is that what I would be doing?"

Owen shrugged. "I don't know. I'm not perfect, certainly."

"I'm not expecting you to be perfect, Owen. I'm not, either. Not by a long shot. But you know that already."

Could he leave it at that? Did she deserve a warning? *I've let down the people I love in the past. Time and time again, badly. My mother. My father. Even my sisters, stuck in Cwmparc living half-lives while I got out. I never even looked back. I wanted to save them but I didn't. Maybe I care about you because I think I can save you.*

Was he actually screwed up enough to think that way? That Emily could somehow be *his* salvation, never mind him saving her? At least he wasn't screwed up enough to say any of it out loud. "Then we sound like a perfect match."

She smiled at that, and looked down, and she was so beautiful and seemed so pure that Owen felt as if he *had* to kiss her. Unfortunately, there was a good three feet between them, and he didn't think a lunge across the sofa was a good idea at this point.

This was Emily's first real date, unbelievable and even criminal as that seemed. He knew he needed to take it slow, even as he'd been itching to pull her into his arms all evening.

"So…" He stretched his arm out along the back of the sofa in a cringingly classic move. "Are you settling into Wychwood?"

"I think I've been forced to settle in, whether I wanted to or not." She gave a soft huff of laughter. "But I'm starting not to mind so much. It actually feels good."

"Good." He let his gaze linger. He was really pulling all the basic moves, but he didn't know what else to do. This was new for him, too. He'd had dates before—dinners, movies, a few lamentable flings that made him cringe with regret now. He'd settled for so little, and now he was finding he wanted so much more, and that scared him about as much as he suspected it scared Emily. Yet here they were, trying.

"What about your mum?" he asked after a moment, when they'd both seemed content to be lost in their own thoughts, the glow of the wood burner casting the dim room in warm shades.

Emily sighed. "She's stable. Still doesn't want to see me."

"Has that happened before?"

A quick shrug, more like a twitch. "She is very up and down. And when she went into hospital in the past, it was not by her own volition. When I don't spring her from the cell, she blames me." Emily's mouth curved upwards in a sad smile. "I understand that."

"What about your father?" Owen asked. He realised he hadn't properly considered her dad, perhaps because his own had been so absent. "Is he around? Involved? I know you said they divorced…"

"He lives in Reading with his second wife and two teenaged children." She spoke matter-of-factly but he heard sadness. Grief.

"Ah," he said quietly.

"We are in touch. I haven't told him about this latest episode, but I called him the week before and said I was concerned about her going off her medication. He said my mum was an adult who had to make her own choices." She shook her head. "I know I can't expect him to sweep in like some knight and rescue everything. They've been divorced for nearly twenty years. He's moved on. Of course he has."

Moved on from his wife…*and* his daughter? Owen disliked the man already. Intensely. Still he kept his voice neutral as he said, "You haven't struck me as someone who's looking for a knight to charge in and rescue her."

She turned to him with a surprisingly playful smile. "Don't I?"

"No, you seem frighteningly self-sufficient. You could run rings around me, I'm sure, in a thousand different ways."

"Well…I don't know how to pull a pint."

"I could show you." There was a flirtatious undercurrent to the conversation, a sensual promise that was making Owen feel as if he were buzzing inside. Emily's smile curved wider, and then he knew he had to kiss her. He couldn't wait a moment longer.

"I look forward to that," she said, and then her eyes widened as he did a slow lunge towards her, intent obvious in every taut line of his body. She didn't move, just waited, quivering a little, as he probably was, because he wanted this so much.

Gently he swept a tendril of hair behind her ear, let his fingers trail across the silky softness of her cheek. She sucked in a quick breath. "May I kiss you?" he asked. "Because I've been wanting to all evening, and it's becoming rather difficult to think about anything else."

She gave a jerky nod of her head. "Uh...yes, I suppose that would be...okay."

"Just okay?" he teased. "I hope it's better than that."

"Maybe..." Her voice trailed away as he came closer, and then he brushed his lips across hers. Just as before, it felt as if he'd been instantly electrocuted, the shock of the feeling nearly overwhelming him. How could he have such a strong physical response to this woman? It was like being burned alive and dipped in ice water at the same time, but nice. Lovely. Absolutely lovely and amazing and all-consuming.

And she seemed to be having the same response back, her mouth opening under his as her hands came up to brace against his shoulders.

The kiss deepened as they fell back against the sofa, and Owen's head blanked completely, leaving only sensation— her softness, her surrender, the little sigh she gave as her arms came around him and he felt all that lovely, pliant warmth beneath him.

Limbs tangled as they stretched out, his body on top of hers, braced on his forearms as the kiss went on and on and his head continued to spin.

And then he felt it, like a light going out. Her body stiffened and her lips slackened under his. Reluctantly, feeling as if it were costing him everything, he lifted his head.

"All right?" he asked gently and she bit her lip. He realised she looked near tears, and in horror and self-recrimination he lurched upright. "Emily...I didn't..."

"No, no. It was... lovely. So lovely." She let out a choked laugh and then, mortified, held her hands up to her face. Owen stared at her in a sort of terrified alarm as she began to cry. This was *not* how he'd hoped this evening would go at all.

"What's wrong?" he asked, wanting to put a hand on her shoulder yet not sure if he should. "Tell me what's wrong, please. Did I... Was I moving too fast?" Although it had felt agonisingly slow to him.

"No, no. It's not that. I don't know if I can explain it." Her hands still covered her face and her shoulders shook. Heaven help them both, she was really crying. This was bad.

"You could try," he offered weakly. "Please?"

She dropped her hands, showing him a tear- and mascara-smeared face. "It's just…I've never. Well, I've never done loads of things."

"I know." Of course he knew. She'd already told him she'd never gone on a bloody *date*. So naturally he assumed she hadn't done a lot of other things, either, including things he was already envisioning with painful clarity.

"I feel like a freak," she admitted baldly. "I'm twenty-six and I'm…well, never mind. And I'm scared. Scared of getting too close, and scared of scaring you off, because I'm so…" She shook her head, leaving him to fill in the unfortunate blank.

Owen leaned back against the sofa as he did his best to relax. "You're not scaring me off."

She searched his face with a sort of hungry desperation. "Are you sure?"

"I'm sure."

"Because I'm sort of scaring myself off."

"Don't do that."

Her mouth quirked in an impossible smile. "I'll try not to."

"Good." Owen released a long, low breath. Maybe it was all going to be okay, even if he felt rather shaky inside. He might have said he wasn't scared, but he sort of was. This was so much more intense than anything he'd ever experienced, and he was so very afraid of letting her down. Still he smiled, just to reassure her. "That's all I need to hear," he said.

# Chapter Fifteen

"DO YOU THINK this rain will ever stop?"

Alice stood by the tall sashed windows as Emily came into the office, the Monday after her date with Owen. She hadn't slept much the night before, her mind insisting on replaying every single moment of the evening, with accompanying in-depth analysis. What had he meant when he'd said... Why had he smiled at her like that... Had she completely freaked him out?

As a result, she was both exhausted and energised, fizzing and fatigued and probably a bit manic, which scared her because it was a little too much like her mother. She wasn't used to feeling this out of control.

"Stop?" Emily glanced at the rain streaking down the windows, bemused. She'd just walked from Willoughby Close through a steady drizzle and she hadn't even noticed, because her mind was pinging around like a ball in a pinball machine. "It has to sometime, I suppose."

"Yes, it's just so dreary." Alice heaved a loud sigh, and Emily cocked her head.

"Is everything okay, Alice?"

"Yes." She shrugged. "Fine."

Which definitely did *not* sound fine. "What's happened?" Emily asked. It couldn't be the baby thing again, could it? Because it was only two weeks since Alice had told her they were trying.

"I don't know. The weather gets me down." Alice wrapped her arms around herself. "It's mid-April and it still feels like winter. And I think I see less of Henry since we started this blasted charity, plus the number of hoops we have to jump through even to have one child come through our doors… I don't know if they'll ever even get here." She shook her head. "Sorry. You don't want to hear all this."

"I don't mind." And, Emily realised, she really didn't. She actually liked hearing someone else's problems, having them confide in her. Being part of someone else's life. It was new and still scary, but she was starting to *like* it. Need it, even. She had friends.

"Well…" Alice slumped into a chair at the table, meant for conference meetings, with a sigh. Emily waited for her to say more. "The thing is," she said after a moment, "I'm not a complainer. I never have been. Even when life is tough—and I admit it has been really, really tough at times—I always made sure to look on the bright side." She drew a raggedy breath. "And yet here I am, married to a wonderful man, living in a beautiful house, and I can't summon that sunny-side-of-life feeling. What's wrong with me?" She looked at

Emily with tears in her eyes, waiting for her verdict.

"Er…" Emily scrambled to think of something helpful to say. "We can't help our emotions," she offered a bit lamely and Alice nodded slowly as she blew her nose.

"I know. But I feel like I'm being a big whinger."

"You're not. You're just saying how you feel, and I did ask."

Alice gave her a watery smile. "Perhaps it's just the weather. All this rain…you haven't had a chance to see the village at its best."

"It can't rain forever."

"I suppose not." Alice heaved a sigh. "Tell me something cheerful or exciting." She smiled wryly. "If you can?"

"Well…" Emily racked her brains trying to think of something, but there had really only been one thing on her mind recently. "I went on a date," she offered shyly, hesitant to admit so much even though she was positively bursting with it.

"You did!" Alice straightened, looking both surprised and thrilled. "Who with? Or is that a secret?"

"I thought it might be posted on the village notice-board," Emily returned wryly. "But apparently not. Owen Jones."

"Owen! Of course. That champagne…"

"Well." Now she was blushing, and yet somehow she didn't mind. "Yes, I suppose."

"So where did you go?"

"He made me dinner at his house."

"Wow." Alice sat back, impressed. "That sounds very special."

"It was, actually." Her face was positively fiery now, and yet she felt like laughing. "But it's early days. *Very* early days."

Alice held up a hand. "I understand completely."

"How did you and Henry get together?" Emily asked curiously. "He's such a…"

"Stuffed shirt?" Alice filled in with a laugh. "I know. I'm not sure how we got together, to be honest. There were always sparks, even if I didn't realise that's what they were." She rolled her eyes. "I have to tell you, before Henry, I had literally zero experience with men. I'd never even been on a date."

"You hadn't?" Emily goggled at her, and Alice gave another wry laugh.

"Nope. As a foster kid, I spent most of my time trying to be invisible, really."

"The date with Owen was my first, too," Emily confessed in a rush, and now Alice was the one to goggle.

"What? But…"

"But what?"

"It's just, well, you're so beautiful. And glamorous. I've been a bit intimidated by you from the start, actually."

"What? No." Emily shook her head, laughing in surprised disbelief. "I've been like you, really. Trying to be invisible to everyone else."

Alice stared at her in confusion. "But why?"

"Well." Emily took a deep breath. Was she really going to keep doing this? Telling people the secrets she'd held closely for so long? "Because of my mother," she said. It seemed she was.

✱

THE RAIN KEPT up all day, and turned into a downpour as Emily hurried home. She'd checked her phone several times—they'd exchanged numbers on Saturday night—and hadn't had any texts or missed calls from Owen, and stupidly, she was starting to feel anxious about the whole thing. At four o'clock she'd recklessly—for her—texted a "thanks for a lovely evening x," deliberating for a good ten minutes over that single x, but there had been no reply, which, an hour later, was starting to make her panic.

What if he'd finally twigged how messed up she was? What if he was regretting everything? The possibility made her chest tighten and fear race through her veins. As scary as all this was, she still wanted it. Wanted *him*.

"Hello, kitten." Her unnamed fluff ball rubbed up against her ankles and Emily scooped him up and pressed her cheek against his tiny, soft head—something she wouldn't have considered doing a few weeks ago. She was changing, whether she wanted to or not, and the truth was, she did.

But when was Owen going to text back?

She fed the kitten and changed into comfortable clothes before making her daily telephone call to the hospital. Her mother had been a patient for eight days now, and yesterday the nurse still believed a visit from Emily would not prove helpful at this point, although today it was different.

"I think your mother might be up for a visitor," she told Emily when she called. "Are you free tomorrow? But ring in the morning to check."

"Oh...okay." Emily couldn't keep the surprise from her voice. She'd been anticipating another gentle no. "That's...well, that's good news."

"Yes." The nurse sounded both brisk and kind, and tears pricked Emily's eyes. Goodness, but she really needed to get her emotions under control.

"Thank you," she managed, and then took a deep breath to steady herself. So her mum wanted to see her, or at least wasn't unwilling for her to visit. Emily had no idea what the level of her enthusiasm would be, and she didn't really want to guess. Better to have low, or even no, expectations.

She checked her phone again, willing Owen to have left a message while she'd been talking to the nurse, but of course he hadn't. She realised she wanted to share this with him, but she wasn't brave or bold enough to call. She wished she was, and she considered ringing several times, but she just couldn't make herself.

Then, at half past six, the doorbell rang. A smile was already spreading across Emily's face as she went to answer it, because somehow she knew who it was. Who it had to be. Even though it could have just as easily been Olivia, or Ava, or Jace...

It was Owen.

"Hello, you." She was positively grinning now, and so was Owen.

"You're in your pyjamas."

"My comfy clothes, thank you very much. You didn't tell me you were coming over."

"Should I have done?"

She shook her head. "I don't know. I don't think it matters, actually."

"Is that a good thing?" he asked, eyebrows raised. "And can I come in?"

"Oh yes, of course." It was still pouring out, and the shoulders of Owen's jacket were soaked. "And yes, it is a good thing. But what are you doing here? I mean...what about the pub?"

"The pub is closed."

"What...?"

"Water has been coming in the cellar. I've sandbagged the place and hoped for the best. But it backs out onto the Lea, so..."

"Oh, no." She looked at him in dismay but he just shrugged.

"Frankly I'm glad for a free evening, and as long as the water stays in the cellar, I should be fine. I put a sump pump in there as well, so there's nothing more I can do. I took a chance you like Indian." He hefted a paper bag, and a sweet, fragrant aroma of almonds and spices wafted out.

"I do like Indian."

"Good."

"Let me get the plates."

It was both strange and wonderful to be fetching two sets of plates and cutlery, wearing her comfy clothes and not even minding. Owen had shrugged off his jacket and then nodded towards the wood burner.

"Do you mind if I get that started?"

"No, of course not. I haven't bothered when it's just been me."

He slanted her a smiling look. "But it's not just you."

"I know." She was grinning again. Like a *loon*.

Owen fetched kindling and wood from the box Jace had provided weeks ago, and soon a merry blaze was crackling away. "Who's this guy?" he asked as the kitten twined about his ankles and he scooped him up in one hand.

"My nameless kitten. The one I told you about before. He was feral—his mother dropped him in the garden and I had to take care of him."

"But you didn't give him a name?"

"Any suggestions?" Emily asked as she started doling out the food.

"Hmm." Owen inspected the kitten seriously, making Emily smile. Again. "How about Tiger?"

"Tigers are white and orange, though, not black."

"Not because he looks like a tiger. Because of the Castleford Tigers." She looked at him blankly and he explained, "A rugby league team from West Yorkshire. Black and orange are their colours."

"I don't know the first thing about rugby of any sort," Emily admitted.

"Somehow that doesn't surprise me."

"You're a big fan?"

"I like to play the odd match. And watch when I can."

"How about Castleford? To be a little different, because Tiger sounds a bit ordinary." She took their heaped plates to the table. "I could call him Cass for short. Although I don't actually know if he's a boy or girl kitten."

"You could check, you know."

"How?"

Owen gave her a look and she started to laugh. He scooped up the kitten, gave a look at his backside, and then turned back to her. "You've got a girl here, so I think Cass fits the bill."

"Cass it is, then." Owen washed his hands and came to the table and somehow Emily couldn't keep from saying, "I'm glad you're here."

"So am I." The look he gave her was warm and lingering, and made her remember exactly how it had felt to be kissed by him. And made her want to be again.

She looked down at her chicken korma and rice, and realised she was still smiling.

✳

OWEN HADN'T BEEN planning to visit Emily tonight. All day he'd been so consumed with sandbagging the pub and moving stock from the cellar, he hadn't even thought about her that much.

And then he'd done all he could do, and locked the doors, and realised there was no other place he'd rather be but here, with her. And so, without caring about how keen he might seem, popping by unannounced the Monday after their date, he'd picked up the takeaway and hightailed it over here. And like Emily, he was glad he'd done it.

"Have you talked to your mum this week?" he asked as they started their takeaways, and Emily shook her head.

"No, although I've rung the nurse every day. She said I might be able to visit tomorrow."

"Might…?"

Emily grimaced. "Depending on how my mum is in the morning, I suppose."

Owen nodded slowly. "How do you feel about that?"

"Truthfully, I don't know." She toyed with her fork, separating a few grains of rice with its tines. "I mean, I want to see her. And of course I want her to get better. But it will feel…tumultuous. And that can be hard."

"I can imagine. Although actually I can't."

"Can't you?" Emily gave him a surprisingly shrewd look.

"You mentioned your dad had a drinking problem. That must have been a bit up and down."

"Ye-es, but it wasn't like your mum, from the sounds of it." He didn't want to equate his situation with hers, and yet Emily wasn't having his rather obvious prevarication.

"But maybe it was, in some ways. I'm realising," she explained slowly, "that I'm not as terribly unique as I thought. All during my childhood and even later, I thought everyone else had a happy family. A normal life. And I never got to know anyone well enough really to think differently. But since coming here to Wychwood...I've realised that everyone has their baggage. Their burdens. And it was arrogant of me to think I was the only one."

"I'd hardly say it was *arrogant*," Owen protested. "Naïve, perhaps."

"Fine. Naïve, then. So tell me what your childhood was like, Owen. I want to know." She looked determined and interested, and here he was, feeling reluctant. It was so much easier to make this about her.

"What do you want to know exactly?" he asked. More prevarication.

"You said you grew up in a small town in Wales..."

"A village, really. A mining village. My father worked in the mines until they closed."

"I didn't even realise people did that anymore. I thought all the mines closed about a hundred years ago."

"Many of them did. Not all."

"And what was that like? Living in a mining village?"

He shrugged, feeling twitchy all of a sudden. "Normal, I suppose, since I didn't know anything else. But also…grim. Everybody wanted to leave, but nobody ever did. And after the mines closed, most of the men were unemployed and bitter. Not a good combination."

"Is that why your father drank?"

"He always drank. He was one of those larger-than-life types, and he was even more so when he'd had a couple of pints. A bit like your mum that way—when he was on form, he was loads of fun. When he wasn't…" He stopped then, because he really didn't want to go into it.

"That must have been hard."

Another one of those twitchy shrugs. "Sometimes."

"What did he do for work afterwards? Once the mine had closed?"

"He did a lot of odd jobs, not all of them legal." A pause. "He used to work as a beater for the lord of the local manor. He had a hunting lodge up in the hills. My dad would flush out the pheasants."

Emily cocked her head, her grey-blue gaze sweeping slowly over him. "Is that why you have a thing against the manor set?"

"I don't have a *thing*."

"You do," Emily insisted. "You said so yourself."

"Fine." Owen sat back in his chair, doing his best to re-lax, or at least look relaxed. He hadn't expected Emily to ask all these searching questions, and neither had he expected to react the way he was, with a prickly self-defensiveness that was more her vibe than his. And yet this was part of the reason he'd come, wasn't it? The whole get-to-know-each-other thing? "The la-di-da lordly type had a son. A spoiled arse, if I'm honest."

"Sounds rather typical."

"I suppose it was. Anyway, during one of the shoots he was larking about, and his father didn't do a damned thing. His gun went off when it shouldn't have, and my father was hit in the leg."

"Oh no!" Emily covered her mouth with her hand, eyes wide with horrified shock. "Was he all right?"

"Eventually, but it broke the bone and he was in hospital for weeks. The lord and his son didn't even care." His throat worked, acid burning in his gut at the memory. "He sent my mother fifty pounds as recompense." Which had been a lot of money for them then, but the injustice, the insult of it, had cut deep, and still did now.

"That's so unfair. I'm not surprised you've got a chip on your shoulder." She paused, seeming to choose her words with care. "But Henry's not like that."

"Actually, he was exactly like that." Emily looked up at him in surprise. "Although it's not for me to say."

"What do you mean?"

Owen knew he shouldn't have said anything. "Ask Jace," he said.

*"Jace...?"*

"He's had some experience with Henry."

"What, Henry *shot* him?" She sounded disbelieving, and yet in some ways she wasn't that far off.

"No, not that. But...something. I'm not saying he hasn't changed, only that seven years ago he seemed as hard and uncaring as my good Lord Westcott did. And Jace bore the brunt."

Emily frowned. "I don't understand."

"I shouldn't have said anything. It wasn't my place."

"If I asked Henry, would he mind?"

Owen shrugged. "I don't actually know. I've lived in Wychwood for nearly fifteen years and I've never spoken to the man."

"Really?" Emily's frown deepened. "That should change."

"Don't worry, I haven't minded." He needed to change the subject before Henry Trent of all people derailed their date.

Emily must have been thinking along the same lines, because she straightened, shaking off her unease about Henry, and asked, "And how did your mother cope with it all? Six children, too..."

Unfortunately that was not the kind of change in subject he was looking for. He didn't want to talk about his mum, either.

"She...struggled." He looked away because he didn't

trust the expression on his face. "It was difficult." And that was all he could say about that. He wasn't going to tell Emily how he couldn't save his mum, how she ended up blaming him for something that had been, arguably at least, his fault. How he'd grown up watching her pain, just as Emily had with her own mother. Nope, he was definitely not going to say any of that.

"I'm sorry, Owen." Emily reached over and put her hand on top of his, a small, gentle touch that he knew instinctively was a big deal for her.

"It's okay." It wasn't, but *this* was, and he was done talking about the drama of families. He squeezed her hand, and she smiled.

They chatted about nothing nearly as intense as they finished their dinner, and then moved over to Emily's rather angular sofa to enjoy the dancing flames of the wood burner. It felt both weird and right when Emily scooted next to him and he put his arm around her, enjoying the feel of her snuggled close, her head on his shoulder. They were silent as they watched the fire, and it felt enough—or almost—to simply sit here with her in the warmth and the dark.

Then Cass scrambled up into their laps, and he let out a laugh. It just felt too perfect.

"I don't think I've been happier," Emily said quietly. She tilted her face up to meet his gaze, a furrow bisecting her forehead. "Does that scare you?"

"Should it?"

"I don't know."

For an answer, because he didn't have another one, he kissed her—a gentle brush of their lips. At least that was what it was meant to be. But as with every time he'd kissed Emily David, it turned into something much more. Her hand crept upwards, her fingers wrapping around his neck as he deepened the kiss and their bodies shifted on the sofa. Blood roared and sang as she pressed even closer to him, and reluctantly Owen lifted his head.

"We should probably stop."

"Should we?" A smile tilted her lips upwards but he saw the hesitation in her eyes and he knew he'd made the right call. "I'm not a child, you know," she added, and Owen let out a laugh that was mostly groan.

"Trust me, I know that."

She chewed her lip, scanning his face. "I'm not fragile, either."

"Emily, you're one of the strongest people I know." And yet strong people could be fragile, too. And the last thing, the very last thing in the entire world Owen wanted to do, was hurt her. "This is our second date, you know. We don't have to rush."

"I know."

"Anyway, I meant to ask about your mum. You're visiting her tomorrow?"

"Assuming she still wants me to, yes."

"Why don't I drive you there?"

She looked at him in surprise. "You'll just sit in the foyer again, you know."

"I know. I'm coming to like that foyer. Very comfortable chairs." He smiled, and she smiled too, and then he brushed a strand of hair away from her cheek. "No one should go through that kind of thing alone. The pub's still closed tomorrow. Let me drive you."

She hesitated, her smile like a flower that had only just begun to unfurl. "Okay," she said at last. "Thank you."

# Chapter Sixteen

THE HEAVY RAIN had downgraded to a misty drizzle by eight o'clock the next morning, when Owen pulled up to Willoughby Close in his van.

"How's The Drowned Sailor?" Emily asked as she climbed inside the passenger side. Owen, she saw, had made somewhat of an effort at tidying up—the paper coffee cups were gone, along with some of the rubbish from the floor.

"Not yet drowned," he returned with a quick smile. He looked and smelled gorgeous—fresh and damp from a shower, wearing his usual rugby shirt and jeans. "There's still water in the cellar, but I think it's under control."

"Good."

"How are you feeling about today?" Owen asked as he drove out of the close.

"I don't know. I'm not letting myself think about it too much, really."

"What happened the last time your mum stopped her medication?"

Emily sighed as she gazed out the window streaked with

raindrops. Spring was coming to Wychwood-on-Lea, daffodils and tulips unfurling under the drizzle, everything muted and grey and yet still coming to life. Spring happened anyway, no matter what was going in life. It was a heartening thought.

"She was doing really well," she began after a moment. "She had a job, which isn't all that usual, teaching pottery at a day centre for the elderly. She was feeling normal, if that's a word I should use. I don't know if it is, or what normal is, for that matter. But she wasn't flattened the way the medication can make her—as if she's viewing everything from behind a gauzy curtain. That's how she's described it. Anyway." Emily blew out a breath. "I think she felt well enough—confident enough—to stop taking the pills. She went cold turkey, which is never a good idea, and it resulted in what her consultant called 'a sudden and severe psychotic episode.' I wasn't there—I got a phone call, just like I did this time. She'd been at work, and she just..." Emily shrugged, her throat tightening as she recalled the consultant's description of what had happened. "Screaming. Throwing things. Hurting herself. It took three aides to restrain her."

"I'm sorry, Emily." Owen's tone was low and heartfelt, and it would have made her eyes sting if she'd let it.

"So am I. It came out of the blue that time. This time I had warning."

"You can't beat yourself up over that."

"It's easy to say that." Just as it had been easy to dismiss her own fears, because she was far away and sometimes she needed a break from worrying about her mother, a realisation that made her feel only guiltier.

"I know how easy it is," Owen said quietly, and Emily turned to look at him.

"You feel guilty."

He shrugged his assent. "Yes. I suppose."

"About your dad?"

A pause, heavy, like a weight in the air. "My whole family, really, but yes, my dad."

"Why?"

Owen flexed his hands on the steering wheel, his gaze straight ahead and yet restless. "For a lot of reasons."

"Will you tell me at least some of them?"

"I got out. I suppose that's the main one."

"From Cwmparc?"

"From that whole way of life."

"That's not your fault."

Owen shot her a knowing look, a faint smile curving his mouth although his eyes looked sad. "Exactly."

It was strange to think that she and Owen were similar, Emily reflected as they drove in silence towards Oxford, and then on to London. She'd assumed from the beginning that they were complete opposites, and that was why they clicked. And they *were* opposites, in many ways, but maybe that was simply because they'd developed different coping strategies.

The traffic increased as they made their way into London, and so did Emily's anxiety. She had no idea what her mother would be like when she saw her; the last time she'd thrown a pitcher of water at her head.

"Nervous?" Owen asked with a small smile, and Emily nodded.

"I have no idea what to expect."

"The nurse wouldn't have asked you to visit if she didn't think it was a good idea."

"I know." Two hours ago, when Emily had rung, the nurse Karen had told her Naomi was "stable"—a word that was reassuring without being terribly encouraging. Emily had no idea what *stable* looked like when it came to a conversation.

Owen parked the van and then took a seat in the entrance hall as usual, giving Emily a wry and encouraging smile. "I really like this chair," he told her, and she couldn't help but laugh, a nervous little giggle that had him reaching over and squeezing her hand. "It's going to be okay," he said. "And I'm here if you need me."

"Thank you."

Emily walked to the ward on watery legs, and the nurse Karen greeted her with a friendly smile. "Naomi has definitely been more stable since we've started her on the new medication," she explained to her as they headed towards her mother's room. "She's on a regular doze of olanzapine, which has helped stabilise her moods, so there are fewer ups and downs."

"Okay," Emily said. "What are the potential side effects?"

Karen gave an understanding grimace. "There's a wide range, as there are with any of these medications. At the moment we've noted that Naomi seems a bit drowsy, and may have some issues with her memory and speech."

*Was that all?* Emily bit her lip to keep from saying something sarcastic. It wasn't Karen's fault, and in any case Emily already knew how the side effects of the medications her mother was prescribed could be almost as bad as the disorder itself. Almost, but definitely not quite. Yet once they started to wear off, and they had to be changed or the dosage upped, then the whole agonising process of adjustment began again. It was a terrible, never-ending cycle that both Naomi and Emily were desperately tired of.

"If you need anything, or your mother becomes agitated, please just pull the red cord." Karen gave her a kindly smile. "I'm sure she'll be pleased to see you. She's been asking for you."

"Has she?" Emily's throat closed and she had to make herself swallow past the lump forming there. "Thank you," she said, and she opened the door to her mother's room.

Naomi was sitting in a chair by the window, her shoulders slumped, her gaze vacant as she rested her chin in her hand. Rain streaked the window like tears, obscuring the grey-on-grey view of a car park.

"Hi, Mum." Emily's voice sounded croaky and she tried again. "How are you doing?"

Slowly, so slowly, Naomi's gaze swivelled towards Emily, recognition flickering in her eyes after an endless moment.

"You came." Her mother's voice was slightly slurred and strangely flat, both undoubtedly results of the medication.

"Yes, Karen said you were up for visitors." Somehow Emily wasn't able to keep herself from taking an awful, jolly sort of tone, like some sort of demented school matron. She hated it, but Naomi didn't even seem to notice.

"I'm not sure I'm *up* for anything. They're all just trying to chivvy me along." Naomi let out a defeated sigh.

"They're just trying to help." Emily took a step into the room, her smile seeming to slide all over her face. "How are you feeling?"

A twitch of her mother's shoulder was the only response she got. Goodness, but this was hard. Emily remembered it all too well from three years ago—the initial rage, and then the horrible flattening out, so it felt as if her mum was gone, even when she was right here, and Emily had no idea what to do, how to be. She felt as if she got everything wrong—her tone, the questions, the way she kept trying to coax her mother along as if she were some sort of sulky toddler. But what else could she do? *Should* she do?

"One week down, just three more to go," she offered hopefully, although she realised belatedly that might not even be true, and it made it sound as if her mother were in prison. "The nurses seem to feel you're making progress, Mum, so that's good. Really good."

"What is progress in a place like this?" Naomi shook her head. "I don't want to be here." She spoke flatly, but her face crumpled and she drew a shuddering breath that sounded like a sob. "I don't want to have to be here. I don't want to be the sort of person who ends up in a place like this, again and again."

"I know," Emily said softly. She was far too near tears herself. She hated seeing her mother like this; sometimes she thought she'd prefer her when she was manic, happiness bordering on hysteria, sometimes frightening but surely better than this *deadness*.

But then she recalled the coming down, that consuming, catastrophic crash, and she knew she didn't prefer it. She couldn't. Even so, this was hard, for both of them.

"Mum, if you concentrate on getting better, you'll be out of here sooner," Emily said quietly. "And you can get back to normal life…" If such a thing existed.

"I'll never be out of here." Her mother sounded both resigned and despairing. "It doesn't matter anyway. Nothing does. If I leave, I'll just end up in here again, won't I? One way or another."

"As long as you manage your medication, that doesn't have to be true," Emily said as firmly as she could. "You can manage this, Mum. You have before, for years at a time."

But Naomi had already turned her face to the window,

away from her. Emily knew the signs; her mother wasn't going to speak to her again. Still, she stayed for another half hour, offering various bits of rather desperate chitchat with her mother remaining stonily silent, before she told her she loved her and said goodbye.

At the nurses' station, the consultant asked if he could speak to her, and with her stomach clenching hard, she agreed and ended up in his office, perched on the edge of a chair.

"Your mother is making good progress," she said with a kindly smile, "and the goal is for her to resume normal life after these twenty-eight days. But it's important for her to be released into a safe situation, and from what Naomi has indicated, that does not exist here in London." A weighty pause, and Emily knew what was coming.

"You want her to live with me."

"If you feel that would be a viable option."

"Yes, of course." Without question. "I have a second bedroom, and lots of my mother's things. I also work very locally, and could work from home if needed." She swallowed hard. It would be a lot of adjustment.

"That's wonderful. I'll make a referral to a consultant in Oxford."

Owen was already rising from his chair as Emily came down the corridor. "How was it?" he asked and she managed a smile.

"It was okay. Not as bad as it could have been, and not

as good as I always wish it could be."

"That's understandable."

"The consultant wants my mum to live with me when she's released from here. I was expecting it, but…" Emily shook her head. "It's going to be a big deal. The last time she came to live with me after being in hospital, I had to take a month of unpaid leave."

"Will you do that again?"

"I don't know. My job is a lot more flexible now, but…" She shook her head, closing her eyes briefly. "I can't think about all that now. Yet."

"It's not for a few weeks," Owen told her. "Look, why don't we do something? Go somewhere?"

"Don't you have to be back…?"

He shrugged. "The pub's still closed. Let's do something fun."

She smiled, something like hope unfurling inside her. "Okay," she said. "Henry said I could have the whole day off if I wanted. That sounds brilliant."

Because it was still raining, they decided to stay inside, and Owen told her he was treating her to lunch at the Fortnum and Mason restaurant in St Pancras. Emily enjoyed avocado on toast while Owen ordered the manliest thing on the menu—a fried chicken escalope.

"Have you ever thought about serving food at The Drowned Sailor?" she asked as she cut her toast into neat squares.

"Certainly not food like this."

"But what about really decent, plain pub grub? I haven't been in The Three Pennies except to ask about the fundraiser, but I know Harriet was saying it had become too fancy. They serve escargot now, apparently." She wrinkled her nose.

"I don't know." Owen shrugged as he stabbed a piece of chicken. "It's not something I've thought about much. Most people come into my pub for a pint, not Pinot Grigio."

"Yes, but everyone needs to eat." She cocked her head as she noticed his slightly defensive stance—shoulders tense, gaze downcast. "What is it? Have I touched a nerve or something?"

"Not exactly." He looked up with a wry smile. "It's just…I've never wanted to pretend to be something I'm not."

"How would serving food be doing that?"

Another shrug. "Just…trying to make The Drowned Sailor anything more than a watering hole, I suppose."

Emily speared a piece of smashed avocado as she considered what he was saying—as well as what he didn't seem to want to say. "Are you afraid people will sneer at you?" she asked cautiously. "For trying to be something more?"

"I'm not afraid."

He sounded so stung, she had to smile. "You know what I mean."

Restively Owen put down his fork. "I grew up poor, Emily. Dirt poor. Until I was twelve, our toilet was in the bottom of the garden."

"Okay." She shrugged right back at him. "I'm sorry about that, but so?"

A smile quirked his mouth at her challenge. "Don't think I'm asking for pity. It's just…I dropped out of school at fifteen, like I told you I didn't even take my GCSEs, and no one bothered to check because too many of us were doing the same. I loafed around, getting up to no good…" He spread his hands. "Frankly, I'm amazed I got this far."

"So am I," Emily said, and he laughed at her honesty. Realising how she sounded, she shook her head with a smile. "What I mean is, you're amazing, Owen. You've risen above so many challenges. If you'd followed the expected trajectory of your upbringing, you'd still be in Cwmparc, struggling to find a job—"

"And drinking my life away."

"Perhaps," she allowed. "But instead you got out, and you made something of yourself. You bought a pub, for heaven's sake! So why not go even further, as far as you want?"

"We are talking about serving bar food, aren't we?" Owen joked. "And not walking on the moon?"

"To infinity and beyond," Emily quipped back. "Or maybe to fish and chips and beyond."

"Maybe," Owen allowed. She saw he wanted to drop it, and she decided she'd pressed enough. But it had felt good, to challenge and encourage, to have their relationship—if that's what they had—be more give and take and not just her desperately needing Owen.

After lunch, they walked to the National Gallery and wandered through the elegant rooms for an hour or two, studying the paintings and then making a game of imagining what the people in portraits were thinking.

"He looks like he really needs to get to the bog," Owen said in a carrying whisper, and Emily had to stifle her giggles.

By three o'clock, they decided to head back to Wychwood to miss the worst of the traffic, and they walked through a steady rain back to the van, getting soaked in the process.

"It's been a wonderful day," Emily said as she pushed her dripping hair from her eyes and Owen started the van. "Even if I'm the one looking like a drowned sailor at the moment." She glanced at him, noticing the furrow between his eyes. "Do you think the pub's all right?"

"I asked Darren to check on the cellar," Owen replied. "And he hasn't texted, so it should be fine." He gave her a quick and lovely smile. "I wouldn't have missed today for anything."

❄

HE'D SPOKEN THE truth, but Owen couldn't keep an anxiety from gnawing inside him as he headed back on the M40. It had been raining steadily all day, and it was now a proper downpour. Plus, although he hadn't told Emily, Darren had texted him an hour ago, apologising that he hadn't had chance to check the cellar.

Even if the cellar was full of water, Owen reasoned, it wasn't the end of the world. He could claim any damage on insurance, and at least the main areas would still be safe. But it had rained a lot, and when he switched on the radio, the news was full of accounts of flooding all across the region, from Oxford to Cardiff. The Severn had burst its banks, and an entire village near it was practically underwater. Owen switched off the radio and concentrated on driving.

As they drove into the village, he noted the rainwater sluicing down the high street with a pang of real fear. Sandbags lined most of the shop doorways, and the trains weren't running.

"Goodness," Emily murmured, giving him a concerned look. Owen's hands clenched harder on the steering wheel. When The Drowned Sailor came into view, he saw Darren out in front, and water streaming out of the door. As he pulled into the car park, an emergency vehicle screamed into the space next to him.

Owen clambered out of the van and sprinted towards Darren. "What's happened—"

"I'm so sorry, Owen." Darren looked shell-shocked. "The water came up from the cellar—the main room has at least three feet in it."

"What—"

"And the ceiling fell in," Darren continued miserably.

"The *ceiling*—" He thought of the damp-proofing he'd been wanting to get around to doing, and shook his head slowly.

"I'm sorry," Darren said again, and Owen stepped back, his mind spinning, as two firemen shouldered their way into the building to deal with the damage.

Emily jogged up next to him, rainwater streaming down her anxious face. "What's happened?"

Owen's chest was tight as he stared at the flooded mess of his pub. He couldn't answer Emily. He couldn't bear putting it into words.

Everything he'd worked so hard for was ruined.

# Chapter Seventeen

OWEN GAZED AROUND the utter, impossible mess of his pub and then at the tumbler of whisky he'd poured and left on top of the bar. He hadn't had a drink in fifteen years, but he was sorely tempted now. In a matter of days, his whole life, which had been starting to shape up rather nicely, was in complete ruins.

It had been three days since he and Emily had driven up to The Drowned Sailor—ironic, the name, now—and he'd glimpsed the devastation. Even then he hadn't realised it fully. He hadn't been able to.

He never should have gone to London, he acknowledged dully as he gazed around at the ceiling rubble, the gaping hole, the water stains on the walls. He'd told Emily he wouldn't have missed it for anything, but he knew now that wasn't true.

He should have missed it for this.

The truth was, in the moment, Emily had been more important to him than the pub. Supporting and even saving Emily had been more important than saving his livelihood.

And here was the result—everything in ruins. His life basically over.

Everyone in the village had been incredibly supportive. An army of volunteers had shown up that first night, sleeves rolled up, ready to work, but there wasn't anything they could do; it was too dangerous and had to be handled by professionals.

Emily had wanted to help, too; when Owen had first run up to his pub, and she'd come to his side, he'd instinctively shaken off the hand she'd put on his arm. He couldn't help it; he'd felt alone, unmoored, unable to do anything but look at what was happening. Roughly he'd told her to go home; she'd looked hurt but had agreed, and he'd told her he'd ring her. He hadn't. Hadn't wanted to, because what had there been to say? *My livelihood, my whole life, has just been destroyed. Want to have dinner on Saturday?*

No. That, just like this, was ruined. Everything was.

Still, Emily had texted, asking how she could help, and Owen had texted back that there was nothing anyone could do. The insurance people had to come in and make their assessments. Now they had and he was left with even less.

Nothing but this tumbler of whisky, the amber liquid glinting in the weak sunlight streaming through the windows, because *now* the rain had stopped.

Owen reached for the tumbler of whisky, his fingers clenching around the glass. He wasn't going to drink it, but he liked to think he had the option of blunting the pain.

Friends were still trying to rally. Jace had offered his DIY services, and Ava had brought food, as if he were an invalid, and Darren had said he would do whatever it took to get the pub back up and running. The trouble was, Owen knew that was impossible. The pub would never open again. Once more he reached for the glass, and then swearing under his breath, rose from the stool where he'd been sitting by the bar.

The insurance company had sent an assessor two days ago, and two efficient, blank-faced workmen had gone through the site. Technically, Owen wasn't meant to be in here, since the place was considered dangerous, what with half the ceiling stoved in. Technically, he didn't care.

The creak of the front door opening had Owen turning as he raked his hands through his hair. "The pub's closed," he called out irritably. "Can't you tell?"

The door opened further, and then Emily stood there. She was dressed in one of her elegant work outfits—a slim-fitting pencil skirt in navy with a pink silk blouse that had little pearl buttons. Her hair was twisted up in some fancy way, and she looked beautiful and sexy and impossibly remote. How could he have thought they'd have a chance, even for a moment?

"What are you doing here?"

She blinked at his surly tone, and then stepped into the room. "I wanted to see you."

Owen spread his arms wide to encompass all the damage—the rubble still littering the floor, the damp walls, the complete ruin. "Not much to see."

Her slate-blue gaze scanned his face. "I'm so sorry, Owen."

"So am I."

She stared at him, and he stared back, and there didn't seem to be much more to say. He dropped his arms and was about to turn away when she asked, "Have the insurance people come to look at it?"

He let out a heavy sigh. "Yes."

"And what did they say?"

He swallowed, feeling like there was a stone in his gut. "They've managed to find a way to keep from paying for most of the damage." Bitterness corroded every syllable, bitterness and guilt, because he knew this was his own damned fault. "The cellar wasn't an approved place for storage, because of the flood risk, so I'm not covered for any of that damage, and the ceiling falling in isn't covered, either, because I hadn't damp-proofed when I'd been told to." Never mind he hadn't had the money. "And because I was cheap, I got the cheapest policy, so all the fixtures and furnishings are covered at their current value, rather than new for like. So that's about a hundred quid, if I'm lucky." He let out another sigh. "It's my own fault. I know that. I should have taken out a better policy, and paid attention to the small print. I should have damp-proofed the upstairs, but I didn't think it was as bad as it obviously was. I *know*."

"I'm sorry." She spoke quietly, sadly, and Owen shook his head.

"It's all right." Even though it wasn't.

"What will you do?"

"I'll have to pack it all in." He shrugged, or tried to, even though the words felt like something physically breaking inside him. "I can't afford to fix it all. I bought this place when it was a falling-down mess, with a business loan I still have to pay back. There's no money for this level of renovation." He kicked at a piece of rubble. "The Drowned Sailor just gave his last gasp."

Emily was silent, and he looked at her, saw her brow was furrowed. Her lips pursed thoughtfully as she scanned the room. "You disagree?" He spoke scoffingly, because to him it was all too obvious.

"No, not necessarily. I just hate the thought of you having to give up."

So did he, yet having her say it made him angry, although he couldn't have said why. "I don't have any choice—"

"I know." She took a step towards him, one hand held out in appeal. "Why are you acting as if you're angry with me? I haven't seen you in three days—"

"I'm not angry with you. I'm just angry about everything." He swallowed. "I'm sorry."

Something flickered in Emily's eyes. "Is that why you've been avoiding me?"

He didn't deny it. "What with all this…" He paused,

still not wanting to say it. Not wanting to feel it. He'd been trying to save Emily, and he was hurting her instead.

"With all this?" Emily repeated. Her voice came out strong, but still with a quaver. "What is that supposed to mean, Owen? With all this, what?"

"I'm not… I can't…" He swallowed. He was such a coward. He couldn't even say it, but then he saw that he wouldn't need to.

Realisation flashed darkly in Emily's eyes and her lips trembled before she pressed them together. "Are you trying to break up with me?"

"I…"

"That is, if there was anything to break up? I know we haven't really been dating—"

"We have." He wasn't going to tarnish or diminish what they'd had, even now. "You've…been important to me, Emily."

"Past tense." The words were bitter. Owen didn't reply. "I don't understand you. Three days ago we were walking around London like we were—like we were in *love*, and now all of a sudden it's all off? How did that happen?" The words burst out of her, radiating with hurt.

"I still care for you," Owen allowed. "I just can't focus on a relationship when my whole life has fallen apart."

"But isn't that precisely *when* you should focus on a good thing in your life?" Emily demanded. "When everything else has gone wrong?"

Yes, if things were that simple. If he felt like he had anything to offer Emily, but now he didn't. He was back to being the roughed-up kid from the wrong side of the tracks, with nothing in his bank account and no job prospects whatsoever. He'd probably end up on benefits, drinking his life away just like he would have done if he'd stayed in the valleys. Maybe there were some things you just couldn't escape.

"I'm sorry, but I'm really not in a place to have a relationship now. I have nothing to offer you."

"Shouldn't I be the one to decide that?"

"No." The word was flat, uncompromising.

Emily flinched, and tried to hide it, and it hurt Owen more than if she'd just taken it on the chin, or gone all prickly, the way she used to. She'd changed, and he'd been part of that. He'd helped her, and now he was hurting her. *The way he always did.*

"So that's it," she said quietly. "That's just it."

"Yes."

She nodded slowly, accepting, her face pale, a dazed yet determined look in her eyes. "Is there anything I can do to help around here?"

After what he'd just done, she wanted to help him? Her kindness and generosity just made Owen feel worse, and more certain that he'd done the right thing. He didn't deserve her. He never had. "No, I don't think so. But thanks."

She gave him a disbelieving look, and Owen imagined what she wanted to say but wasn't. Thanks for nothing, you arse.

"Emily..." he began, but then trailed off to nothing because there was nothing to say.

"I guess this is goodbye," she said.

"I'll see you around the village," he offered, although perhaps that made it all worse.

She gave him another eloquently silent look and then, without saying anything more, she turned and walked out of the pub. As the door closed behind her, Owen swore out loud.

❄

SHE WAS NOT going to cry. At least, she was not going to cry until she was back in her cottage, and no one could see her start to sob. Emily walked quickly away from the pub; the warm spring sunshine spilling from the sky felt like an insult, after all the rain. *Now you shine. Too little, too late.*

She drew in a steadying breath to keep the tears at bay as she walked back to Willoughby Close. It was Friday afternoon, and she'd left work early, so unlike her, but she'd *needed* to see Owen. Three days of silence and she'd really begun to worry. She'd had reason, it seemed.

*I'm not in a place to have a relationship.* What did that even mean? She'd seen the grim resolve in Owen's eyes, and known better than to argue. Not that she would have. She felt far too uncertain and inexperienced to fight for something she barely trusted or understood herself. They'd had a handful of dates, after all, even if it had felt like so much more than that.

From the first moment she'd met him, her relationship with Owen had been intense and overwhelming. And now it was over. He couldn't have made it clearer just then that he'd wanted her out of his pub, out of his life.

*Why?* Why did this have to make a difference? Her life was messy and complicated too, but she'd still wanted Owen in it. Why was he pushing her away? Maybe *she* was the problem, Emily reflected despairingly as she let herself into her cottage. Cass trotted up to her faithfully, and with a sigh she scooped her up, kicked off her heels, and headed upstairs to the rocking chair in her bedroom, with its view of the wood and the river.

Maybe she was too complicated for Owen. He couldn't handle her problems along with his own. She could hardly blame him for that; she knew she was difficult, and touchy, and fragile. She had a mother in a psychiatric hospital who was coming out in sixteen days, and going to have to live with her. She didn't even know how to do relationships, never mind fight for them. She was at a complete loss.

So maybe Owen was right, and it was better this way, at least for him. She was too much work. Too much effort. And even though it didn't feel right now, it might eventually. She could go back to the way she'd been, because she'd been happy like that.

*No, you weren't.* The blunt voice in her head could not be ignored. *You might have tricked yourself into thinking you were, but you weren't. And you can't go back, at least not easily.*

But she could try, because at least the way she'd been had been a whole lot safer. Closing her eyes, Emily buried her nose in Cass's fur and let the tears come.

❄

AN HOUR LATER a persistent knock at the door had her rising from the rocking chair, her heart leaden and her limbs aching. She didn't know how long she'd been staring into space, reliving the best moments she'd had with Owen, even though every one felt like sticking a needle into her eye. Gone. All gone.

She opened the front door warily, knowing she looked a fright and not really caring. Ava stood there, looking so sympathetic and sorrowful that Emily struggled not to burst into tears. She already looked a mess, anyway, so she supposed it didn't matter all that much.

"Oh, Emily."

Ava stepped into the cottage and put her arms around Emily for a quick, hard hug, which felt exactly like what Emily needed. It was a hug to bolster rather than one to fall into, and Emily gave a big sniff as she turned to put the kettle on.

"How did you know?"

"Because I just rang Owen to ask if I could help and he

gave me a typical man's pity party, invitation for one." She shook her head in exasperated disgust. "He is being so very *stupid*."

"I don't know what I did wrong," Emily said in a woebegone voice. She couldn't help it; the words slipped out of her.

"You didn't do anything wrong," Ava said firmly. "It's just Owen, being a typical man, thinking he has to save the world."

"Or just me," Emily said softly. She'd been thinking a lot about that over the last miserable hour, how Owen had swept in on his charger and changed her life. He'd been so kind, so understanding, so very patient, but maybe at the end of the day she really was too much work.

"Most men have some sort of complex," Ava said after a moment, her lips pursed and her hands on her hips. "They can't help it, bless them. Owen's is of the save-the-world variety, it seems, so you might be right there."

The kettle clicked off and Emily dolefully plunked teabags into two mugs. "What with his pub and his livelihood up in smoke, it's no wonder he doesn't want to bother with me, as well."

"Well that's even stupider than what he said," Ava returned robustly.

Emily splashed milk in the mugs and then handed Ava hers. "What did he say?"

"That's for him to say to you, not me," Ava said after a

moment. "I'm not going to gossip." Which piqued both Emily's curiosity and her anxiety.

"I don't think he'll say anything to me ever again," Emily said, knowing she was being melodramatic and unable to help it. "At least not anything important."

"The thing you need to realise," Ava said as she sipped her tea, "is that you don't need saving."

Emily stared at her uncertainly. "What...what do you mean, exactly?"

"I've been where you are," Ava said matter-of-factly. "As I've told you before. Different situations, of course, and we reacted differently, as well. But I've felt...damaged. Different from everyone else."

"Yes..."

"And then Jace came along and saw me for who I really was, who I could be. And that felt like the most wonderful thing in the world. But he didn't save me." Ava paused. "He simply thought I was worth saving."

A tear threatened to drip down Emily's cheek and she blinked rapidly to keep it back. "Evidently Owen doesn't think I'm worth saving."

"He does," Ava replied with sudden ferocity. "I know he does. It's just that he's too stupid and proud to see it." She shook her head, giving a long, frustrated sigh. "Give him some time and space. I'm sure he'll come round. You know Jace was the same? Too proud, especially when everything was taken from him."

"Everything was taken from him? When was that?"

Ava hesitated, and then shrugged. "I don't think he'd mind me telling you. A long time ago, Jace got in a fight in a pub and punched a bloke. Unfortunately the bloke died, and Jace was sent to prison for seven years."

Emily's eyes widened. "I had no idea…"

"Well, he doesn't go around shouting about it," Ava said dryly. "For obvious reasons. And part of the story is that the bloke in question was Henry's younger brother."

"*What…*"

"Which is why he got such a stiff sentence. But that's Henry's story to tell, not mine."

"Actually, Owen said something about all this," Emily said slowly. "About Henry and Jace. He didn't say what, but he referenced it."

"Jace got the job here at Willoughby Manor because Lady Stokeley thought Henry had been unfair. And Jace and Owen became friends because they'd had somewhat similar experiences, although Owen never went to prison." Ava smiled wryly. "But don't you see, Emily? Everyone's got stories. Sorrows. Regrets and things that make them feel less than, like nobody would want them. You're not the only one."

"Yes, I do realise that," Emily said. She'd been learning it since she'd moved to Willoughby Close.

"But do you really realise it?" Ava persisted, her tone both gentle and challenging. "Do you really believe it, deep down inside, that you are worth not just saving, but fighting for?"

"It's whether Owen believes it…"

"I know he believes it about you. Whether he believes it about himself is another matter."

"About himself! But…" Emily shook her head. "He has everything together."

Ava rolled her eyes. "Have you not been listening to a single thing I've said?"

Emily let out a little laugh. "Sorry," she said. "I guess I have a lot to think about." She just hoped Owen did, too.

# Chapter Eighteen

"YOU'RE LOOKING WELL, Mum." For once Emily managed not to inject her voice with that manic note of cheerfulness. She sounded normal, and more amazingly, she felt normal.

It had been a week since Owen's devastating decision to end their fledgling relationship, and Emily had worked hard on coming to terms with a lot of things. Fortunately she had amazing friends to help her along, something that felt like a miracle. She had Ava's brisk but loving talking-tos, and Alice's sympathy and amazing muffins, and Olivia's kindly chats. Emily had apologised for getting cross with her a few weeks ago, and Olivia had apologised again for interfering.

"Actually, I need people to interfere," Emily had said frankly. "I'm hopeless on my own."

"Aren't we all," Olivia had returned with a laugh and a smile.

She had Cass, who was growing bigger by the day, and a job she was really starting to love, and even Henry's brisk cheerfulness to keep her on track.

Yesterday she'd mustered her courage to ask Henry about his relationship with Jace.

"You've heard about that, have you?" he'd said with a sigh. "I'm not surprised. Wychwood-on-Lea really is a small place."

"I think I already know what happened," Emily had told him. "And I know it was a long time ago. But how do you feel about it now?"

Henry was silent for a long moment, staring at the ceiling as he reflection on her question and how to answer it. "The truth?" he finally said, and his voice held a timbre of sadness she'd never heard from him before. "I feel regret. At the time, I was so angry, and so sure I was right. And most people who knew me would have thought I could never, ever change from that position." He dropped his gaze to look at her directly, the expression on his face both bleak and wry. "But I did, with Alice's help. With a lot of people's help. And I realised that everyone can change—myself included. Which was quite a big thing to grasp, for someone like me."

*Everyone can change.* It meant that she could, and was, and she didn't even need Owen to do it. And it meant Owen could change, as well, which she hoped he would, at least in relation to his feelings or lack of them for her. But just as Ava had said you couldn't save anyone, Emily realised you couldn't change them, either. And so she'd spent the last week working and waiting, hoping and healing, and here she was, visiting her mum, six days before she was due to come back with her to Willoughby Close.

"I am feeling a bit better," Naomi allowed with the smallest of smiles. She still looked worn and somehow faded, as if something essential had been leached out of her, but there was a faint spark to her eyes that hadn't been there a few weeks ago.

Emily put the bunch of pink tulips she'd brought in a vase by the window. It was the end of April and spring had finally sprung, complete with blue skies, lemony sunshine, and warm breezes. Too late for The Drowned Sailor, but Emily was trying to enjoy it anyway...even if every time she walked past the now-dilapidated pub filled her with sadness and longing. So much had changed, in such a short amount of time.

"I've been getting your room ready," Emily said as she turned back to her mum with genuine cheer. "I had quite a few of your things—that crochet blanket you made a few years ago? And some of your books on pottery."

"I did like pottery," Naomi mused.

That, along with a lot of other things, had been one of her mother's phases. "There's a few of the vases you made as well," Emily said. "I've put them in the window. You have a lovely view of the meadow, and the Lea River beyond. I know it's not London, but I've come to enjoy living in the country."

"I think country living suits you," Naomi said unexpectedly, and Emily looked at her in surprise. Her mother so rarely took any sort of interest in her life.

"Do you?" she asked.

"Yes, you seem more relaxed, despite all this." Naomi gestured around the room, encompassing everything that had happened to both of them. "You were always so anxious, Emily. I suppose that's at least partly, if not all, my fault." Naomi sighed, and Emily sensed her retreating, as if that engaged part of herself were sinking back into the swamp of her lethargy.

"I have been anxious," she said quickly. "It's true. And controlling. But I'm learning not to be, and that is definitely a good thing." With a self-conscious smile she willed her fists to unclench.

"Well, that's something good, then," Naomi said after a moment. "But I don't know if country living will suit me. When your father took me out to Reading, I felt like part of my soul started to wither. He never understood." She turned to look out the window, a sad smile curving her lips.

"I didn't know that." Her mother never spoke about her failed marriage, how she'd walked out of the family home one evening and hadn't returned for three days. Or so Emily's father had said; Emily couldn't remember it herself. Perhaps she'd blocked it out. She perched on the edge of the bed, waiting for more, but Naomi stayed silent. "What happened, Mum?" she asked after a long, still moment. "Between you and Dad?"

"It's not his fault." Naomi's voice was distant. "The truth

is, I never should have married him. I wanted someone to steady me, but it wasn't fair to ask another person to do that for me."

"Steady you…?"

"Yes." Naomi turned back to Emily. "You can't know how it feels, to know you're out of control and unable to help it. To crave a feeling you know could destroy you. To feel like your life is never your own."

"I didn't realise…" It had never occurred to Emily that her mother might fight against her condition. Sometimes it seemed as if she wasn't even aware of it. And yet here she was, lucid and honest and full of weary despair. "I'm sorry."

"So am I. I know I've put you through a lot."

"It wasn't your fault, and it made me stronger." Emily knew she couldn't be angry with her mother for the way she was, the way her own life had been. It wouldn't be fair or right. And in this moment, she was thankful, in a strange and unexpected way, for everything that had brought her to this moment, this place, this understanding. "We're going to get you home soon, Mum," she said, reaching for Naomi's hand and giving it a squeeze. "It's going to be good. Really good."

On the train ride back to Wychwood, Emily gazed out at the rolling fields streaming by, bursting with buttercups, the grass a vibrant, almost fluorescent green. Sunlight streamed across the meadows, glinting on the puddles still left by the rain. It was all so impossibly beautiful, and it made Emily wonder how she could have ever lived in London, with its grimy streets and choking pollution, everyone busy and uninterested. She'd craved that once, but she didn't anymore. Now she was really looking forward to getting back to Wychwood, even if the thought of Owen, and his absence in her life, made her heart feel as if it were being wrung in her chest.

She faltered in her step as she passed the village green and saw the big, black-and-white "for sale" sign outside The Drowned Sailor. What would Owen do without the pub? It felt as if it were part of him as well as part of the village, his very lifeblood. It saddened her that she couldn't even talk to him about it; he didn't want her to. In the week since they'd had their last conversation, Owen hadn't reached out at all. They weren't going to date and it didn't seem like they could be friends, either.

As Emily came into Willoughby Close, Olivia popped her head out the door. "How was your visit?" she called.

"It was actually okay." Emily paused in the courtyard, her keys in her hand. "My mum's coming back to stay with me for a while next week," she added. She'd told Ava and Owen, but she hadn't got around to telling everyone about what was happening. Saying it out loud made it feel more real, more immediate.

"How do you feel about that?" Olivia asked with a look of compassionate concern on her friendly face.

"Better than I expected," Emily answered honestly. "I

love my mum, and I've enjoyed her company in the past, but it can be very up and down. I feel more prepared somehow, this time. And I've already got a lot of her things here. I've been unpacking them, trying to make things welcoming."

"I saw the pottery in the window. Is that hers?"

"Yes, it is."

"It's beautiful. I love the vibrant colours. Is she very artistic, your mum?"

"She is, actually," Emily said with some surprise. She hadn't really considered her mother's wild and different hobbies as anything other than a manifestation of her mania, but now she realised, along with Olivia, that the pottery bowls and vases were really quite lovely.

"You know my mum lives in the village, as well?" Olivia told her. "There's a terrific day centre in Witney she goes to. Lots of different people there."

"That's a thought," Emily said, although she couldn't imagine her mother sitting around watching telly or playing Scrabble with a bunch of pensioners. She was only fifty-four.

"I don't mean that she would go there as a visitor," Olivia said with a laugh. "That would be a bit much. No, I meant she could offer classes, perhaps. Pottery or painting. They're always looking for volunteers."

"Oh, I never thought…" And she wasn't sure she could imagine it. Would her mother be able to handle something steady? Emily couldn't remember the last time she'd had anything close to resembling a regular job.

KATE HEWITT

"Think about it," Olivia said. "And if it's something she might like, I'll have a word with the manager."

"Okay, thanks. That could be a really good idea."

As Emily let herself into her cottage, her phone buzzed with a text from Ava, checking how the visit had gone. And Alice had left her a casserole already warming in the oven, as well as feeding Cass. Emily read the note with its loopy, cursive handwriting and couldn't help but smile.

She wasn't doing this alone. She didn't have to manage her mother by herself; she didn't have to manage her mother at all. They could have a proper relationship, in a supportive community, and it could be good, even if it was hard. She truly believed that now, and she was thankful...even if she still desperately missed Owen.

❄

"IT'S A BEAUTIFUL day and you should be outside."

Emily blinked at Harriet's rather firm tone. It had been a week and a half since Owen had ended things, and her mother was coming home in just a few days. Emily had been busy trying to get things ready for her, as well as keep on top of her job, although Henry had been expansive in his understanding, and told her she could take as much time off as she wanted. Emily appreciated the sentiment, but she liked her work, and the fundraiser was now less than two months away.

And now Harriet was here, hands on hips, expression

stern, telling Emily she needed to get out. Emily hadn't seen her except in passing since that first night at the pub, which felt like a million years ago. She had no idea why Harriet was here now.

"Ava told me about Owen," Harriet said in her brisk way. "And I'm truly sorry. Men can be really amazingly stubborn and stupid. I can't do anything about Owen, but I can help a bit. I've got the kids and the dog in the car and it's a glorious day. I thought we could walk through the bluebell wood on the other side of the river, by the big estate. The rain and then the sunshine have brought them all out, and they're truly gorgeous. I've even packed a picnic."

"And you want me to come?" Emily said, unable to keep the disbelief from her voice. This was most unexpected. Yes, she'd made friends in Wychwood, and inroads into the community, but she was still more than a bit intimidated by Harriet Lang.

"Why not? Ava said you might spend the day by yourself mooching about, otherwise."

Emily let out a huff of laughter, although there was some truth in the statement. As determinedly optimistic as she was trying to feel, a Saturday on her own could still feel rather long, especially when everyone else was busy with their families. "I don't *mooch*," she said.

"Mince, then?" Harriet suggested, eyebrows raised. "I don't know. It's a lovely day, and the kids are getting restless. Why don't you come with us?"

In fact, Emily had been planning on spending the day tidying her already tidy kitchen, and perhaps doing some batch cooking, maybe going for a walk. Activities that would have satisfied her perfectly well in the past, but felt just a little bit empty now. Or even a lot empty. It was the strangest thing, but she didn't actually *like* being alone anymore.

"Well?" Harriet asked in her schoolteacher voice, a glint of challenge in her eyes, as if she was daring Emily to be brave enough.

"All right," Emily said with both a sigh and a smile. "Thank you for the invitation. Let me just get my wellies."

Three pairs of eyes regarded her curiously as Emily climbed into the passenger seat of Harriet's estate a few minutes later, and was introduced to her children—fourteen-year-old Mallory, who had a bored, worldly-wise air; eleven-year-old William, who was full of manic boy-energy; and eight-year-old Chloe, a blonde cherub who didn't stop talking. Daisy, an enthusiastic spaniel, barked rapturously from the boot, tongue lolling out.

At least Harriet's car was clean. Spotless, in fact. Emily noted the plastic pouches with the children's names fastened to the backs of the seats with approval. Harriet was clearly a woman of organisation.

"So how is the fundraiser going?" Harriet asked as she pulled out of Willoughby Close. "It's only two months away?"

"Yes, end of June. I think I have everything organised,

but there is still a lot of detail work to do." She'd spent the last week confirming vendors, arranging the proper licences and inspections, and was now looking for a PR firm to do the publicity and posters. Work had become a necessary and welcome distraction from thinking about Owen.

"We're all looking forward to it, aren't we?" Harriet said with a glance back at her brood, who gave a variety of responses, from Chloe's enthusiastic chirp to Mallory's bored sigh. William had started kicking the back of Emily's seat with methodical determination, something she was trying not to let bother her.

"I hope it will be a success. A true community effort. I've got to get the posters up soon, so everyone knows about it."

"I might be able to help with that," Harriet said. "I do some PR work freelance, and I'd do it for free, if you liked. I'll give you my card with my website and you can have a look. No pressure."

"Oh, wow." Free PR by a local businesswoman would be ideal. "Thank you."

Harriet gave her a quick smile. "It would be my pleasure, honestly." She turned in to a gravel drive on the edge of a pastoral-looking meadow, a wood skirting on one edge and a tranquil pond glinting on another. "Right, time to exercise this lot," she announced.

"I don't need to be exercised," Mallory complained, while William hurled himself out of the car as soon as Harriet had put it in park.

"This bit is open to the public although you have to pay for the formal gardens," she explained as she slapped her National Trust membership card on the dashboard. "And dogs are allowed off lead, thankfully, or Daisy would go mad."

Harriet helped Chloe out of the car as Mallory slunk behind and William ran ahead with a ball. Harriet clipped on Daisy's lead as Chloe slipped her hand into Emily's, looking up at her with wide blue eyes.

"Where are your children?"

Emily let out a surprised laugh. "I don't have any."

"Why not?"

"Well…I'm not married, for a start."

"You don't have to be married to have children," Chloe stated matter-of-factly. "My friend Izzy's mum isn't married. She doesn't even have a boyfriend."

"Oh. Well." Emily met Harriet's gaze in a laughing plea for help.

"Emily might have children one day," Harriet said as she rounded them all up and directed them to a narrow path that wound through a deep wood. "She's a bit young."

"How old are you?" Chloe asked.

"Er, twenty-six."

"Izzy's mum is only twenty-five—"

"That's enough, Chloe." Harriet gave her daughter a gentle push. "Go kick the ball with William. Mallory, no phone."

Emily glanced behind them to see Mallory sulkily tucking her phone in her jeans' back pocket. Did Harriet have eyes in the back of her head? That must be a mother thing, except her mother had never been like that.

Chloe's words continued to rattle around in her head—*where are your children? Why don't you have any?* Questions she'd never considered for herself before, because the whole concept of children, family, husband, all of it, had been completely out of her experience and even her imagination.

Yet now...now she felt differently. Now she felt that a relationship could be possible, if not with Owen, then maybe, one day, with someone else. And yet just the thought of "someone else" made her heart twist inside her. She didn't want someone else. She wanted Owen.

"So how are you, really?" Harriet asked in a gentler voice as Mallory lagged behind and William and Chloe raced ahead. They'd crossed the sunny meadow and were now walking through the wood, the path twisting through the trees among pools of sunlight and wells of shadow. The air smelled of damp earth and freshness, and despite her sadness about Owen, Emily's spirits lifted just a little.

"I'm all right, I suppose," she said.

"Ava mentioned your mum's in hospital, but coming out soon?"

"Yes, in just a few days." Of course the Wychwood grapevine was sizzling with the news. Emily wasn't surprised, and she tried not to feel raw. She certainly didn't feel anywhere near as prickly and defensive as she once would have been.

Harriet laid a hand briefly on her arm. "It's not gossip, it's concern," she said quietly, seeming to see the struggle Emily still felt. "Although I know one can feel like the other. But we've all been through rough times, and we want to support each other. No one's an island, you know."

"I am learning that, actually, thanks to everyone here." Emily managed a smile. "You've been through rough times?" Harriet seemed so confident and capable, Emily had trouble imagining it.

"Yes, I have," Harriet answered frankly. "I've had my whole life upended, actually, and while it turned out to be a good thing in the end, it certainly didn't feel that way at the time. It felt absolutely horrible." She heaved a sigh of memory before continuing, "My husband Richard lost his job...we lost our house...I lost my friends, or at least the people I thought were my friends. It felt as if I had absolutely nothing. That's why I ended up in Willoughby Close for a time. Richard and I separated for a few months."

"I'm sorry," Emily said quietly. "I didn't know any of that."

"It was very humbling," Harriet continued, her face set in grim lines of memory. "I thought I had it all together. In retrospect, I was a bit arrogant, and I needed taking down a peg or two. I probably still do." She gave Emily an abashed smile. "I don't think we had the best start, and I know I'm a bit bossy, but I do want to help, you know."

"Thank you," Emily murmured. She was grateful for Harriet's honesty, but she wasn't sure now how she could help. Owen was still uninterested. No matter how capable she was, Harriet couldn't make him change his mind.

"So, Owen," Harriet said as if making an announcement, and Emily looked at her warily.

"Yes…"

"I've been where he is," she continued with relentless determination. "Losing everything. Feeling as if you have nothing to offer anyone. And let me tell you, it hurts when you've always been the one who takes care of things. Who's used to being in charge, and having all the answers, and bailing people out of their own scrapes."

"I know that is how you are," Emily said with a small smile, "but do you really think that is how Owen is?" She realised she hadn't had a chance to find out.

"He was with you," Harriet said bluntly, and Emily grimaced. *Ouch.* "I don't know the ins and outs of course, but I know how hard it is for a man who likes being seen as the veritable knight in shining armour to suddenly lose his steed and his shield. That's how Richard felt, and I was too angry and hurt to see it. I don't want you to be the same."

"So is Owen like you or like Richard?"

"Both of us in different ways?" Harriet answered with a laugh. "I don't know. The analogy falls apart at some point I'm sure, but all I'm saying is, be patient. Give him a chance."

"Give him a chance?" Emily shook her head. "I think you're talking to the wrong person. I'd give Owen a million chances. He's the one who isn't giving me one. He said he's not in a place to have a relationship."

"Because he doesn't think he has anything to offer you. So you need to decide if he does, and then you need to tell him so."

Emily stayed silent as she considered that terrifying prospect. Owen had been so very clear about what he did and did not want for her. Could she really be brave enough to put herself out there, to fight for what she wanted? What if Owen rejected her again? Emily didn't think she could take that, not after everything else. "I don't know…" she began, but Harriet shook her head.

"I think you do. I know it's scary. That makes it worth doing." She touched her arm. "Look."

Emily looked up to see bluebells stretching in every direction, a living, violet carpet that was breathtaking in its pure beauty.

"Wow," she said softly. She'd been so intent on their discussion she hadn't seen the beauty all around her. The possibility as well as the promise.

Ahead of them Chloe let out a squeal, and William gave a cackle. Mallory heaved a dramatic sigh. "There isn't even any signal here," she complained.

"You're not meant to be on your phone," Harriet shot

back. She gave Emily an encouraging smile. "Think about it."

"Okay," Emily said. She gazed out at the bluebells in the shadowy wood, the sky impossibly blue high above them. A day full of hope, of optimism. Maybe even of second chances.

Maybe it was time to start taking some risks.

✳

SHE WAS STILL considering Harriet's words on Monday, when she headed to work and spent a full eight hours at her desk, working on the fundraiser details as well as the appeal Henry wanted sent out to five thousand potential donors.

The weather had stayed warm, and she'd enjoyed spending most of Sunday in her garden, weeding the flower beds and then just sitting in the sunshine. Her mother was coming home tomorrow, and Emily had got her room ready, everything spotless, tidy, and hopefully welcoming.

The sun was still shining as she headed back to Willoughby Close at half past five, the air balmy and full of birdsong. Since Saturday she'd been dithering about doing what Harriet had suggested—finding Owen and telling him to give her—*them*—a chance. Yet every time she actually thought about doing, walking to his house and knocking on his door, her insides froze with terror. She *couldn't*. She couldn't risk the rejection.

Then, as she rounded the corner to the turn-off for the

close, her heart seemed to clang in her chest like a bell because there was Owen right in front of her. *Had he come to find her?* He faltered in his step, looking as surprised to see her as she was to see him.

"Hey." His voice came out in something close to a croak and he gave a crooked smile.

"What are you doing here?" Emily asked. Too late she heard the hope in her voice, and saw the guilty look flash across Owen's face. In an instant she knew he wasn't here for her. Nothing had changed.

"Jace and Ava invited me over for supper. I'm just using the shortcut through the wood."

"Oh." Disappointment and something close to grief swamped her. Of course he was.

Owen jammed his hand in the pockets of his jeans. "How are you? How's your mum?"

"She's coming back here tomorrow with me." Emily decided to sidestep the first question, because the only answer she could give was that she was missing him terribly.

"Is she? That's great news, at least, isn't it?" A lopsided smile curved his mouth and made Emily ache. Everything about him was wonderfully familiar and yet impossibly remote.

"Yes, it is. She's doing well and I hope she'll be happy here."

"How are you getting to London and back?"

"I'm renting a car."

He looked torn, and Emily knew he was thinking of suggesting he give her a lift, just as she knew he wouldn't. "I should tell you," he said after a moment, looking even more uncomfortable, "that I'm moving."

"Moving?" She stared at him in shock. "Where?"

Owen shrugged. "Not sure. I kept going east from Cwmparc and ended up here. Maybe I'll keep going— Oxford, London? Wherever I can find some work."

"What about your house? And the pub?"

"I'm selling the pub, and I'm letting my house."

Emily could scarcely take it in. He was just *leaving*? Because of her? "When?" she finally managed faintly.

"I don't know. A few days, maybe a week. When I have everything in order. I've still got to finish the insurance claim for the pub, and arrange the house let. Not too long, though."

"But...you've lived in Wychwood for fifteen years."

Owen hunched his shoulders. "Time to move on, then."

"I hope you're not thinking of moving just because of me," Emily blurted. "I'm not going to make a nuisance of myself or something, Owen. You don't have to leave on my account."

"It's not just you."

"Why, then?"

"It's everything, Emily. I've lost everything."

*You haven't lost me,* she wanted to say, but couldn't. She felt too shocked, and too stung by his news. He wasn't just walking away, he was running. And she wasn't brave enough to fight for him to come back.

"I should go," he said as Emily struggled for something to say. "Ava and Jace are expecting me."

She nodded, mechanically, and still stayed silent as Owen walked past her, down the lane, and then cut through the wood, until the trees swallowed him in darkness.

# Chapter Nineteen

"YOU ARE A complete git." Jace gave him a frank look over the rim of his beer bottle. "You do know that, don't you?"

Owen shifted on the sofa in Jace and Ava's conservatory with an irritable sigh. "No, I don't."

"Moving from Wychwood? You're part of this community, Owen. You can't just leg it when the first thing goes wrong."

"The first thing? Try everything."

"Even so. Why not stay? You have friends here to help you get back on your feet."

But he didn't want that help. He didn't want to need it. Owen stayed silent as he took a sip of his seltzer water. He could have really used something stronger to drink, especially after seeing Emily just now, looking so fragile and beautiful and yet somehow strong. Wonderful, basically. He missed her more than he could put into words. More than he wanted to.

Jace leaned forward, intent now. Ava had made herself

scarce as soon as Owen had walked through the door, which made him realise that this was a complete set-up. He was going to get a proper talking-to, whether he wanted to or not. The only reason he'd agreed to the meal was because he thought Jace and Ava deserved to hear it from him that he was moving on. He supposed a dressing-down was fair payment for his unwelcome news.

"Owen, don't make the same mistake I did."

"What? What are you talking about?"

"When Henry Trent came back to Willoughby Manor, he was set to fire me. You remember? It was over two years ago now."

"Yes, I remember."

"And I was ready to hightail it out of here, leave Ava and everything behind, because I didn't want her resenting me for holding her back. I had nothing, Owen. I had even less than you."

"I don't—"

"I didn't have a house," Jace cut across him, his voice hard. "Or a pub to sell, or a clean record. I was—I am—an ex-con. Remember?"

Abashed, Owen looked down. "I remember," he said quietly.

"But Ava showed me that loving someone isn't about getting yourself together so you're good enough to love and be loved. It's about finding the person who accepts you as you are: messy, complicated, broken. And then holding on to them because out of everything in this life, that is the thing most worth fighting for." Jace sat back in his seat and took a long swallow of beer. "And that's enough soppy emotion from me for one day," he said with a quirk of his lips. "For one year. But come on, Owen. Don't run away. Not just for your own sake, but for Emily's and everybody else's. We need you here, man."

Owen shook his head. He appreciated everything Jace had said, his honesty as well as his emotion, but it was different when you were applying those home truths to your own situation, and the fact was he couldn't.

"Really?" Jace said, eyebrows raised. "You're just going to take everything I've said and toss it in the bin?"

"It's different with me."

"Yeah, because you're not an ex-con."

Owen sighed and raked a hand through his hair. "Emily has enough to be dealing with already—"

"So did Ava. She was pregnant."

"It's different," Owen insisted, because he didn't have anything else.

"It really isn't."

Owen shook his head again. He didn't want to explain everything to Jace, even though he suspected his friend would understand. He couldn't tell him about his family, all the disappointments and failures he'd left behind, and how he couldn't bear doing that again with Emily, even though he knew he already was. Better to run. To run and try to forget.

Even if he already knew he never would.

✱

"AND THIS IS Willoughby Close."

Emily kept her voice cheerful as she pulled the rental car into the little courtyard and parked. It had been a long day already, and it was only a little past noon. She'd arrived at the Huntley Centre for eight o'clock, which had meant getting up at the crack of dawn—not that she'd slept much, anyway—and then there had been several hours of paperwork and consultations in order for her mum to be released. An appointment had been made with a psychiatrist in Oxford for next week, and Emily had taken all her mother's prescriptions along with her notes.

Naomi had been strangely docile, mostly silent, for the entire morning, so Emily had no idea how she felt about anything. But at least they were here now, and she could show her mother her room, find a rhythm to their new life together.

"We're in number one, right here," she said as she opened the car door. Naomi undid her seat belt and stepped out of the car. Her expression was bland, even blank, and she said nothing as she waited for Emily to unlock the cottage door. "Here we are," Emily called out cheerfully, and she opened the door and stepped aside so her mum could go in first.

Naomi stepped into the cottage, taking in her surroundings with that same bland look. Emily tried to see the cottage from her mother's eyes—it had changed a bit, since she'd first moved in six weeks ago. There was a jug of pink tulips on the table, and Cass's feeding bowls by the French windows. Olivia had given her a colourful afghan throw that Emily had spread over her grey sofa, to make it look a little less utilitarian. She'd put a few of her mother's pottery vases on the windowsill, and the effect, while still spare and tidy, was a bit more welcoming than it used to be.

"And your room is upstairs," Emily continued, trying to fill the void of silence with cheer. "Would you like to see it?"

Naomi gave a tiny nod, and Emily led the way. "Here we are." Once again she stepped aside so her mother could come into the little bedroom Emily had tried to make as homey as possible. Another one of Olivia's afghan throws covered the bed, and she'd framed some of her mother's watercolours—they were really quite good—and hung them on the walls.

There was more of her pottery on the windowsill, and a bookshelf with some of the books she'd left behind—a guide to essential oils, a few hippy how-to books. And last but definitely not least, Emily had lugged the rocking chair into the room and put it by the window. It was a little big for the space, but it had felt important somehow.

Naomi didn't speak as she looked around the little room, and then, still saying nothing, she walked towards the rocking chair and laid one hand on the carved arm.

"Do you like it?" Emily asked hesitantly. "I borrowed it from the manor. They had a bunch of furniture in storage. I'm not sure why, but it reminded me of you for some reason."

"There was a rocking chair in your bedroom, when you were small," Naomi said, her voice so soft Emily strained to hear it. "I used to sit you on my lap and read to you there."

"*Goodnight Moon*," Emily whispered. Her eyes filled with tears she didn't completely understand.

"That was one of your favourites." Naomi turned around, a look of such despair on her face that Emily couldn't keep a couple of tears from trickling down her cheeks. "We were happy then."

"Oh, Mum. We can be happy now, too."

Naomi shook her head, and then she covered her face with her hands. "I've made such a mess of things," she said in a muffled voice. "How can you not hate me? I know I made your childhood a misery. I've known it all along."

"Oh, Mum." Emily's heart ached to hear her mother's confession. "I don't hate you at all. I love you, and I don't want there to be any regrets. Let's live in the present, and for the future." Emily crossed the room to put her arms around her mum. "I've made a mess of things too sometimes, but I'm learning not to, and to see my way through the mess. You can too, Mum. We can do it together."

Naomi let out a shuddering sound. "I don't know if I'm strong enough."

"Together," Emily insisted. "We can be strong enough together."

Her mother remained in her embrace for a moment longer, as Emily held her gently, wanting to imbue her with her strength and love. Then Naomi moved away, wiping her face, trying to smile.

"What a pair we are," she said.

"Yes," Emily agreed. "We're a pair."

❄

THE NEXT FEW days were challenging as both Emily and her mother tried to find a new normal. Emily worked half the day from home, to keep her mum company, and then spent the afternoons in the office.

Olivia had stopped by with several meals, a dozen freshly made scones, and an offer for Naomi to visit the day centre where her mother went—to do some watercolours.

Naomi had brightened at that possibility, and although it made Emily a bit anxious, she agreed her mum should at least give it a try.

A week slipped past without her seeing Owen; she didn't even know if he'd left Wychwood already. Every time she thought about talking to him again, begging him to give her a chance, she told herself there was no point. It was already too late. Maybe that made her a coward, but then he was one, as well. Or, the far worse possibility, he was indifferent and over her.

On Saturday Harriet arranged for everyone to go out—
Alice and Ava, Olivia and Ellie, Emily and Naomi. They all
gave the shuttered façade of The Drowned Sailor a poignant
look before heading to the only pub in town, turning their
noses up at The Three Pennies' la-di-da atmosphere.

"White truffle chips?" Ava said in disgust. "Who *eats*
those?"

"Actually, I think they're delicious," Harriet admitted
with a grin. "But the 'roast cod loin with balsamic crumb' is
a bit much. Why not just call it fish and chips and be done
with it?"

"I wish The Drowned Sailor had done food," Ava said
with a sigh. "Good, plain pub fare—that's what this village
needs."

"I told Owen the same thing," Emily said, even though it
hurt to say his name. "Nothing fancy, just plain, good food."

"Exactly." Ava nodded her approval. "And I suppose he
said no because he's a man?"

"What does being a man have to do with it?" Ellie asked
with a laugh.

"Men can be so stubborn. They don't want to fail, or be
seen as failures." Ava shook her head. "Owen really needs to
learn that lesson."

A silence fell that made Emily shift uncomfortably in her
seat. Her mum glanced at her, noticing her unease. "Who's
Owen?" she asked.

The silence stretched on as Ava gave her a significant

look, and Alice, Ellie, and Olivia all waited to see how Emily would answer. The trouble was, she had no idea what to say.

"He owned the other pub in the village—" she began weakly, only to have Harriet cut her off with a strident tone.

"He's only the love of your daughter's life," she pronounced. Naomi looked at Emily in surprise.

"What…? You haven't mentioned him."

There was a lot she hadn't mentioned. Over the past week Emily and her mum had been making strides, finding a new and welcome intimacy to their relationship, but she hadn't told her about Owen…or her broken heart.

"It's over," she said numbly.

"Only because you're both as stubborn as one another," Harriet flashed. "You've got to fight for him, Emily."

"Perhaps he should fight for me," Emily flashed back before she could think through her response.

"He has," Ava said softly. Everyone turned to her in surprise. "All along, he has. Maybe now it's your turn. Isn't that how relationships—how love—is supposed to work?"

Emily was silent, her eyes stinging as she realised the truth of Ava's words. All along Owen had supported her, encouraged her, been gentle and patient with her in so many ways. Yet at the first trial, when he'd been the one to falter, so had she. She'd taken her lead from him, instead of trying to fight, like Harriet and the others had encouraged her to.

"Owen's planning to move on tomorrow," Ava stated. "At least, that's what he's told Jace. He hasn't found a buyer for the pub, but he figures he can handle that from afar. He's putting his house on Airbnb."

Emily stared at her. "What…what are you saying?"

"I'm saying tonight is your chance, Emily David," Ava stated. "Your last chance. Go get him." This was meant with a chorus of approval, and Emily pressed her hands to her heated cheeks.

"I can't…"

"You can."

Naomi put her hand on her daughter's. "Love is worth fighting for," she said quietly. "There are a lot of things I don't know. Things I've done wrong. But I do know that. Don't live a life with regret, Emily, like I have."

"Oh, Mum." Emily drew a shaky breath. For the first time she was actually, seriously contemplating doing something. Not in the hypothetical way she had before, but in an I-might-walk-to-his-house-right-now way. It made her heart race and her mouth dry; she had that swooping feeling inside she used to get as a child, when she was about to jump off a diving board.

*I might really do this.*

"Do it, Emily," Ava said, her voice low and urgent.

"Do it! Do it!"

"You can, you know. What are you risking? A broken heart? You've already got one." This, of course, from Harriet.

Emily looked around the table at all her friends—yes, her friends, and felt her heart fill and then overflow. Then her mother squeezed her hand and smiled, and Emily knew she really was going to do this.

"Okay," she said, and everyone bellowed and cheered their approval, which caused the bartender to give them all a quelling look. Clearly they were not The Three Pennies' desired—or usual—clientele.

Emily rose from the table on shaky legs, the one glass of wine she'd had swirling in her stomach and making her head spin. "I'm doing this," she stated, and everyone cheered again, causing a waitress to tut.

"Go for it, girl!"

"Go get him!"

Naomi gave her a fleeting smile. "I'm proud of you," she said softly, and Emily smiled.

"Thanks, Mum."

Outside the pub the air was soft and warm, a sunshine-filled drowsiness left over from the afternoon. The high street was quiet, tumbling down towards the village green and The Drowned Sailor, and up towards the other side of the village, and Owen.

Taking a deep breath, Emily squared her shoulders and started walking. With each step she took, both her certainty and her anxiety grew.

Was it really only six weeks ago that she'd walked disconsolately up this high street, terrified to ask people if they'd be part of the fundraiser? Six weeks ago that she'd met Owen and the sparks had begun to fly?

What if he said no? What if he rejected her…again?

But like Harriet had said, that didn't matter. Her heart was already broken. And, Emily realised, she needed to do this as much for her sake as for Owen's. To prove to herself, as well as to him, that she was worth fighting for. Their love, fledgling though it had been, was worth fighting for.

Onward she went, as the sun sunk towards the horizon and golden light spooled across the sky. She'd only been to Owen's house the one time, and as she came to the top of the village, she wondered if she'd even remember how to get there. Several residential streets branched off from the high street, all looking the same, with semi-detached houses of Cotswold stone and neat, narrow gardens in front.

She went down the first only to discover it dead-ended, and then a second that fell away to farmland on either side, not a garage in sight.

As she tried the third street, her courage began to fail. Was she ridiculous? Pathetic? Yet how she could turn around now? She had all her friends rooting for her. Her mother cheering her on. She needed to do this.

She ventured down the street, wishing she might see something familiar, but she'd been in such a tizzy when Jace had driven her last time, not to mention she'd had a lot of gin, and so now she didn't recognise anything.

But she didn't *not* recognise anything, either, and she knew his place was around here somewhere, and so she kept walking down the street, past neat houses with bikes and trampolines in the garden, a couple of kids still out who looked at her curiously as she passed. Emily had no idea what the expression on her face was; she probably looked constipated or something. One step, then another, and another.

And then the houses petered out and she saw them—a set of dilapidated garages that hardly looked as if one might house a beautiful home. She recognised Owen's house immediately, the first garage of the set, the stairs on the outside heading up to the first floor.

She was here.

Emily took another buoying breath and climbed the stairs.

At the top she raised her hand to knock, conscious of the import of this moment, and how so much was held in the balance.

"Here goes everything," she said aloud, and then she knocked on the door.

# Chapter Twenty

OWEN WASN'T EXPECTING anyone at this time of night. He had a duffel bag on his bed but he hadn't yet had the heart to fill it. A couple of empty crates were in the kitchen area, to pack away his personal stuff. He hadn't done that, either. And now someone was knocking on his door, and he really hoped it wasn't Jace, giving him what-for again. He'd had enough of being told what a cowardly jackass he was being. He already knew.

"Hello...?" The single word trailed away as he saw Emily standing there, her face pale and her eyes bright, her fists clenched at her sides. "Emily...what's wrong?"

"What's wrong?" she repeated rather shrilly. She sounded both nervous and angry, and Owen had no idea why. "Everything and nothing, I suppose. May I come in?"

"Yes, but..." He didn't know what protest he could make, only that he really hadn't been expecting her here. He stepped aside and she walked past him along the mezzanine towards the spiral staircase that led to the living area. Her shrewd gaze clocked the bag on his bed but she made no comment.

Owen followed her down the stairs, wondering what on earth was going on, and yet at the same time realising, to his own shame and weakness, he was glad to see her. Really glad.

"So you're leaving tomorrow, Ava said," she said flatly, her back to him as she walked towards the sofa.

"Yes."

She whirled around, one hand on the back of the sofa to steady herself. "Where are you going?"

"London, I think. I have a mate who says there might be construction work for me there."

"Construction work?" She sounded disbelieving, and Owen tried not to flinch.

"I need a job."

"Have you worked in construction before?"

"No, but I've got a strong back and willing hands."

She shook her head slowly. "Where will you live?"

He shrugged. "Sofa surf for a bit, I suppose, until I can get my own place."

"Sofa surf?" Now she sounded even more disbelieving. "Owen, is that really what you want?"

Of course it wasn't. How could she think that for a minute? A *second*? He just shrugged, because he had no real response, at least not one he was willing to give.

"Why are you doing this?" she asked, and now her voice sounded quiet and intense, and that made him squirm inside. He didn't want to have this conversation, this reckoning, and yet he knew Emily deserved it. She deserved more of an answer than he'd given her so far.

"I told you before. I'm not in a place to be in a relationship." Even now, when he knew she deserved more, he prevaricated. He just couldn't help it. He didn't want to have to admit his failings, and yet he sensed from Emily's quiet tone, the determined tilt to her chin, that he would have to. She would make him.

"Why not?" Emily asked baldly. "Why is running away to London better than staying here and fighting for something? For us?" The words rang out, wobbled, and fell to the floor. Owen looked away. "Don't I deserve an answer, Owen?" Emily asked, her voice softening. "I know we weren't—we weren't *together* for very long, but it felt important to me."

"It was important to me too," Owen couldn't help but say. She deserved that much. She deserved so much more.

"Then why are you willing to throw it away at the first hurdle?" Emily asked, her voice breaking right in half. "Don't you think we're worth more, Owen? What we had? Because I do."

"It's not that simple…"

"But it can be, surely? If we let it? I know you don't have the pub anymore, and you feel like you can't offer me something. I don't even know what." The words were coming faster, tumbling out of her so Owen couldn't interrupt, even though he wanted to. He wanted her to stop listing his weaknesses. His failures. "But I didn't fall in love with you because of your job, Owen, or your bank account. I don't care about those."

He blinked. "Fall in…"

"Yes, I've fallen in love with you," Emily declared recklessly. "Or maybe I'm in the process of it, I don't know. When is it complete? Does it last your whole life? Because I want to keep doing it, if you'll just let me. If you'll give us a chance." She paused, her lips trembling. "If you're falling in love with *me.*"

Owen let out a groan as he sank onto the sofa, his head in his hands. "It really isn't that simple."

"Then tell me why not."

There was no other choice now, he knew, not when Emily had been so honest and vulnerable. Not when she'd told him she loved him.

"Because I can't bear letting you down," he said heavily. "And I know I will."

"You're letting me down now, Owen, by walking away from me. Nothing could be worse than that."

He lifted his head to gaze at her bleakly. "Are you sure about that?"

❄

EMILY REGISTERED THE grim, despairing look on Owen's face and swallowed hard.

"Yes." At least she wanted to be sure, although she felt,

just by looking at Owen's face, that she was going to have to steel herself for whatever came next. "I am," she added for good measure.

Owen let out another heavy sigh. "I never wanted to hurt you."

"The only way you've hurt me is by walking away," Emily stated quietly. "I really do mean that, Owen. No matter what you tell me now." She did believe that. At least she *hoped* she believed it. What could he possibly say that would change her mind? That would be so terrible? She couldn't think of anything, and yet the look on Owen's face made her wonder.

He didn't reply and Emily went to sit beside him on the sofa. She took his hand, lacing her fingers through his.

"You've been strong for me," she said. "Let me be strong for you."

Owen was silent for a long moment. Then he said, his voice strangely flat, "I tried to save you, Emily, because I couldn't save anyone else."

Emily stiffened at that admission as she remembered Ava's words—you can't save anyone, you can only believe they're worth saving. "Who couldn't you save, Owen?" she asked gently.

"My mother. My father. My sisters."

"How…?"

He drew a shuddering breath. "I told you my father was a drunk. He could be a happy drunk, the life of the party, and so much fun to be around…until he drank too much, and then he turned mean. Really mean." Emily waited, her hand in his, knowing there was nothing she could say. What she needed to do now was listen.

"When he was mean," Owen said, the words carefully distinct, "he hit my mother." Emily couldn't keep herself from giving a soft gasp of distress. "I started to realise when I was around twelve. And I didn't do anything about it until I was sixteen. I was too scared of him."

"You were a child, Owen."

"At thirteen I was tall as he was. The truth was, I loved him. He was fun. And I wanted him to love me."

She heard the bitter guilt corroding every word, and her heart ached. "That's understandable," she said softly.

He lifted his lowered head to give her another bleak look. "It gets worse."

"All right."

"When I was sixteen my mum ended up in A&E with a couple of broken ribs and a black eye. I went at my dad, giving him all I had. I was stronger and faster than he was, and I beat him up pretty badly. When my mum found out…she was furious. She didn't want him to be hurt. She wanted him to be home with us. And the next day, when she was still in hospital, he left. Less than a year later he was dead in a stupid brawl. My mother never forgave me."

"None of that was your fault."

"I ruined my family," Owen stated bluntly. "First my

dad, and then my mum, and then my sisters. One of them ended up on the drink like my father."

"Not your fault—"

"I saw it happening, and I didn't do a damned thing because I was heading the same way myself. In fact, I gave her her first drink when she was only thirteen. She's never recovered. And then there's my other sister, Carys. When I left at seventeen, she begged to come with me. She said she'd die in Cwmparc. She was sixteen, a year younger than me, and desperate. I left her there. And she's still there—with no husband, four kids going wild, and an addiction to prescription painkillers. Is that not my fault, Emily? I didn't save any of them. I got myself the hell out and they're lucky if they get a telephone call from me once a year, because I can't stand the guilt."

"Then make amends," Emily said steadily. "Set it right."

He gave her a look of mingled hope and despair. "*How?*"

"By calling them more. By helping them—"

"How? Because I've got nothing now. I sunk everything I had into that pub, and the insurance payment is barely going to cover my debts. I've got no job—"

"So you can get a job," Emily returned. "You have fifteen years of experience in owning and running a small business. Why shouldn't you start again and succeed? Plenty of other people have." She pointed a finger at him. "You know what your problem is? Your head is stuck in Cwmparc. You think you can't amount to anything even now, when you've already done so much. People can change, Owen. They can grow stronger and braver and better. Look at Henry. He made a huge mistake with Jace—and yes, I know all about that—but he changed. Look at Ava. She turned around her life around. So did Jace, and Alice, and even Harriet… I don't know a single person in Wychwood who hasn't had some sort of hard time! It doesn't have to be different for you." She felt a sudden, surprising spike of anger. "Stop feeling sorry for yourself."

"What?" He stiffened in shocked affront. "I'm not…"

"Yes, you *are*. You think you're the only one who has made mistakes, has regrets? You think I don't regret shutting people out of my life for years and years, and then letting my OCD tendencies control me? *Huh?*" Her voice rose, strident and powerful. It felt good to shout at him, to shake him up. Good and necessary.

"Emily…" Owen looked shell-shocked by her outburst.

"And what's with your saviour complex, Owen?" she continued relentlessly, on a roll now. "You wanted to save me? Well, guess what, I don't *need* saving. I need someone to understand, and encourage me, and be there, but I don't need someone, even you, sweeping in on your white horse and *saving* me. All I wanted, all I've *ever* wanted, is what Ava said. For someone to think I'm worth saving."

"I do think that—"

"Then let go of all your guilt because it's not helping anything. How is running away again going to solve anything?

You feel guilty for getting out of Cwmparc. Do you think you'll feel better getting out of Wychwood?"

"It's not like that," Owen said with some fire in his voice. "I can't stay."

"Why not?"

"What do I have to offer you?"

"I told you, I don't need for you to have a fat wallet or an impressive job. I don't care about those things."

"And if I'm a useless plonker on benefits?"

"That's not who you are," Emily answered steadily. "If you have to go on benefits for a bit, fine. Plenty of people do. My mother is. But you'll get back up on your feet, Owen. You've come this far. Why put a ceiling on what you can accomplish, especially when you have so many friends to help you? When you have me by your side?" Her heart beat hard as she said the words. She meant everything she said, but she was conscious that she was really putting herself out there. If he turned away from her now…

She'd be devastated. She'd also be blisteringly angry.

Owen was silent for a long moment. He was still holding her hand, so that was a good thing, but Emily sensed the indecision in him. The torment.

"Owen, I meant what I said—you've been strong for me," she said quietly. "*So* strong. But now it's my turn to be strong for you. I don't want to be the only one who needs help and support. That's not the point of a relationship. Let me be strong for you. Let me…" Her voice caught. Now she was laying herself bare, offering herself up on an altar. "Let me love you."

Still Owen didn't speak. Emily didn't either, because she'd said everything she knew to say. His head was lowered so she couldn't see his face. Her heart was thudding so hard she felt sick. She realised she was squeezing his hand as hard as she could, and she tried to relax—and failed.

"Do you really love me?" he finally asked in a low voice and Emily's breath rushed out in a gasp she couldn't keep herself from.

"Yes. At least, I think I do. I've never fallen in love before so I don't know how it feels, but these last weeks without you have been miserable, even as I've been finding my way. I've realised that I can live without you, but I really don't want to."

Owen let out a soft huff of laughter that made Emily's heart tumble in her chest. "Yeah, that about sums it up."

"Do you mean…"

"How can you still love me, when I've let you down so badly?" He lifted his head to look her full in the face, waiting for her verdict.

"How can you love me when I've been all over the place, prickly and stupid and touchy and tense?"

"You're not—"

"And you haven't let me down. We can work through this, Owen. We are working through it. That's a good thing, right?"

A smile curved his mouth slowly, like a sunrise creeping over the horizon, flooding the world with light. "Yes," he said after a moment, an ache in his voice. "It is."

"Then…" She hardly dared to hope. To believe.

"I'll stay, if you'll have me. I don't know what I'm going to do, or how it's going to work out, but for once I'm not going to run. I want to fight—for you, for me, for us." He squeezed her fingers before he leaned forward and pressed his forehead against hers.

Emily closed her eyes, breathing him in, her whole body feeling shaky and weak after such an intense few minutes. She thought she might cry, but she didn't. It felt too deep for mere tears.

"Thank you," he whispered, his forehead still against hers.

"You don't have to thank me."

"I love you, you know. I should have said it before. I should have said it first."

"It's not a competition."

"Good thing." He leaned back, still smiling, his eyes crinkled. "I'm glad you were willing to put up with me, Emily David."

"Likewise."

She smiled back, still feeling shaky, and then he kissed her and oh, it felt so sweet and so right, like flying away and coming home all at once. The future was still uncertain, but this wasn't. This was rock solid.

"I've got a few people waiting to hear what's happened," Emily said when the kiss finally stopped. "We were having a drink and Ava and Harriet and even my mum all encouraged me to come here and talk to you. They'll want to know what happened."

"Are they slumming it in The Three Pennies?" Owen asked, eyebrows raised, and Emily laughed.

"And hating every minute. We need you back."

"I'll drive you down there. That should satisfy them."

"Then you must not know them very well," Emily returned with another laugh. "They're going to want more than that."

In fact, her friends were exuberantly delighted when they saw Owen's van trundling down the high street, his window rolled down as he waved at them all.

Ava threw her arms wide before blowing them both kisses, and Ellie was jumping up and down. Harriet was clapping and hollering, and Alice looked teary. Best of all, her mother had the biggest grin on her face that Emily had ever seen.

"Yes, you *queen!*"

"You go, girl!"

"Owen, you lummox, you finally saw sense!"

"Now, now, ladies," Owen admonished, smiling, and Emily found she couldn't stop smiling—or laughing. Life had never felt so sweet, or so promising.

"You are going to kiss her now, aren't you?" Harriet demanded, and Emily looked through the window to see every single one of her friends—as well as her mum—mock-glaring at them both, hands on hips.

"Yes," Owen told them, "as a matter of fact, I am."

And so he did.

# Epilogue

THE DAY OF the Willoughby Holidays fundraiser was as perfect as a promise—lemon-yellow sun, washed blue skies, and air as soft as a kiss.

The grounds of Willoughby Manor were full of people, and laughter, and fun—a proper Victorian arcade of amusement, include an impressive Ferris wheel, stalls and stalls showcasing every local business, including The Three Pennies' elegant marquee—and Man with a Van, Owen's new venture providing a pop-up pub.

Naomi had been the one to have the idea, having spent the better part of a year in a van about five years ago, when Emily was at uni. With the sale of The Drowned Sailor—it was now going to be a kebab shop—Owen fixed up his van and invested in some folding tables and chairs and a liquor licence.

The pop-up pub proved to be a huge success, not just in Wychwood but in many of the smaller, outlying villages that didn't have a pub of their own, and welcomed the van's visits, often with a pleasingly long queue. Owen had discovered he enjoyed being on the open road, and he was thinking of adding food to the pub's offerings as well. All in all, it had turned out far better than he'd ever expected.

As Emily walked through the crowds at the fundraiser, surveying all her handiwork, she was pleased to see a long queue winding away from Man with a Van, while The Three Pennies was catering to a smaller and slightly older, more well-heeled crowd.

The last two months hadn't been without their challenges. Naomi had to have her medication adjusted twice, and while she'd been warmly embraced by everyone just as Emily had, she'd struggled to find her place. She was now volunteering at the day centre in Witney, offering both watercolours and pottery classes, and enjoying both.

Emily had been in touch with her dad again, and while their relationship hadn't changed yet, she'd suggested visiting with Owen, and her father, surprised, had agreed. No date had been set, but Emily was hopeful that her relationship with her dad could be, if not fully restored, then at least improved.

Things with Owen had had their challenges too. Life wasn't a fairy tale, even when it had a happy ending. Owen had had his doubts about his business, his past, especially when he'd brought Emily back to Cwmparc and his family hadn't exactly greeted him with open arms. It had been a tense, painful few days for everyone, but then one of his sisters had reached out by email, and another one was now talking of visiting. Small steps, early days for everyone, but still progress.

Emily also had challenges of her own. Her OCD tendencies still reared their controlling head, and the anxiety she'd struggled with all along hadn't simply disappeared now that she was finally happy. But again—small steps, early days. Progress. She loved Owen, and her mum as well as her dad, her friends and her job, and of course her kitten. Life, for the first time ever, felt full. Full of busyness, hope, and joy.

"Emily, this is *marvellous*," Harriet exclaimed as she strode towards Emily. "Really it's a million times better than our usual boring old fete. How have you managed it all?"

"I had a lot of help—"

"I think I've done just about everything—the only thing left is a sample dance with that new teacher. She's a gorgeous Amazon. She intimidates even me."

"Even you?" Emily teased. "Her name is Belinda and she just moved to Willoughby Close last week. She lives in number two."

"I had no idea! I've been so busy with the kids and work and everything... Well, now I'll have to try the dance class. I'll give her a proper Willoughby welcome."

Emily watched, smiling, as Harriet strode off again, towards her new neighbour, who was teaching a couple of kids how to jitterbug. She *was* a gorgeous Amazon—at least six feet tall, with long, wavy hair and blue-green eyes and what Emily would call a full, generous figure. Despite her height, or maybe because of it, she was incredibly light on her feet.

Emily hadn't yet had a chance to get to know her properly—the last few weeks had been completely consumed by the fundraiser—but she looked forward to making a new friend.

"I'd say this is definitely a success." She turned in surprise to see Owen walking up to her. He slid an arm around her waist and she leaned her head against his shoulder.

"I thought you'd be busy all night."

"I left Darren in charge." His second-in-command had gone in as partner on the pop-up pub venture, and they were considering buying another van and expanding the enterprise. "You must be exhausted."

"I am," Emily answered. She'd been working sixteen-hour days for the last week, supervising all the set-up and other last-minute details. "But I'm happy."

"So am I." He wrapped his other arm around Emily and drew her more snugly against him. "*Very* happy."

A sudden squeal erupted from the top of the Ferris wheel, and Emily looked up to see Olivia and Simon grinning from the highest car on the wheel. Olivia was holding up her left hand in triumph.

"I think," Emily said, "Olivia and Simon have just got engaged."

"So it would appear." Owen sounded both wry and pensive. "And Ava's expecting...but I suppose you've already heard?"

"Of course I have."

"I wonder who will be next with the big news," he mused. There was a smile in his voice and Emily leaned back against him as she smiled too.

"I suppose," she said thoughtfully, "we'll just have to wait and see."

"That we will."

They hadn't talked about those big questions yet, but sometimes Emily felt they didn't need to. Life was unspooling like a golden thread, shimmering with promise. She wasn't afraid of what it held, or what uncertainty or challenges might lie ahead. Not now. Not with Owen, and her mum, and her friends.

Not when everything was right with the world.

"Come on, you two!" Harriet called from the makeshift dance floor where she was gyrating rather wildly. "Let's do the lindy hop!"

## The End

*Read Belinda's story next, and catch up with all of your old friends, in* **Christmas at Willoughby Close**

Want more? Check out the first Willoughby Close book, A Cotswold Christmas!

If you enjoyed *Welcome Me to Willoughby Close,*
you'll love the next books in....

## The Return to Willoughby Close series

Book 1: *Cupcakes for Christmas*

Book 2: *Welcome Me to Willoughby Close*

Book 3: *Christmas at Willoughby Close*
*Coming November 2020!*

Book 4: *Remember Me at Willoughby Close*
*Coming January 2021!*

*Available now at your favorite online retailer!*

# More books by Kate Hewitt

## The Willoughby Close series

Book 1: *A Cotswold Christmas*

Book 2: *Meet Me at Willoughby Close*

Book 3: *Find Me at Willoughby Close*

Book 4: *Kiss Me at Willoughby Close*

Book 5: *Marry Me at Willoughby Close*

## The Holley Sisters of Thornthwaite series

Book 1: *A Vicarage Christmas*

Book 2: *A Vicarage Reunion*

Book 3: *A Vicarage Wedding*

Book 4: *A Vicarage Homecoming*

## About the Author

After spending three years as a diehard New Yorker,
**Kate Hewitt** now lives in the Lake District in England with
her husband, their five children, and a Golden Retriever. She
enjoys such novel things as long country walks and chatting
with people in the street, and her children love the freedom
of village life—although she often has to ring four or five
people to figure out where they've gone off to.

She writes women's fiction as well as contemporary romance
under the name Kate Hewitt, and whatever the genre she
enjoys delivering a compelling and intensely emotional story.

Thank you for reading

## *Welcome Me to Willoughby Close*

If you enjoyed this book, you can find more from all our great authors at TulePublishing.com, or from your favorite online retailer.

Made in the USA
Monee, IL
24 January 2021